Fowl Play

A Bellavista Cooperative Mystery

BY IONA LAM

Fowl Play
published by Iona Lam
This is a work of fiction. Names, characters, places and incidents are products of the author's imagination or are used fictitiously and are not to be construed as real. Any resemblance to actual events, locales, organizations, or persons, living or dead, is entirely coincidental.

Copyright Iona Lam 2024

All rights reserved. No part of this publication may be reproduced, stored in a retrieval system or transmitted in any form or by any means, without the prior permission in writing of the author, except in the case of brief quotations embodied in critical articles and reviews.

For my family - with all my love.

Chapter 1

> "No one else will do it for you."
> - Raquel DeWitt, *The Smart Woman's Guide to Getting It Done*

"May I have your attention please?"

Mallory McKenzie-Chu stood at the head of the twenty-seat formal dining table and rapped the walnut surface to bring the meeting to order. To her chagrin, the room continued to hum with animated conversation.

"My dear, that won't work with this crowd," said Georgie Vandervoss, Bellavista Manor's oldest — and original — resident. She put two fingers to her mouth and blew out an ear-piercing whistle, startling Mallory, who stumbled into the projector screen. Everyone stopped talking at once.

"Thank you, Georgie," said Mallory gratefully.

Straightening the screen and her glasses, she smiled brightly as the five residents took their seats. To give herself a confidence boost, she silently repeated the affirmation she'd read that morning: *You're awake and caffeinated. Time to slay the day!*

"Good morning, everyone! Welcome to the inaugural meeting of the Bellavista Housing Cooperative!"

The table broke into applause.

"Now that the cooperative has been established, we're ready to move ahead with the redevelopment that will transform Bellavista Manor. I'm so pleased to be working with you on this project and to be back at Bellavista."

"And we're so happy to have you back after so many years," interjected Cora Sherman, Bellavista's owner. "And to entrust our dearest dream to your capable hands. We have every confidence you'll accomplish amazing things!"

A trickle of sweat rolled down Mallory's back. More than anything, she wanted this project to be a success. Her future depended on it. "Thank you, Cora. And thank you, Kiki, for being our official minutes taker," she continued, gesturing at Kiki Lee, who was sporting a Red Sox cap over her ponytail, and sitting with hands at the ready in front of her laptop.

"Before I start the presentation, Cora is going to say a few words."

"Hold on a sec," said Kiki, fiddling with the power cord. "My battery's low, and I can't connect to power. Oh, it's back. We're good."

"My goodness, this feels so official!" said Cora, as she stood, beaming at the assembled group. Though her loose topknot was now a brilliant white, and her steel-blue eyes were framed by stylish tortoiseshell bifocals, Cora looked unchanged from when Mallory had met her as a student on Vancouver Island twenty years earlier. "We don't usually bother with minutes."

Unfortunately, this was true. Bellavista operated with a cheerful disregard for formal procedures. Mallory had plans to change all that.

"When my brother Nathan and I purchased Bellavista all those years ago from dear Georgie, we knew we had found someplace very special. A Samuel Maclure masterpiece in Victoria's oldest neighborhood."

The overhead light flickered and went out. Lucas, the property's twenty-something resident handyman, jumped up. "I'll check the breakers!" he said. A few minutes later, the lights came back on.

"Ah, much better!" said Cora with a wobbly smile. "Where was I? Oh yes, now that our intentional community is operating as the Bellavista Housing Cooperative, we can do so much more with this unique property."

Cora grew animated as she spoke. "Victoria is well-known for its retiree and senior population…"

"Newlyweds, nearly deads and garden beds," muttered Etta Hoskins, the second-oldest resident and Cora's longtime friend, who was seated next to Mallory.

"…but the options for retirement living follow the same tired model — sterile apartments, three bland meals a day and a shuttle to the local mall. Where's the adventure? Where's the life? As we've all discussed, retirees want alternatives to the institutional option, and we can turn Bellavista into that! Building affordable homes on Bellavista's grounds while maintaining the house to heritage standards is right on target with the city's density-positive initiative. If we all work together, we can make this dream a reality!"

"Thank you, Cora," said Mallory. "Inspiring words indeed."

A loud gurgle followed by an ominous rumble overhead drowned out what she was going to say next. She glanced up at the ceiling.

"Nothing to worry about," chirped Cora. "Old plumbing in an old house!"

"Okay, then," said Mallory. "Let's proceed with the PowerPoint presentation of the redevelopment. Kiki, can you press play?'

"I would like to say something first," piped up Georgie.

Reluctant to let her agenda slip so early, Mallory said, "Georgie, we'd love to hear from you, but do you mind if we do the presentation first? There'll be plenty of time for input afterwards."

"No, no, let Georgie have her say." Waving her hand graciously, Cora resumed her seat.

Georgie leapt from her chair with a nimbleness that belied her years. Mallory wasn't sure how old Georgie was, and her defiantly red curled bob wasn't revealing any secrets, but she must be more than eighty. Bellavista Manor had been built originally for Georgie's family at the turn of the twentieth century. When the house and its entire contents were sold to Cora and her brother Nathan at a liquidation sale, Georgie came as part of the package— or rather, Cora didn't have the heart to ask her to leave.

"When my grandfather, Cornelius Vandervoss, hired the great Sam Maclure himself to design our family home, he wanted Bellavista Manor to be the brightest jewel on the hill. This magnificent house has witnessed glittering extravagances and heart-wrenching tragedy. But through it all, Bellavista has remained unchanged."

"Apart from falling roof tiles and sagging floors," grumbled Etta *sotto voce*. "I could do without the original plumbing."

"I take seriously my role as the keeper of my family's history," continued Georgie. "The caretaker of its secrets. I know well the ghosts that wander these halls..."

Mallory couldn't suppress an involuntary shudder.

Tears filled Georgie's eyes and rolled down her cheeks as she appealed to the group.

"Promise me that this redevelopment will not change the core of Bellavista, the heart of who we are. If Bellavista changes, how will I ever feel at home again?"

Georgie clasped her hands to her chest. "If I have to lie, steal, cheat or kill, as God is my witness, I'll never be homeless again!"

When Mallory stared open-mouthed at Georgie, Kiki leaned over and whispered, "Georgie's been practicing that line for weeks. She's the lead in the Silver Thread Theatre's production of *Gone with the Wind!*"

"Take it down a notch, Scarlett." Etta wasn't having any of Georgie's dramatics. As Georgie flounced into her seat and Etta struggled to her feet, Mallory regretfully bid goodbye to her carefully timed agenda.

"You're never going to be homeless, Georgie," said Etta, not unkindly. "But we must be ready to make changes. However, I have serious reservations about this redevelopment plan. It's not realistic."

When Cora protested, Etta cut her off. "It's all very well to talk about converting tennis courts into housing, but all that costs money. How are we going to pay for this?"

Undeterred, Cora said, "Metchosin Barnes at city council is very supportive of our project and has been telling me about funding options. The city wants properties like Bellavista to develop their grounds. How can the city refuse us?"

A gust of wind slammed one of the windows shut, and everyone froze as the walls trembled. When nothing happened, they all relaxed, until a chunk of plaster crashed onto the table.

"That funding won't make a difference if Bellavista collapses around us before we get it!" said Etta, coughing.

Lucas nodded, his sandy-brown curls bouncing. "Yeah. We gotta put real money into this place for real repair work. I do what I can but as I keep saying, we're looking at some major repairs. Major."

He whipped out a sheaf of documents stapled together and handed it to Mallory. "Here's a breakdown of the repairs we need. See, I've marked the urgent projects in yellow." Based on her quick skim, Lucas had highlighted practically every item.

"I've done what I can with the plumbing," Lucas told her, "But it's not gonna last. The light flickering, that's a sign something's up with the wiring. The roof, well that's a whole other problem."

"You see?" said Etta. "Yesterday a clay pot fell over the edge of the veranda and shattered while I was painting below. We need to check the railings."

That got Mallory's attention. The clay pots Cora collected were large and very heavy. "Were you hurt?"

"No, but if we don't act now, there'll be an accident," said Etta.

Seeing Cora's face fall, Etta softened her tone. "The reality is, we're getting older, Cora. We — I — don't have the energy to take on a renovation, let alone a massive property redevelopment. Bellavista needs a complete overhaul just to keep it running. Getting rid of the rodent problem alone will be a huge undertaking."

Mallory glanced down in horror, pulling her feet up tightly under her chair.

"With the property already heavily mortgaged, we need real investors," Etta continued. "People who are interested in taking on this kind of property. If we open ourselves to what they're offering, we could negotiate an interest in exchange for keeping our suites and getting essential work done. We could leave the additional development to the developer. That way, the redevelopment would be more manageable for us."

"If you're talking about that smarmy, smooth-talking Nate Narkiss, I'm not interested." Cora's face reddened. "He wants to buy Bellavista to expand his luxury condominium development into our land! He's not interested in our cooperative! What would happen to our intentional community, hmm?"

"We'd survive!" Etta wasn't backing down. "We'd get reliable plumbing, a roof that doesn't leak and a beautiful home without vermin, which, if you ask me, sounds really good right now!"

While Cora and Etta's discussion grew heated, Mallory checked how the others were reacting. Georgie twisted her long strand of pearls, while Lucas bounced his knee against the table. Amira Hassan, the newest member of the co-op, whom she was told had arrived the year before with her son as a Syrian refugee, watched the two women with a worried frown on her brow.

"Cora, I know you don't want to sell to Nate Narkiss, but at least hear him out," Etta was saying. "He has the crew and skills to take care of the restoration work."

"Nate Narkiss would be great!" agreed Lucas. "I know him from my old job; do you want me to give him a call?"

The rapid tap-tap-tap of Kiki's keyboard filled the silence as once again, Cora slowly got to her feet, her face flushed.

"Are you seriously asking me to consider Nate Narkiss?" she said, her voice rising at the end. "He's completely wrong for

Bellavista! Once Nate Narkiss gets his hands on this property, what do you think would happen to our greenhouse and vegetable gardens? Do you really think Nate's going to allow the Kitchen Cooperative to keep its operations here?"

Amira looked up at that, her face pale under her dark brows.

"Cora..." Etta began.

Cora held up a hand. "Let's not overload Mallory on her first day or hold up her presentation any longer."

With that, Cora brought the meeting back on track. Mallory's heart sank. So much for being a "cooperative." Cora had hired her to steer the redevelopment through the zoning process. Now it looked like her main task would be corralling residents into consensus about what the redevelopment would be, and she had less than two weeks to do that.

༺ ༻

Still operating on East Coast time, Mallory couldn't ignore her hunger pangs once the meeting wrapped up. She needed more sustenance than the granola bar she'd scarfed down right before the meeting. In the kitchen, she found Amira and a group of women filling large trays with a variety of shaped dough.

"Hi Mallory. Can I get you anything?" asked Amira with a strained smile. She gestured to the women beside her. "These are my friends, all part of the Kitchen Cooperative. We're doing large-batch production today."

A middle-aged woman with a short, sturdy frame, dark eyes and a wide, welcoming smile introduced herself as Reem, while a statuesque woman with closely shorn curly hair and a warm, brown complexion shyly told Mallory her name was Bishaaro.

"Hey, Mallory!" Kiki was enthusiastically beating a large bowl of cream with a whisk.

Amira offered Mallory a triangular-shaped pastry baked to a golden crisp. "Please, try a *fatayer* -- this is a very popular pastry from my hometown."

She happily took a bite, tasting something green and savory. Spinach, mixed with onions, herbs —mint, she guessed— and a sharp, salty cheese.

"Thanks," she said. "This is delicious."

Reem glanced over at Kiki, industriously whipping the cream. "Kiki," she exclaimed, reaching for the bowl. "You will make butter soon! We need more eggs and some green onions. Take Mallory with you and show her the greenhouse. We will have coffee ready when you return."

"Sure!" Kiki agreed, motioning to Mallory to follow her out the back door. As she left, Mallory glanced back at the three women whose heads were now together in intense conversation, no doubt about the cooperative meeting earlier.

With a confident, springy step, Kiki led them down the hill away from the house. After arriving for her first visit twenty years ago, Mallory had fallen in love with Bellavista Manor on sight. The grand old house, with its reddish-brown exterior, striking white trim and mortared rock walls, wouldn't have looked out of place in a Golden Age mystery. Towering rhododendron shrubs created a riotous canvas of fuchsia, peach, and lilac, while the multiple gables and dormers of the sprawling British Arts and Crafts home provided spectacular views over the Georgia Strait. However, there was no denying the place was showing the wear of its years; the roof shingles were precariously loose and the triple chimneys that supported the numerous fireplaces were missing more than a few bricks.

Cora had fashioned the extensive gardens into a bucolic paradise, making Bellavista an outlier among the neighboring subdivided estates and mid-century bungalows. Over to the left, the Garry oaks, unique to Vancouver Island, sent their scraggly, grey branches into the air. Below the Garry oak grove, a verdant lawn sloped gently down to an orchard, where the plentiful spring blossoms promised an abundant harvest. Farther down, where the land leveled off at the base of the property, were an overgrown tennis court and dilapidated stables that used to house the Vandervoss family's carriage and horses. Mallory could easily visualize the changes to be made based on Cora's development plans. No doubt the proposal was ambitious, but it would also be transformative.

"How did you get involved in the Kitchen Cooperative?" she asked as they made their way towards the greenhouse. Kiki looked a lot younger than the other women.

"My mother helps out with the cooperative, but she's not been well the last few months, so I've been coming instead."

"That's nice of you. I'm sure the women appreciate the help."

"I enjoy it. And I'm learning so much from them. They're all immigrant and refugee women supporting their families through their shares in the cooperative. Amira really knows how to organize a kitchen and our team so we're super-efficient. I can see how she was once the chief-of-staff at a major hospital."

"Really?" asked Mallory. "Why's Amira running a catering company instead of practicing medicine?"

"She told me there were no opportunities for her to retrain in medicine in Canada."

"Still…." It wasn't her business, but there must be some opportunities for Amira. Canada – and the island in particular – was in dire need of medical professionals. Amira's skills would be in high demand; it would be a great shame if they weren't put to use.

As they walked past the chicken coop, Lucas came out of the gate and caught up to Mallory with long, gangly strides.

"Have you had a chance to look at the repair list?" he asked.

"I'll go through it later today," she told him. Lucas reminded her of a wind-up toy, with compressed energy coming out in bursts.

"And you'll talk to Cora about Nate Narkiss? She really needs to get his company involved."

His insistence surprised her given Cora's clear opposition. "I can't promise that I'll change Cora's mind, but I'll see what I can do."

Lucas didn't look happy, but it was the most she could commit to doing. Mallory and Kiki continued down the steep path bordered by moss-covered terrain. As the mist of the early morning cleared, revealing a glorious day, she took a deep breath. After the tense atmosphere of the meeting, it was exhilarating to be outside in the invigorating ocean air.

"Do you mind if I ask you something personal?" asked Kiki. "Are you Chinese? I was born in China and came to Canada when I was a baby, but I don't speak Chinese. Or maybe you're biracial? Japanese or Korean?"

People, especially those of Asian heritage, often asked about her background, trying to guess the origin of her light brown hair and tapered hazel eyes. Usually, Mallory rolled her eyes at the nosiness of others, but she didn't mind Kiki's curiosity.

"I don't speak Chinese either," she said. "I've been trying to learn Cantonese so I can talk to my Ahmah. The "Chu" in my family name is Chinese and the "McKenzie" is Scottish from my mother's side; my family is a multi-cultural smorgasbord. We even have Swedish and a bit of Japanese in the mix."

"My family's a smorgasbord too." Kiki grinned in kinship, her brown eyes shining in her heart-shaped face. Probably in her twenties, Kiki looked not much older than seventeen.

Kiki pulled out a set of keys, fumbling with the lock to the greenhouse door. Damp, warm air swirled around them, contrasting with the cool morning air as Kiki pointed out with pride the rows of young tomato plants and emerging herbs.

"We try to use everything we grow in our products, with as little waste as possible. Lucas is researching how to build some beehives so we can harvest our own honey. I can't wait. Amira was so happy when we received the professional kitchen certification."

Kiki's smile faltered. "It would be really sad if the Kitchen Cooperative couldn't operate at Bellavista. I've no idea where they could relocate."

With access to an abundance of organic ingredients, from fresh eggs to fruits and vegetables, the Kitchen Cooperative ran an impressive operation. Would an active business enterprise on the property be a selling point for investors... or a deterrent?

ଓଃ

After the garden tour, Mallory left Kiki collecting produce in the greenhouse and walked back to the main house, noting with concern the state of the roof. Bellavista had certainly seen better days. Still, the entry hall, with its wainscoting and Persian rug runners, showed off the manor house's enduring elegance. Heading up the winding staircase, she caught the comforting scent of lemon wax polish, underscored by a hint of cumin and coffee.

Cora had put her back in the second-floor room she used to share with Cora's niece, Saffron, on weekend visits from Lester B. Pearson World College. From the much-loved, faded green-and-blue William Morris wallpaper to the twin beds with matching floral duvets, the room looked unchanged since the days she and Saffron had stayed up all night talking. That first week at LBP, Saffron Kalinsky, confident, super-friendly and opinionated, had immediately befriended an overwhelmed Mallory newly arrived from Montreal, and had promptly invited her to Bellavista when the campus emptied out on the weekend and the threat of homesickness loomed large. Saffron's friendship and the warm welcome Cora and the other residents had offered Mallory had provided her with a ready-made home-away-from-home that first year. *So odd to be here without Saffron. I wonder if she even knows I'm back?*

Cranking the bedroom window open, she breathed in the salt-tinged ocean breeze. She loved this view. From this vantage point, she could see all the way past the Fairfield neighborhood, with its quaint mix of heritage homes and mid-century additions, to the whitecapped waves along the Dallas Road waterfront, and further out, to the thin layer of mist gathering across the horizon.

She sat on one of the beds with Lucas's repair list, but the length of it made her head hurt. Every item indicated a major issue with the property. The last few days had been a whirlwind of learning about the housing cooperative and poring over development plans and spreadsheets. The property might be worth millions, but that was only on paper; without an investment infusion, Bellavista's financial future looked bleak. Instead of building her confidence, Cora's public declaration of faith in Mallory's abilities triggered anxiety and self-doubt. How was she expected to live up to Cora's expectations? *Okay, don't panic. You got through the first meeting. One step at a time.*

Abandoning the repair list, Mallory stretched out on the bed. How was she going to unite the residents on a redevelopment plan? The future of her fledging consulting business depended on the project's success. While Raquel DeWitt had paid her a generous severance when the family outgrew the need for her services, she didn't want to dip into that nest egg without first securing an income. She had moved out of the DeWitt home and into the drafty loft over her parents' garage to save money. Her fee for taking the Bellavista project through development approval was three thousand dollars, including free room and board at Bellavista, but that fee had to cover all of her overhead, including travel. The pressure was on to deliver the project on time; there was no room for failure.

It didn't help that her father, Walter, was emailing her law school applications. He had never understood why she had worked for so long as a house manager for the DeWitts. Why waste a perfectly good business degree catering to the needs of privileged people?

But Mallory's mother, Fiona, had tactfully given her daughter the space to grieve the loss of her close-knit work family at the DeWitts, while suggesting she consider working for herself. On one of their early morning power walks up Mount Royal to the lookout, Mallory had shared her struggles with finding a new career.

"I miss my early morning coffee with Monty and Phyllicia and hearing how the DeWitt twins are doing in school," she'd told her. "I miss working with Raquel on her book tours. I've thought about working for another family, but I know I could never recreate the relationship I had with the DeWitts." Mallory had smiled wistfully. "They were their very own brand of kooky and I fit right in."

"They were certainly unusual," Fiona had remarked dryly. She'd tolerated Raquel DeWitt in small doses. "What about going back into the hospitality industry? Raquel hired you straight from the front desk at the Chateau Champlain. Are there any jobs that appeal to you?"

"Plenty!" Mallory had told her. "But apparently, working as a concierge to a single family for more than two decades doesn't count for much, even though I managed a staff of ten and hosted more social events than most hotels. Even with that experience and a business degree, I'm being offered entry-level jobs. I'm too old to start at the bottom again."

Her mother had disagreed. "No, you're not! Many women reboot their careers later in life! Look at me, would you ever have thought I'd be getting my psychology degree after all this time?"

Mallory remembered poking her mother affectionately in the arm. "You've been an armchair psychologist my whole life. How else would I have survived adolescence?" As they reached the lookout, they'd both taken a moment to catch their breath. Leaning against the weathered stone banister, Mallory looked out over the Montreal cityscape.

Fiona had looked thoughtfully at her daughter. "What about starting your own business? You've joked that working at the

DeWitts turned you into a 'Jane-of-all-trades;' you can do anything you set your mind to do."

Mallory had laughed. "That's me — a 'Jane-of-all-trades' and a master of none."

"That's not true, as you very well know," her mother had told her. "You've spent years catering to other people's needs. When you start paying attention to your own needs and trusting your instincts, you'll find out who you are and what you want."

"Is that your psychological insight for the day?" Mallory had teased. "How much for that nugget of wisdom?"

Fiona had given her daughter's arm a gentle squeeze. "Consider it on the house."

When Mallory had launched her private consulting business, she'd wanted to prove to herself and her family that she could flourish without being in Raquel DeWitt's orbit. She could hardly believe her good luck in landing a project managing Bellavista's heritage redevelopment, not to mention getting to work with an old friend like Cora as her first client. Spending the spring in Victoria, British Columbia instead of the slush-filled streets of Montreal was also a definite perk. Mallory didn't want to mess up this opportunity.

Her mother had brought up something else that day. When the psychology course Fiona was taking did a section on neurodivergence, her mother had come home armed with worksheets. She'd coaxed Mallory into completing one and presented her daughter with the results. Mallory had stared at the assessment: strong likelihood of ADHD.

"You're kidding, right, Mum?" she'd said. "Attention Deficit Hyperactivity Disorder? Isn't that what Jesse Donovan next door had growing up? The kid couldn't keep still— he bounced off the walls. I'm not like that."

"ADHD isn't actually all about kids who are hyperactive," Fiona had responded. "There's a type of ADHD diagnosis that describes people who have trouble with attention and focus without being hyperactive. A lot of times, girls who have inattentive ADHD don't get diagnosed until they're a lot older because they're quiet and seem like they're daydreaming a lot. But they can also get super focused on things that really interest them and it's hard to tear themselves away. That sounds a lot like you."

The McKenzie-Chu family had a special word for Mallory's constant daydreaming: *boketto* — a Japanese word meaning, "staring off into the distance without thinking about anything."

"Mum, I don't have ADHD!" Mallory didn't know why she was being so adamant. Something about the ADHD label unnerved her. "Don't you think I would have been diagnosed in school?"

"I'm not saying you have it, as I'm no expert. But a lot of people — especially women — are discovering they have it later in life. I think you might want to ask your doctor to run a proper assessment. It could help you better understand how your mind works."

Sitting up, she brushed away the memory of her mother's concerned face, just as she had brushed away her mother's suggestion that day. Sure, she was forgetful, who wasn't? She ran late to appointments, but with an elaborate phone alarm system, she was managing to be on time. Working for Raquel DeWitt had been high-stress, high-demand, but she'd performed well. So what if she had problems in her personal life with misplaced papers and remembering to pay bills on time? That was life. Not ADHD.

Cora popped her head around the door, interrupting Mallory's reminiscences. "Oh, good, you're here. Can I have a word?"

Embarrassment flitted across Cora's expressive face as she perched on the bed next to her. "I'm sorry you had to witness that clash of opinions. Not the best impression to set on your first full day."

Mallory waited. She'd learned that not saying anything often led others to fill in the silence and reveal more information than if you peppered them with questions.

"Don't let Etta's doomsaying worry you," said Cora. "Etta was a bookkeeper long before she was an artist, so she can't help overthinking every little decision we make. She's always asking me about expenses and gets annoyed when I file anything as "miscellaneous."

Having run across a few of those miscellaneous files during her review of the cooperative's documentation, Mallory empathized with Etta's frustration. It was time to be direct with Cora.

"I'm worried that this late in the process, not everyone is in agreement with the redevelopment plan," she said. "The development hearing is in a few weeks, so I'll need to understand what changes you're prepared to make and how I can help the group reach consensus."

Cora sighed. "I don't know what's gotten into everyone suddenly when we've been discussing this plan for months! Georgie will come around, so long as we leave her suite and the common rooms as they are. Amira wants to keep her kitchen and the greenhouse. As for Etta, she'll come around too. This is the direction we need to go in as a cooperative. I'm certain of it."

Cora's response told her everything she needed to know about the Bellavista Housing Cooperative; it was Cora's way all the way. It seemed she was a lot like Saffron after all.

As if reading Mallory's mind, Cora patted the bedspread and remarked, "On our first trip to Italy, Saffron and I picked up these bedcovers at a market in Tuscany." She traced the elegant, patterned spread. "She fell in love with the country. I never thought she would end up going to Milan every year for fashion week."

"How is Saffron doing?" Mallory asked. She couldn't avoid mentioning Cora's niece, not when Cora knew they used to be so close. After graduation, Saffron had been scouted by a modeling agency and whisked away to London. According to a gushing profile she'd read in Elle magazine, Saffron had recently swapped a lucrative career as a model for the business side of the industry, making a name for herself as a visionary stylist and advocate for high-quality, plus-sized fashion. She was happy for Saffron's success, but it had felt like a gut punch to learn about it secondhand. She hadn't spoken to Saffron in years, not since their graduation year when Saffron had invited her boyfriend of the moment on what was supposed to be a girls' trip to Hawaii. With no desire to play third wheel, Mallory had pulled out of the trip, and Saffron had flounced off on her own. When she came back, they'd ended up having a terrible argument that blew up their friendship, not to mention their roommate situation. While she felt regret about the way their close friendship had abruptly ended, she couldn't see a way back. Without trust, there was no relationship left.

"We hardly see her these days because of work," Cora told Mallory. "Saffron will be so sorry that she missed you."

When she didn't reply, Cora tilted her head and looked keenly at her. "I get the sense you two don't keep in touch as much now, do you?"

Flustered, she turned back to the view to hide her discomfort. "It's been a while."

"What a pity, when you were inseparable in school. Well, I'm glad to have you back again and I'm very grateful you're helping with this project."

"I'm happy to be here too," said Mallory. She *was* happy to be back on the Island and at Bellavista, even if the memories were bittersweet.

Suddenly, loud cries and squawks shattered their peaceful moment.

"Oh, what now?" muttered Cora. She hurried out of the room, with Mallory following close behind.

Chapter 2

> "Never trust a man with two first names"
> - Raquel DeWitt, *The Smart Woman's Guide to Getting It Done.*

"Get off me! Shoo!"

Near the chicken coop, a man in coordinated pastel golf gear leapt about as a flock of irate chickens swarmed his feet. Etta and Amira were doing their best to corral the chickens back into the coop, but the feisty flock evaded their efforts.

"Call off your attack hens!"

Cora glared at the man who continued to dodge the chickens. "What are you doing here, Mr. Narkiss?"

A red- and-blue-feathered rooster attempted one last vicious peck at the man's tasseled loafers before Cora shooed the indignant bird away with her foot. Freed from poultry interference, the man smoothed back his thick, ash-blond hair and regained his composure.

"Since you haven't returned my calls, I thought I'd pay you a visit."

"I thought I made it clear that we've nothing to talk about," began Cora.

"I invited Nate."

Cora turned in shock. "Etta! Why would you do that?"

"Nate has made changes to his proposal, and you should hear him out before rejecting it. Nate, this is Mallory McKenzie-Chu, our project manager."

"Delighted to meet you, Ms. McKenzie-Chu," Nate said with a wide smile. "Nate Narkiss, Sand Dollar Developments. May I call you Mallory? Such a fetching, old-world name."

Mallory prided herself on being open-minded, but Nate's attempts to charm her put her back up. Men like Nate Narkiss often underestimated her because she was small – a smidgen over five foot three – female and Asian. For Etta's sake and out of curiosity about Nate's proposal, she put on a polite smile and shook hands. Cora pursed her lips, her arms crossed tightly in front of her.

Nate made a show of handing Mallory a glossy, coil-bound folder labeled in a fancy script: "Sand Dollar Developments Presents the Rock Cliff Resort."

Mallory flipped through the glossy, professionally printed brochure. The design plans showed a luxurious-looking building with multiple levels and spacious terraces overlooking beautifully landscaped grounds.

"My reputation speaks for itself," said Nate. "I've been responsible for many of Victoria's premiere property developments, but in my humble opinion, the Rock Cliff Resort surpasses them all. We're talking the highest quality construction, spacious suites with spectacular views, professional staff to cater to your every whim..."

Cora let out a snort of derision.

"And access to world-class amenities, including a spa, sauna and gym and an on-site doctor and personal chef! What more could you ask for?"

"What more indeed? And the cost of living in this lap of luxury?" asked Cora witheringly.

"Nothing for you to worry about," said Nate. "What I'm proposing is for our mutual benefit, as neighbors. Bellavista is hanging together with duct tape and Gorilla Glue, but it won't much longer. You can't keep up with all the repairs. I hear your plumbing needs redoing, and"—he glanced up and shaded his eyes— "looks like your roof is going to follow suit pretty soon."

To underline his point, a shingle toppled to the ground, narrowly missing Nate's head. He jumped out of the way, brushing off his shoulders.

"That's an occupier's liability lawsuit waiting to happen. Okay, so here's my proposal. You sell me Bellavista, and I'll guarantee you a worry-free future."

Cora bristled. "I've told you before — Bellavista is not for sale."

"Ah, but I can offer you something no other buyer can. Please, hear me out." Nate gestured toward the wicker table and chairs set out on the patio. "Give me ten minutes." At Etta's pleading look, Cora reluctantly took a seat. Nate pulled up a chair next to Cora and Mallory and Etta rounded out the table. At this point, Amira murmured her excuses and returned to the house.

Taking charge of the discussion, Mallory said, "You've made it clear you'd like to purchase the property. What kind of numbers are you offering, Mr. Narkiss, and what arrangement do you have in mind?"

Nate grinned. "Call me Nate. I like your style. Considering the current decrepit state of the property, I'm offering a more-than-generous $8.5 million."

Before she could respond, Cora expostulated, "You must be joking! What kind of insulting offer is that?"

Mallory interjected calmly, "You must be aware that the property assessment alone is $12 million, and we expect that the property would fetch much more on the open market. Bellavista offers extensive grounds with an original Maclure design, all within walking distance of downtown Victoria. As you pointed out, there's nothing else like it."

Nate pulled out a duplicate of the brochure he had handed to Mallory and spread it out. "What I'm proposing is an exchange of interests that guarantees all the current residents a lifetime, fully paid-up interest in brand-new custom suites at the Rock Cliff Resort. I'll even throw in membership to our clubhouse —with dues paid for the next decade— and access to all amenities."

He turned to Cora. "All you and the current residents would need to pay for is your meals, and since the suites will be self-catering, you could opt out of the meal plan, should you choose to do so. Think about it. You would all get a worry-free lifestyle because I'd take care of everything."

"I bet you would!" muttered Cora.

"By fully-paid up interest do you mean rent-free *and* maintenance fees-free?" asked Mallory. Maintenance fees could be as much as rent. When Nate nodded, she quickly did the math in her head based on the five current residents. If she estimated a minimum twenty-year life interest, at market rent and average condo fees, Nate was offering a discount of $2.5 million. "By my calculations, your offer still comes up a couple of million dollars short."

Nodding approvingly, Nate pointed his finger at her. "Cora, you've got yourself a smart one here!" Mallory grimaced at the condescension. He didn't pat her on the head, but he might as well have.

"That's not all I'm offering; I'll also take on full responsibility for bringing Bellavista up to code and restoring the house to its former glory."

"What kind of restorations?" asked Cora. "Georgie doesn't want material changes to the house."

"I'm prepared to renovate to the highest historical standards," said Nate. "I've access to top-notch woodworkers and craftsmen. We'd repaint the exterior and interiors, fix the roof and anything else that needs repairing or replacing. From what I hear, you need a complete overhaul of every major system: plumbing, gas, electrical wiring and a new roof. I can take care of all that. Bellavista would become the Rock Cliff Resort's heritage clubhouse, the centerpiece of the property."

Nate was spot on with his assessment, based on Mallory's brief review of Lucas's repair list. Her heart had dropped when a Google search revealed that a new roof in Bellavista's British Tudor shingle style could cost a minimum of $250,000. If Nate was committed to restoring Bellavista, the total cost could well be in the millions, way beyond the cooperative's reach.

Cora frowned. "What's the point of renovating if we don't get to stay at Bellavista? I can't see Georgie moving into one of your fancy modern suites and leaving behind her beloved home."

"There'll have to be some compromise," answered Nate. "I'll be saving Bellavista by transforming it into a phenomenal clubhouse that will draw all of Victoria, preserving its legacy for generations. Would Georgie rather the property crumble to the ground from neglect? That's what will happen in a few years if you don't take drastic action now."

Mallory raised her eyebrows. "If you want to convert Bellavista into a clubhouse, how will you comply with the city's heritage requirements? I can't see how Bellavista would work without making significant structural changes to accommodate those kinds of amenities."

"Other areas of the estate will supply fitness and wellness facilities," said Nate, waving his hand dismissively. "I want to make Bellavista, with this spectacular view, into an old-world clubhouse, a place where residents can browse the library, smoke a cigar in the cigar lounge, play a game of billiards. Many of the main rooms will accommodate these activities since they were designed for them. And having converted units upstairs means we will have ready-made guest suites once our interior designer makes them over. Look, details are in plans I have back at the office. Why don't you come over to check them out tomorrow?"

Cora flipped through Mallory's brochure, shaking her head. "What about the plans we had to turn the tennis court into modular housing built around an open courtyard? What about the renovation of the carriage house so we could rent it out as an Air BnB? There's nothing about the conversion of the stables into a communal space for events and morning yoga."

"Cora, think of the advantages Nate's new plan offers. We wouldn't need to do any further development if Nate covers the costs of fixing Bellavista," said Etta earnestly. "Developing the property was a last resort to fund the crippling maintenance costs of the house. Now we don't need to take on such an enormous project."

Cora shook her head even more adamantly. "We had a vision to develop affordable homes and maximize the potential of this property! What's the point of the cooperative if all we do is turn Bellavista into a glorified country club for privileged people?"

"You'd be preserving a work of art that is part of the history of this city," said Nate. "Isn't that part of your vision?" He unfolded his six-foot frame from the wicker armchair and stood. "Look, I've a meeting I can't miss so I have to get going. I'll be presenting the development proposal to city council tomorrow night, so I hope you'll seriously consider my offer."

Cora grabbed the folder from Mallory and thrust it back at Nate.

"We're. Not. Interested." she hissed. "Take your sketchy business plans elsewhere. I've heard stories about how you treat the people who buy into your developments. We don't share the same values or vision, so I want no part of your ghastly resort next door. Bellavista is not for sale."

Nate's face darkened, his charm evaporating like water droplets on a hot skillet.

"I wouldn't act so sure if I were you," he said, looming over Cora. "Don't count on council supporting your hippy-dippy co-op plans, not when my development has the mayor's own backing. I played a round of golf with him this afternoon and he was very supportive. Watch what you say about my business."

Mallory responded sharply. "Is that a threat, Mr. Narkiss? Because I don't care for your tone."

"Call it a friendly warning. If my application doesn't get the green light, don't think that means yours will."

He swiveled around, scanning the property. "This property is incredible and it's right in the heart of Rockland, the most historic neighborhood in the city. Where else can you live on an actual estate and still be within walking distance of downtown Victoria? What a waste if you do nothing with it." Nate thrust the folder back at Cora. "I'd think carefully before you reject my offer, if I were you." He sauntered off.

"Over my dead body! Or yours!" shouted Cora after his departing figure.

Cora threw the folder down, where it landed on the ground with a puff of dirt. "Etta, you're no fool. You know as well as I do that Nate Narkiss is a self-promoting showboat who can't be trusted. Why are you giving him the time of day?"

Mallory reached down to pick up the folder that had fallen open and dusted it off. To her astonishment, the middle pages featured Bellavista Manor at the heart of the Rock Cliff Resort. That was a little presumptuous.

"We don't have any other options, Cora!" Etta was saying. "We need to consider the possible, not the impossible! Yes, I would love for Bellavista to become a self-sustaining community, but we are in no position to make that happen."

"I've got plans; I've got it all under control."

"No, you don't!" Etta turned to Mallory. "Did Cora tell you we have investors lined up? Well, there are none."

"That's not true!" objected Cora, "Agatha and Edith are both interested, as is Flora. And...and lots of other people!"

"Cora, I don't want to see you put your entire heart and future into this expansion only for you to lose everything! There's too much at stake!" Etta's voice shook as she pleaded with her friend.

Cora looked at her with dismay. "Why have you lost faith in me, Etta?"

Etta pressed her lips together, holding back her emotion. "Let Mallory look over Nate's proposal. And you need to let Saffron in on your plans. She has a right to know what we're doing."

"We'll have to make sure that the chicken coop gate is properly secured," said Cora to Mallory, her voice trembling. "How did the chickens get out in the first place?"

"I'll ask Lucas to have a look," said Mallory.

"Lucas is usually on top of things like that and he's always around the chickens—doesn't like anyone else feeding them. But we do need him to see to that latch right away. If the chickens get out again, we'll never hear the end of it from Pierce Wexford next door."

Cora headed back toward the house without saying another word to Etta.

"Cora must see reason," said Etta fiercely, grabbing hold of Mallory's arm. "Mallory, you must make her see reason! If we don't partner with Nate, our development project is doomed!"

When Lucas came back an hour later, Mallory mentioned the sticky latch on the chicken coop to him, and he rushed out to fix it. He might be a bit high-strung, she thought, but he had a decent work ethic and took his responsibilities for the chickens' well-being seriously.

In the kitchen, Amira was setting the table with the mismatched willow ware and silver thrift-store cutlery Cora loved to collect. The members of the Kitchen Cooperative had left, having cleaned up the kitchen until every surface shone.

"I hope you are not alarmed by your first meeting with the cooperative," said Amira. "You will see we all have strong opinions and share them openly."

"I'm here to listen and help as much as I can," said Mallory.

"When you have some time, I would like to share my ideas about the redevelopment."

"Any time," said Mallory. "I'd be happy to hear them."

Amira smiled with relief, and together they brought the rest of the prepared dishes to the table. Something about Amira put her immediately at ease as they worked silently together; the woman held herself with a quiet confidence that didn't require Mallory to make small talk.

Lucas arrived, making appreciative noises. "This looks great, Amira." It was indeed an inviting spread, featuring hummus drizzled with olive oil, a colorful chopped vegetable salad and a platter of grilled chicken skewers.

Amira beamed at the compliment. Lucas helped bring in the water carafe while Amira arranged the glassware on the table. "I'll put a tray together for Etta. She prefers to eat in her room in the evenings," Amira explained to Mallory.

Lucas took a seat across from Mallory. "The best thing about living here is Amira's cooking," he said, helping himself to some skewers.

"Does Amira cook every night?" She wasn't sure how the cooperative ran. Each resident had their own self-contained suite that included a small kitchenette.

"Amira cooks on Sundays and makes bread for the week. Cora cooks on Fridays, and the rest of the time we fend for ourselves. Etta lives off boiled eggs, as she's always wrapped up in a creative project."

Cora came in looking frazzled. "Lucas, I can't get the washing machine to shut off. Can you take a look at it?"

Lucas obligingly got up. Cora sighed heavily as she took a seat at the head of the table. "The machines are probably getting close to needing to be replaced. They're very solid but we can't find parts for them any longer."

Mallory winced. Yet another outlay to add to the growing list of essential items needing to be replaced.

"Mallory, my dear!" *Joy* by Patou enveloped Mallory as she was enfolded in a hug and given an exuberant kiss on each cheek. Resplendent in a silver, beaded, floor-length gown, Georgie still believed in dressing for dinner.

"Sit next to me." Georgie insisted. "I've lots to tell you. You must convince Etta we don't want to sell to that nasty Nate Narkiss!"

Etta appeared, taking a seat on the opposite side of the table from Cora. "Didn't want to miss Mallory's first dinner," muttered Etta. Mallory was touched by the effort.

Georgie patted Mallory's hand. "We're so glad you became part of our little family. We loved having you girls come visit when you were students, and now here you are again, running your own business!"

Etta snorted. "We never got any sleep when you two were in town. Always using the intercom to order hot cocoa and cookies to be sent up in the dumbwaiter and using up all the hot water."

"I promise not to buzz you unless I'm in desperate need of hot cocoa," Mallory teased.

With a dramatic sigh, Georgie interjected, "Enjoy the intercom while you can. Nate Narkiss is going to rip it out and anything else with value from this house once he gets his hands on the property."

Cora banged the tabletop with her fist. "We need a strategy for dealing with Nate Narkiss. We can't be the only ones who object to his flashy, over-the-top mega-complex. His tacky development is a blot on the landscape. No one wants that kind of facility here, not in Victoria and certainly not in Rockland."

"Hear, hear!" cried Georgie, pounding her small fist on the tabletop, bangles jangling. "Yesterday, as I was going past the Sand Dollar lot next door, I spotted a protester! He'd set himself up with signs and everything. One of them said, "Sand Dollar Development Sucks —Ask Me Why!"

"See? Nate's got a terrible reputation." Cora gained steam. "I bet the heritage society has something to say about the monstrosity going up next door."

"The society held protests when Nate tore down the original building a few months ago," said Georgie.

"That's it. I'm going to the council meeting to object to Narkiss's application!" announced Cora.

"Cora, do you think that's a good..." began Mallory, as Lucas said, "Wait a minute..."

"If you publicly oppose Nate's application, you'll make an enemy!" cried Etta. "Please see some sense, Cora."

"Yeah, you don't want to cheese off Nate!" said Lucas, looking perturbed.

"You're being naive if you think Nate is going to follow through on his offer." Cora threw up her hands. "Why are you pushing Nate's proposal so hard, Etta? You too, Lucas?"

"And I don't understand why you're refusing to listen to anyone!" countered Etta. "These decisions...they affect all of us, but you won't acknowledge any of our concerns. Ask Saffron what she thinks. She has a stake in this decision too."

This was news to Mallory. "Do we need Saffron's agreement before we submit the development application?" she asked Cora, feeling a pool of anxiety at the thought of having to engage with her former best friend. The last time Mallory had seen Saffron at graduation, they had avoided each other. Mallory had no idea if Cora had even told Saffron that Mallory was working as the project manager for the cooperative development.

"Saffron is happy to leave Bellavista for me to manage; she doesn't have the time, with her busy career and constant travel. Besides, when Saffron called me a few weeks ago, I ran the development proposal by her, and she was fine with it." Cora was breezily unconcerned.

Etta shook her head. Cora's response wasn't giving Mallory a lot of comfort. Nate's application gave her the perfect opportunity to see council in action, but Cora's "burn it to the ground" attitude was giving her palpitations. "Cora, let me handle any statements you want to make at Nate's development hearing, okay? You hired me to be your representative, so let me do the talking."

When Cora reluctantly agreed, Mallory sighed with relief. Mallory didn't want to admit how nervous she was about the cooperative's hearing. *Was it wise to let Cora attend?* The risk of Cora getting into another argument with Nate nearly made her change her mind. She would have to figure out a way to keep Cora from going rogue.

Chapter 3

> "Always be where the action is."
> - Raquel DeWitt, *The Smart Woman's Guide to Getting It Done.*

The next afternoon found Mallory scanning the packed council room at city hall, making sure to secure seats for Etta and Georgie. Despite Mallory setting three alarms to arrive on time, they'd had a hard time finding parking. All the residents were in attendance except Lucas, who said he needed to fix the busted light over the *porte cochère*.

"Hey, Mallory!" Kiki waved to Mallory from where she was running the refreshment table.

"You seem to pop up everywhere," said Mallory, as she perused the tea selection. There must be something with caffeine other than coffee. After a long day poring over development plans and walking around every inch of the property with Cora, Mallory's energy needed a pick-me-up if she was to get through the council meeting without nodding off.

Nate Narkiss, his athletic frame poured into a sharply tailored blue suit, stood nearby, chatting to a fellow attendee. "I hope Cora Sherman can finally see sense," he was saying loudly. "Bellavista is going to waste. She's turning it into an urban farmyard. Complete with a chicken condo!"

"Better built than most of your developments, Nate," said a striking blond woman with enviably toned arms as she approached the refreshment table. Mallory recognized Metchosin Barnes from her headshot on the city's website. Curiosity getting the better of her, Mallory lingered to pour herself some tea, as Nate's plastic grin wavered for a moment before he recovered his composure.

"Mets, always a pleasure. I see you're here fulfilling your civic duty as council woman. And trying to drum up support for your re-election campaign, I'm guessing? I hear you're in for a fight."

Ouch. If looks could kill.

"Much like you've been drumming up support for your next development? Had any cozy golf games with the mayor recently?"

Nate shrugged, but his face flushed red, and his jaw tightened. "The Rock Cliff Resort will be the crown jewel of the Rockland neighborhood. It'll set a standard that the city hasn't seen before. I'm not worried about my application getting the green light. Good seeing you, Mets."

He nodded curtly and walked away, his face once more flashing his trademark smile.

"The day you kicked that excuse for a man to the curb was a very good day," said Cora, coming up behind them. She gave Metchosin's arm a comforting pat.

Metchosin smiled. "I couldn't agree more. Now, let's see what delicious treats the Kitchen Cooperative has prepared for us."

Mallory leaned forward. "I'm curious about your name —I used to go to Lester B. Pearson in Beecher Bay. Were you born in Metchosin?"

"Oh, forgive my manners," said Cora. "Metchosin, this is Mallory McKenzie-Chu; she's our new project manager. Councillor Barnes has been helping me navigate the grant options at city hall."

"Nice to meet you, Mallory. As for my name, well..." Metchosin smiled wryly. "My father thought Metchosin was such a beautiful word and place that he insisted I be named that when I was born there. He didn't realize that, translated from the local First Nations language, 'Metchosin' means 'Place of Stinking Fish!'"

Mallory laughed. "That's quite the origin story."

"It worked out well during my campaign for city council. The Stinky Fish campaign received tons of attention. Listen, I'm very excited about the plans Cora has put together for Bellavista. Affordable housing, especially for seniors, is a cause I'm passionate about. Please feel free to drop by my office anytime. Or you can also find me at Bend Studio, on Fort Street."

"Mets is the owner of Bend — it's a hot yoga studio," added Kiki. "Hi, Mets."

"Hey, Kiki. See you there on Tuesday?"

"I'll be there."

"Do you do hot yoga?" Mallory asked Kiki, as Metchosin and Cora caught up.

Kiki laughed. "No!" she protested. "I hate getting sweaty. I work at the reception desk at Bend Studio on Sundays and Tuesdays. Metchosin is a good boss; she's very understanding when I need to take time off to care for my sister's kids."

How many gigs did Kiki work? Raised voices caught Mallory's attention. A bowtie-wearing gentleman whose weathered complexion spoke of a longstanding appointment with a tanning bed was gesticulating wildly before Metchosin. The councillor answered him calmly, but that infuriated the man even more. He turned abruptly, ending the discussion. Metchosin shook her head.

Suddenly, a squealing microphone made everyone cover their ears.

"Uh, sorry about that. Could I have your attention, please? We're about to start the council meeting, so we ask that you please turn off your phones. No recording of any kind may be done. The official recording will be posted on the city's website in a few days."

As everyone took their seats or went to stand along the back wall, the mayor welcomed attendees and acknowledged the traditional territory of the Lekwungen people. After council adopted the agenda and dealt with housekeeping matters, Nate Narkiss stepped up to the podium.

"Mr. Narkiss, you're welcome to start any time."

Mallory observed the panel of council members, identifying the mayor, Tony Petrucci, and others easily. Years of memorizing faces and names from the society pages for Raquel's charity fundraisers had honed Mallory's skills.

"Your Worship, Council members," began Nate, his voice easily reaching into the far corners of the room. "Thank you for your time. In front of you, you'll find an information package setting out all the details for my proposed development. The Rock Cliff Resort is destined to be the grandest luxury complex this city has ever seen! With breathtaking views and resort-like amenities, we'll set a new standard in retirement living as the ultimate destination for retirees."

"Does he really want to describe a retirement home as the 'ultimate destination?'" remarked Cora in a loud whisper to Mallory. "Unnecessarily morbid, don't you think?"

"Picture this — an unparalleled retirement experience drawing people from around the globe. We're talking a deluxe resort experience, but instead of vacation, you live there year-round! Now I know that some people were upset when I tore down the old Richardson home, but Sand Dollar Developments took great care to rescue as many original elements and architectural features as possible. We've kept some brick work and carved wooden posts, as well as the original mantels and light fixtures, even the tiling. All these items will be incorporated into the new builds so that the history will be retained. Not only that, but we also have plans to rehabilitate the decrepit property next door into a clubhouse that will be open to the public through membership."

"Is he talking about Bellavista?" Cora whispered urgently to Mallory, who was trying to follow the presentation. "What's he saying?"

"I wonder if council understands the current state of Bellavista and what a favor I would be doing to the community to take over this dilapidated property?" mused Nate into the microphone.

"Leave Bellavista out of this!" cried Cora, face flushed, and hands clenched into fists. "We're not selling to you, Narkiss!"

"Order, order!" shouted the mayor, banging his gavel. "You must wait your turn."

Nate concluded with a video presentation showing an aerial tour of an artist's rendering of the Rock Cliff Resort set to a swelling score, as slick and polished as himself.

Mayor Petrucci leaned forward. "Mr. Narkiss, thank you for that wonderful introduction to your stunning development. I'm sure I speak for all of us at city council when I say that the Rock Cliff Resort is exactly the kind of upscale, quality development our city needs. Now, unless anyone on the council has any questions, we can move to the vote for..."

"Your Worship," Metchosin Barnes interjected. "I have a few questions for Mr. Narkiss."

Grudgingly, the mayor nodded.

Metchosin locked eyes with Nate. "Mr. Narkiss, why should city council approve your high-end development when there is a critical affordable housing shortage in Victoria?"

"Ms. Barnes, I'm well aware that adequate rentals are a big part of your election platform. The Rock Cliff Resort will offer a wide range of pricing, but we are first and foremost a luxury development."

"So, you're saying you have no intention of including any rental units or more affordable units?"

"I didn't say that," answered Nate, his smile becoming a little bit more forced. "The resort will welcome everyone to our state-of-the-art facilities, both residents and non-residents.

Metchosin switched tacks. "What about the lawsuits filed against Sand Dollar Developments? How are you addressing those?"

Nate's smile became a little less steady. "We're working hard to resolve any issues."

"We've every confidence you'll do so," interjected the mayor as Metchosin frowned. "Now, if there are no more questions from council members, the floor is open for members of the public."

Approaching the podium, the man whom Mallory had seen accosting Metchosin adjusted the microphone down to his height.

"My name is Pierce Wexford and I'm submitting a formal objection on behalf of the Victoria Heritage Society for Architectural Preservation. Sand Dollar Developments has ignored every single one of the Society's very reasonable recommendations, including preservation of the Italianate villa that once graced the Richardson property. After reassuring city council that he would do everything possible to save that villa, Nate Narkiss tore it down! He's not to be trusted. Council must reject this application!"

"Reasonable?" expostulated Nate. "The society wanted me to restore a condemned building riddled with termites because Emily Carr's monkey once bathed in the bathtub!"

"Sand Dollar's latest monstrosity will be a blot on the character of our historic neighborhood!" Pierce's face turned red as he gripped the podium with both hands.

"I'd say we're saving the character of Rockland by turning the decrepit property next door into a centerpiece of the community," responded Nate coolly. "Preserving Bellavista Manor before it deteriorates beyond all hope must be something that the society can support, right?"

"Nate Narkiss has no claim to Bellavista!" said Cora, rushing up to the podium and pushing Pierce aside. "He's misleading you!"

"State your name and the reason for your objection," said the clerk, trying to gain back control of the meeting.

"Cora Sherman, owner of Bellavista Manor and member of the Bellavista Housing Cooperative," said Cora loudly. She reached and pulled Mallory upfront. "This is Ms. McKenzie-Chu, our representative."

Mallory stumbled into the podium. She hadn't expected to have to speak at this meeting. Channeling the time she'd faced down a room of belligerent parents after the DeWitt twins filled their school's swimming pool with bubble bath right before a swim meet, she gathered her thoughts.

"Um, thank you, Mr. Mayor, council members. The Bellavista Housing Cooperative will be making a fulsome presentation at the next council meeting in two weeks' time. For this hearing, we need to clarify that Sand Dollar Development has no legal claim to Bellavista. The owners haven't reached an agreement with Mr. Narkiss…"

"And don't intend to do so! Ever!" added Cora.

"Really? Have you cleared that with your niece?"

Cora turned to stare open-mouthed at Nate. "Saffron? What are you talking about?"

"I had an interesting conversation with Ms. Kalinsky the other day. Turns out that she's much more open to my offer than you are, and I believe she's the majority shareholder in Bellavista, correct?"

It was Mallory's turn to stare open-mouthed at Nate.

"As I said," continued Nate. "Ms. Kalinsky is looking favorably on my proposal, so favorably that I feel confident in telling this council that the Bellavista property will be part of the new Rock Cliff Resort."

Cora banged on the podium, shouting into the microphone, "Not if I have anything to do with it! I'm going to do everything in my power to stop you, Nate Narkiss! You're never getting your hands on Bellavista!"

"I think council would be interested to hear about the asbestos problem," sneered Nate. "And the fire hazards, the plumbing and roof leaks, and didn't I hear that you recently had Pests Be-Gone out to deal with a rodent infestation?"

"How do you know about that?" gasped Cora, covering her mouth as Nate grinned triumphantly.

The mayor banged the gavel again, getting a workout. "Order! There will be a five-minute recess before council votes."

In the ensuing din, Mallory pulled Cora away from the podium. "Let's get you a nice cup of tea," she said. She didn't like how shaken

Cora looked after the confrontation. Nate's revelation that Saffron held a majority stake in Bellavista and that they were close to a deal was news to Mallory. *What else am I not being told?* Two days into her job and she had even less of an understanding of what she was supposed to be doing. She left Cora with a sympathetic Kiki, while she looked around trying to spot Nate. She had to find out what he had discussed with Saffron.

Mallory caught sight of Nate sauntering toward the exit and hurried over to him. As he approached the door, Georgie blocked his way. Nate looked up, startled.

"I won't let you touch Bellavista!" cried Georgie. "If you dare to disturb my family ghosts, they will take their revenge on you!"

While he shrugged off her words, Nate couldn't hide his annoyance. "If you're worried about your family ghosts having a roof over their heads, then sell to me. Bellavista is falling to pieces and I'm the one that can save it."

"If I have to lie, steal, cheat..." began Georgie, working herself up. Heads turned to take in the spectacle.

Don't say it!

"...or *kill*, as God is my witness, I'll never be homeless again! Get your greedy hands off my home!"

Georgie's face crumpled. Whispers broke out around them as Mallory and Amira pushed their way toward a now-sobbing Georgie.

"I'll take Georgie home by taxi," said Amira to Mallory, her arm around her weeping friend. Mallory nodded with relief. It was the best thing to do. But where was Cora?

Back at the podium, Nate waited as the council members took their seats again. But before the clerk could reconvene the meeting, a commotion erupted at the doors.

A helmeted rider on a souped-up red mobility scooter zipped across the floor, sending people scrambling to get out of his way. As a loudspeaker blared, "Sand Dollar Builds Crappy Homes," the driver revved the engine and aimed his speeding scooter... straight at Nate.

The scooter screeched to a halt, inches in front of Nate, who stumbled backwards and fell to the floor.

Whipping off a helmet to reveal a shock of white hair, the driver shouted, "Don't be fooled by Sand Dollar's slick marketing! Buyer beware!" He pulled out a bundle of pamphlets from his knapsack and threw them in the air. Before security could reach him, the driver quickly pulled on his helmet, turned around and drove back through the open doors.

The mayor banged his gavel again. "Order! Order!" shrieked the clerk.

Nate got to his feet, shaking with rage. "That guy nearly killed me!"

In the ensuing pandemonium, Mallory lost track of Cora. Talking to Nate would have to wait until she found her. As Mallory scanned the panicked crowd, Kiki appeared with a flustered Etta.

"That was Art Papatonis," Kiki shouted to Mallory over the din. "The protestor next door? He must have rigged up his mobility scooter — I didn't think they could go that fast!"

With the meeting doors closed and now guarded by security, the clerk called the council meeting back to order, everyone resumed their seats and the council hurriedly voted. Metchosin was the sole "no" vote. Nate nodded in satisfaction as his development was approved before striding from the room.

There goes my chance to talk to Nate about his discussion with Saffron. She stood, craning her neck past the dispersing attendees to see if she could locate Cora. As the sole of her shoe skidded on something slippery, Mallory looked down to see one of the tossed pamphlets under her foot. After picking it up, she tucked it in her jacket pocket. "I still can't find Cora," she said to Kiki. "I'm worried she got disoriented in the commotion."

They found Etta a seat while they separately searched the meeting room and adjoining hallways. By the time they regrouped, the hall was empty except for a few stragglers.

"She's not answering her phone," said Mallory, checking hers for the hundredth time. "What should we do?"

"Knowing Cora, she's likely taking a long walk to work off some steam," said Etta. "She's probably halfway home by now; the walk takes less than an hour, and it's still light out. Since I have a set of spare keys to the car we should head back — we might spot her on the way."

Mallory drove Cora's ancient hatchback, first dropping Kiki off at the Cook Street Community Centre for yet another gig, before heading up Rockland Avenue to Bellavista. As they crested the hill, they passed the Sand Dollar site, where she could see that Art Papatonis had set up camp, his sandwich board lying beside a folding deck chair piled with books. But Art and his scooter were nowhere to be seen.

The sky was still light by the time she pulled into the drive. She could feel a headache blooming. Cora hadn't shown up at Bellavista, but Etta didn't seem worried. Georgie and Amira appeared to have gone to their rooms, so Mallory put together an easy supper of pantry items for Etta and herself. After helping an exhausted Etta to her room, she excused herself and escaped into the gardens.

Streaks of red and orange marked the evening sky as she took the path that led to the fountain. In the hush of the early evening, the orchard let out a gentle fragrance as she wandered through the trees, her headache now full-blown. She sat beside the bubbling stone fountain, letting her fingers drift in the water, breathing in the scent of cherry blossoms. Peace and quiet at last. This was the first moment during the whole day that she had spent alone.

What a day! So much for getting a read on how council operated. She needed to find out what Saffron was planning. By including Bellavista in his proposal, Nate had upended the value of the cooperative's entire proposal.

As the last rays of the sun faded from the sky, the temperature dropped. Mallory was about to head in when her phone vibrated. It was her mother.

"Mum, it's late for you; you're not usually up at this time."

"I had to hear how your first few days on the job went, but your phone was off earlier. How's everything going?"

Mallory filled her in on events at Bellavista and the disastrous council meeting. "My job feels impossible — the Co-op members can't agree on anything! What was I thinking, taking this project on?"

"I'm sure Cora finds it a comfort to have you involved," said Fiona encouragingly. "You're great at problem-solving. Take it one step at a time. You can do this!"

Mallory wasn't so confident. The stress of not knowing what was going to happen next was putting a severe strain on her composure. "After seeing everybody else let loose with their emotions, I feel like throwing a tantrum myself!"

Fiona clucked sympathetically. "Don't stretch yourself too thin. There's likely a lot that's been percolating beneath the surface for some time, and now the pressure of moving the project forward is bringing those conflicts to the surface. You can't expect to figure it all out at once."

Suddenly, a cry of distress shattered the evening quiet. Mallory jolted to her feet, straining to hear where the noise had come from. The chicken coop. Her mind flashed to coyotes.

"I have to go, Mum. Something's up!"

She raced toward the chicken coop, heart pounding, not thinking too clearly about what to do if she did find a coyote.

A visibly distraught Amira emerged from the chicken yard as Mallory crested the hill.

"Amira, what's wrong? Did a coyote get one of the chickens?"

Amira couldn't speak. She was trembling and gripping her hands together. The chickens were going berserk.

The last thing Mallory wanted to see was a scene from a non-PG rated version of Wild Kratts. She pushed open the wire door to the chicken yard, careful to shut it behind her, and went to peer inside the coop. Sprawled across the ground was a figure lying on its back. She gasped and moved forward. Those tasseled loafers…

"Mr. Narkiss?" she called out. "Nate?" Mallory reached out a hand to touch his leg. He didn't respond. She looked closely at his face. She jumped back, hand to her mouth. Nate's unseeing eyes stared blankly at her.

Chapter 4

> "Avoid messy situations… if you can."
> - Raquel DeWitt, *The Smart Woman's Guide to Getting it Done.*

In shock, Mallory stumbled out of the yard.

"It's Nate Narkiss," she told Amira. "I think he's dead!"

Amira nodded, calmer now. She had pulled herself together and let the medical professional in her take over.

"I checked for a pulse — there was none," she said to Mallory. "There is nothing more we can do for him." Amira grabbed her arm, "Come, we must call the police."

They ran back to the house. As they opened the back door, they found Cora inside, removing her shoes. "What's wrong?" she cried, seeing their faces. Amira ran wordlessly past to get to the phone.

Mallory came in and closed the door. "Amira found Nate Narkiss in the chicken coop. He's dead."

Cora's eyes widened in shock. "What are you talking about?"

"He's lying in the chicken coop, not moving. Amira tried to find a pulse but couldn't." Mallory shuddered. "She's calling 911. We need to tell the others before the police get here."

Cora swung into action. By the time the police arrived minutes later, the residents at home — Cora, Amira, Mallory, Georgie and Etta— were all gathered together in the library. Lucas's truck wasn't in the driveway, and he didn't respond to his phone. Georgie sat on the sofa wrapped in a velvet bathrobe, looking small and tired. Etta sat next to her, her hands trembling around the milky cup of sweet tea Amira had made.

As Mallory accepted a cup, Amira looked at her with concern. "I'm fine. Really. It was the shock of seeing him lying there and realizing that he was dead."

Amira's face clouded. "It was a very difficult thing to discover."

Did seeing Nate's lifeless body bring back unpleasant memories of the war for Amira? She had been so shaken when Mallory had found her, but she had recovered her equilibrium.

When sirens signaled the arrival of the police, Cora turned to Amira. "The police will want to talk to you first as you found Nate's body. Mallory, would you go with her? I'll stay here with the others."

Mallory and Amira stood at the front door as a police car, fire engine and ambulance pulled up to the house. All of Victoria's emergency services had responded to the 911 call. As they watched two police officers come up the gravel drive toward them, Amira shivered. Mallory quickly fetched a wrap from the hall, which Amira gratefully accepted. The first officer, heavy-set, with a mournful-looking face that reminded Mallory of a basset hound — if a basset hound had a bristly blond mustache — made introductions while his much younger, much taller companion took notes.

"I'm Detective Blair, and this is Detective Grover, from the Victoria PD. We understand that someone named Amira Hassan in your household reported finding a body in your yard."

"Yes, that was me," responded Amira. Her face beneath her floral hijab looked tense. Mallory introduced herself to the officers and they asked to be taken to where the body was found.

"Please, follow me." Amira walked ahead of the police officers down the slope to the chicken coop, hugging her wrap around her shoulders. The outside lights had switched on and now gently illuminated the chicken coop yard. Inside the fenced area, a figure emerged from the shadows.

"Police. Who's there?" Detective Blair called out sharply. "Show yourself and state your name."

Lucas stepped into the light, a sheen of perspiration on his brow and his breath coming short and quick.

"I'm Lucas Turner. I -- I thought I heard something and came to check on the chickens."

"He works here," Amira quickly vouched for him. "Lucas is our handyman."

"Did you touch anything?" asked Detective Blair sternly.

"No. I-I just got here. What's going on?"

"Don't move. We're going to need a statement from you."

Detective Blair pushed past Lucas into the yard, the paramedics carrying gear right behind him.

Lucas stared as the team entered the coop, chickens clucking at their feet.

"Did someone get hurt?" he asked urgently. "What happened?"

"I found Nate Narkiss in there," whispered Amira. "He's dead."

Lucas pushed his hair back with a shaking hand, his eyes going wide. Before he could ask any more questions, the team filed out again. The paramedics conferred briefly with Detective Blair who nodded grimly. He took out his cell phone and spoke quietly into it as the paramedics left, carrying their unused equipment. The reality of the situation hit Mallory. It wasn't her imagination. A man was dead.

Detective Grover turned his alert brown eyes to Mallory, Amira and Lucas. In the light shining from the outside lamps, he appeared to be South Asian, in his late-twenties, young for a detective.

"Ms. Hassan, Ms. Chu — er, McKenzie-Chu — I'll need to get witness statements from both of you, and Mr. Turner here, as well as anyone else on site. If we can find somewhere to conduct the interviews and take statements, it will save everyone a trip down to the station."

"Everyone is in the library. There is a small study next door that you can use," said Amira. "I will show you if you follow me."

After the introductions were made in the library, Detective Grover turned to Amira. "Ms. Hassan, if you don't mind, I'll take your statement first. Then, Ms. Chu—sorry, McKenzie-Chu —if you could join me next after Ms. Hassan returns?"

As soon as they left the room, Cora hurried up to Mallory. "What do the police think happened? Did Nate have a heart attack?" she asked breathlessly.

Mallory shook her head. "They didn't tell us anything. The paramedics came but there was nothing they could do."

Someone had lit a fire in the hearth. Lucas joined the others in the library, standing with his back to the fireplace, watching the door. He looked like he had seen a ghost, although Mallory didn't think he'd had time to get a glimpse inside the coop. Perhaps he was squeamish about the very idea of being near a dead body. Mallory shivered, feeling ill herself at the recollection.

"What was that man even doing in our chicken coop?" asked Georgie crossly. "Stealing eggs? Wouldn't put it past him."

"Shush, Georgie," said Etta sternly. "The man has died, after all."

"Surely, you're not going to pretend to be devastated?" asked Georgie, raising a skeptical eyebrow. "He likely got scared by a chicken and had a heart attack."

"Nate died on our property; that makes it personal," answered Etta. "Although we had nothing to do with it, I can't help but feel responsible in some way. I invited him to consider our project and now he's dead." Etta looked shaken, her hand trembling on her cane.

"It feels very wrong for Nate to have died here," admitted Cora, "After I argued with him in public."

A strangled sound caught Mallory's attention. It came from Lucas; he looked terrible, his eyes darting to the door, as if he were afraid of who might enter. *What was going on with him? Could he possibly know something?*

"Lucas, are you alright?" Cora asked. She must have noticed how unwell the handyman was looking. It might be time to round up more refreshments.

Amira returned, looking strained, but giving Mallory a reassuring smile.

"Detective Grover asked for you next," she said.

In the study, Detective Grover asked Mallory several questions, giving her time to respond and taking down notes. After she had finished signing her statement, she asked, "Can you tell us anything about how Nate Narkiss died?"

He shook his head. "I'm afraid we'll need to wait for the coroner's report. Could you ask Mr. Turner to come in?"

After Lucas finished his interview and came back looking even worse than he had before, Det. Grover interviewed Etta, Georgie and finally, Cora. Meanwhile, Mallory and Amira made more tea. It helped to do something useful to distract from the gravity of the situation. She had never been part of a sudden death before, so she'd no idea if the length of time it was taking to wrap up the interviews was standard.

"Did Detective Grover ask what you were doing at the chicken coop?" asked Mallory as she put teabags in the warmed teapot.

"I went to bring Gregory Peck in for the night."

"Doesn't he stay in the coop?" she asked in surprise.

Amira poured hot water into the teapot and said, "Our neighbor complains about his crowing, so we take turns bringing him in for the night, when we remember. Georgie went out to feed the chickens around 6 p.m. since Lucas was out, and she asked if I could bring him in later."

If Georgie had fed the chickens at 6 p.m., and Amira had gone to take Gregory Peck out by 8 p.m., that left a two-hour window for Nate to have ended up in the coop. Mallory had been in the gardens around half past seven before her mother's call. Something must have happened to Nate between six and seven that night.

As they served the tea, Mallory asked whether anyone had heard or seen anything unusual. While Bellavista was a massive house and the grounds were extensive, someone might have heard something, even if they dismissed it at the time as insignificant.

"Nothing," answered Amira. "After we returned home from the council meeting, I made up a tray for Georgie and we each had dinner in our rooms, and later, I was on a Skype call with my son. I heard the chickens when I approached the coop, but nothing else."

As Amira's suite faced the front of the house and the chicken coop was down in the gardens at the back, it wasn't that surprising she hadn't heard any disturbance.

"I never heard a thing either," said Etta. Etta's ground-floor suite faced directly onto the terrace and was the nearest to the chicken coop. "I was working on a piece and had music on. It helps me focus. The volume bothers Cora when she's in her study, so I wear headphones. I didn't realize anything was wrong until Cora knocked on my door to tell me the police were coming. What about you, Georgie? Did you notice anything unusual when you went to feed the chickens?"

Georgie made a rueful face. "My hearing is not what it used to be. I have hearing aids, but I took them out to go to bed when I turned in, around seven-thirty. I didn't notice anything before then except for the peacocks making a ruckus. See, that's why I think it was a heart attack. I bet Nate was being a busybody, snooping around our property, and a peacock scared him. I told Detective Grover that when I went out to feed Gregory Peck after dinner, I could hear them cawing."

"I do not think it was a heart attack," said Amira. "There was blood on the ground, but I couldn't tell where it was coming from."

"Blood?" gasped Georgie as Etta's brow contracted with concern. Before Mallory could follow up, Cora came back into the library and pulled Mallory to one side.

"They've called in the Major Crimes Unit," she whispered agitatedly, "I heard the officer say it was a suspicious death. They're saying Nate was murdered!"

☙

Before Mallory could respond, Detective Blair came into the library and called for everyone's attention, cutting through the buzz of conversation. "While we have not yet determined the cause of death, due to the extent and nature of Mr. Narkiss's injuries, we are treating his death as suspicious."

General consternation broke out at the news, as Cora asked the detectives, "What kinds of injuries?"

Detective Blair cleared his throat. "We're not at liberty to say anything more until the coroner confirms the cause of death. An officer will secure the chicken coop and surrounding area overnight, as it's now a crime scene. We'll need to relocate the poultry."

He paused. "I understand that you all live here in some sort of communal arrangement, right?"

"Yes," said Cora, her brow furrowed, "Bellavista is a housing cooperative; we share the common areas and have our own suites."

"We'd like your permission to carry out a search of the grounds and the house tonight, including your individual units."

"You think the killer could still be here? In our home?" shrieked Georgie. A deep chill overtook Mallory, and she wrapped her arms around herself to keep from shivering.

Ignoring Georgie's outburst, Detective Blair continued. "With your consent, we can complete our search tonight and be out of your way. I'd appreciate it if you would stay in this room until we're finished."

"Officer, it's getting late, and we've all had an exhausting evening," objected Etta. "Can't this wait until tomorrow?"

As the others murmured in agreement, Detective Blair raised his voice over the din. "You don't have to consent to a search tonight. However, I believe I have grounds to obtain a special warrant tonight and will do that if necessary." As everyone fell silent at that comment, he added, "Before you agree, let me note that you should understand what I'm asking to do, and you should understand what might happen if we go ahead with the search."

"What do you mean?" demanded Cora. "Detective, are you saying *we* are under suspicion?

"We'll need to review your statements and confirm your whereabouts tonight as well as your relationships to the deceased. I'm saying you're all persons of interest until we determine otherwise."

Protests broke out immediately, Cora's the loudest. "How can you even think any of us is responsible? A man like Nate Narkiss must have had enemies. Shouldn't you be looking into that?"

Detective Blair looked annoyed that Cora was questioning his investigation. "We'll be looking into every aspect of this case. As I said, as persons of interest, you are not to leave town for the moment."

"So please don't fly the coop," added Detective Grover. When Detective Blair shot him a look, Grover grinned sheepishly. *Unusually perky for a homicide detective.* This situation was getting worse and worse. A violent death and now they were suspects?

"Can you at least tell us what you're looking for?" asked Mallory. "You said we needed to understand what you're going to do, and now you're entering our private spaces."

"We suspect that some kind of weapon was used to inflict injury on Mr. Narkiss," Detective Blair admitted reluctantly.

"Well, then you should go ahead and search," said Cora, "We've nothing to hide!"

"Is that wise?" asked Mallory in a low voice. "I think we should talk to a lawyer first."

Cora jutted her chin out. "I'll give Becca a call tomorrow, but I'm not worried. No one here is." Cora spoke confidently, but the others exchanged looks. Lucas looked like he was about to pass out. *Does he know something about what had happened to Nate?*

Taking Cora's declaration as general consent, Detective Blair directed his officers, who spread out over the house.

Cora dragged Mallory into the kitchen and shut the door. "I felt that we had no choice but to agree to the search; it would look so odd if we refused, don't you think? Do you think they heard about the incident at the council meeting? I didn't mean it literally when I said Nate was a dead man!"

Mallory tried to reassure her. "Let's not speculate until we learn more. The police are being thorough; that's likely all this is."

What would happen once the police found out about Cora's and Georgie's very public confrontations with Nate Narkiss? Would the police jump to conclusions? She wished she had more trust in the criminal justice system, but she'd heard too many stories of innocent people being caught up in flawed investigations.

"What am I supposed to do with the chickens?" Cora asked, breaking into Mallory's thoughts. "They can't all stay on the veranda."

"What about the carriage house?" asked Mallory. Cora had given her a tour of the carriage house and discussed the plans to turn it into a deluxe apartment that the co-op owners could rent out to guests and as a vacation rental. The building was structurally sound, and the door could be secured.

"I'll have to check with Lucas," said Cora. "He's been using the loft for personal storage."

Lucas had no problem with their suggestion; in fact, he looked relieved to have something to do besides wait for the police to finish their search.

"Thank you. That sets my mind at ease," said Cora with relief. "You know what the chickens need – feed and water and such? Can you pull that together?"

Lucas nodded and headed out.

"We're going to have to round the birds up," said Cora. "It's not going to be easy."

It wasn't, but with the help of Lucas and a couple of reluctant police officers, they managed to herd the chickens out of the coop and into their temporary home. Mallory overheard the CSI officers muttering under their breath about compromised crime scenes. Lucas wouldn't let anyone else move the bags of feed and made sure the chickens had water and places to roost for the night.

When the group finished transferring the chickens, they came out to see yellow crime scene tape being extended around the coop and chicken yard with an officer standing guard. The sight brought home the reality that the police suspected foul play. Mallory shivered, feeling sick at the thought. *Who could have done this, and why?*

"I've checked with the officers, and they said I could stay and make sure the chickens are settled," Lucas told Mallory and Cora. He seemed to have regained his composure. "I'll come right back in after that." Gratefully, they left him to it.

Back in the library, Mallory glanced up at the clock over the mantlepiece. It was a few minutes past eleven. By the noise overhead, the officers were wasting no time. Hopefully, they'd be done shortly, and everyone could go to bed. Georgie had sprawled out on the sofa, and Etta looked bone-weary. Tea only helped so much. Mallory sat back in an armchair and closed her eyes, her mind wandering. It would have to be this night of all nights that everyone had been doing their own thing instead of their usual gathering in the lounge after dinner. Her eyes flew open as the implication sank in; not one of them had an alibi that could be confirmed.

☞

Mallory woke up from her doze when Detective Blair gruffly addressed Cora, letting her know that they'd finished searching the grounds and common areas and were accessing the private suites. The fire had long burned down, leaving a small pile of gently smoking ash. *How much longer was this search going to take?* It was already three a.m. If she couldn't go to bed, she could at least get some fresh air.

Cora had the same thought. "Does anyone want to join me on the veranda? It's chilly out but it would be better than being stuck in here."

Mallory ran upstairs to grab a jacket. As she passed by Georgie's open door, she could see her standing in the middle of her room, clutching a dark green silk shawl about her shoulders as officers rummaged through drawers and threw open closet doors. Catching Mallory's eye, Georgie hurried out to the landing.

"Mallory dear, this is most distressing. I hate anyone touching my things."

On the veranda, they found Cora and Etta seated in the Adirondack chairs. The thirty-foot-long open space spanned the entire back of the house and offered spectacular views over Fairfield, the Strait of Juan de Fuca and the Olympic Mountains. Along with a mishmash of comfortable rattan seats and throw-draped Adirondack chairs, one of Etta's easels was set up in one corner.

The chill in the air bit through as Mallory zipped up her jacket. It was barely light out and as the sun rose, it cast everything in a warm, golden light.

"I thought we could all do with fresh tea," said Amira, setting down a tray with a teapot and cups. Everyone gratefully accepted a steaming cup of vanilla rooibos, even Mallory although she was already swimming in tea. She found it comforting to hold the cup of fragrant brew to warm up her hands.

"Where's Lucas?" asked Cora, looking around.

"They let him stay in the carriage house with the chickens," said Amira. The morning quiet was broken by sounds of furniture being shoved aside and doors and drawers being opened and shut.

"I hope they don't leave too much of a mess," muttered Cora. "If they go through my study and disturb my filing, I'll never find anything again."

"Would you be able to tell?" scoffed Etta. "It's already a disaster in there."

As the two of them bickered back and forth, it was clear they both were trying to distract themselves and the others from what was going on inside the house and the questions they were all asking themselves. How did Nate die? And were any of them really suspects?

Mallory tried to remember what she had seen that night. In her mind's eye she pictured Nate's outstretched form, his unseeing eyes, and what looked like a bruise or blood on his cheek. Was that the blow that killed him and if so, were the police looking for a blunt instrument? Amira had mentioned seeing blood. How could the police suspect that any of them had the strength to hit Nate, let alone fell him to the ground? She tried to focus on the logistics of the crime, pushing to the back of her mind for the moment the thought that kept intruding; how big of a threat had Nate been to Cora and her beloved Bellavista community?

"How long are we staying out?" asked Etta. "The police should be done by now. I'm cold and my knee is acting up. What on earth are they looking for?"

"A weapon," answered Amira matter-of-factly. "There was a lot of blood on the ground. I suspect an artery was hit because of the extent of hemorrhage."

As they all adjusted to the implications of that, Detective Blair came out onto the verandah with Detective Grover and another officer, both of whom were wearing gloves and holding items wrapped in plastic. Amira gave a start as she spotted what they were carrying.

Detective Blair stopped in front of Amira and gestured to Detective Grover, who presented what looked like silver utensils. "Ms. Hassan, we found these items in your rooms. Would you mind telling us what these are and what you're doing with them?"

Amira returned his gaze steadily, but she'd gone pale, and her voice shook as she answered. "I was a surgeon in my home country, and these surgical instruments were part of my kit."

"Aren't such items supposed to be stored at a clinic or the hospital?" asked Detective Blair. "Why would you need to have a set at home?"

"I'm no longer practicing, officer, but I kept them as...as a memento."

Detective Blair lowered his chin. "Ms. Hassan, I'm asking you to please accompany us to the station. We have a few questions to ask you."

Cora looked like she was about to protest, but Mallory put her hand on Cora's arm to steady her. The police were now approaching Georgie, who was standing at the edge of the verandah with her back to the view. With the early rays of the sun highlighting her silhouette and the fringes of her shawl, Georgie looked like an old-school flamenco dancer.

Detective Blair held out an item. "Miss Vandervoss, we found this in your room. Would you mind identifying it for us?"

Georgie considered the proffered object, a large red and black fan, folded shut. "Why, it's a fan, Detective. A gift from a dear friend in Spain many years ago."

"Would you care to demonstrate how it works?"

Georgie took the fan and with one fluid motion flicked it open. She waved it gracefully in front of her.

"May I?" asked Detective Blair, holding out his hand for the fan. When he held it away from him and pressed the embossed edge of the fan, the edge fell back to reveal a razor-thin stiletto.

There was a collective gasp. Georgie's hands flew up to her cheeks. "Oh, my goodness. I had no idea. How did you ever figure that out?"

Detective Blair's cheeks colored. "I have, um, an interest in antique weaponry and I've seen this kind of fan before, in a museum. When I spotted the distinctive handle, I thought it prudent to check it out."

He pressed the edge again and the sinister-looking blade slid from view. Handing the fan back to Detective Grover to bag, he asked formally, "Ms. Vandervoss, I'm afraid you'll need to accompany us as well."

"Oh, my goodness, officer," murmured Georgie, clutching her hands together.

"What about me, detective?" called out Etta brusquely. "Are you going to bring me in because you found a palette knife in my room?"

Detective Blair grunted. "Not at the moment, Ms. Hoskins."

As the officers escorted Georgie and Amira into the house, Cora announced, "I'm going too!" and strode out after them.

Chapter 5

> *"Prepare for the unexpected."*
> *- Raquel DeWitt, The Smart Woman's Guide to Getting it Done.*

"Let me go instead," said Mallory, following Cora out into the hall. "You've been up all night."

"Would you mind staying with Etta? I'm concerned about how she's taking this, and we need someone who can handle any reporters who might show up." Cora gave her hand a reassuring squeeze and rushed out.

Detective Grover was escorting Etta inside, saying, "We apologize if you find your personal belongings out of order. We tried to minimize the disruption as much as possible."

The police had been respectful for the most part during their search, but it could not be denied that the house was in disarray. Drawers had been pulled out and emptied. Cupboard doors were left ajar. Etta headed to her suite, a determined look on her face, while Mallory did what she could to restore order to the main floor.

As Mallory tidied up, her mind ran on an endless loop of questions. *Did the police really suspect that Amira had killed Nate with her surgical instruments? What would have driven Amira to do so? Was the fear of potentially losing the Kitchen Cooperative and her home so great that it clouded all reason and drove Amira to act impulsively?* Although she'd only known Amira for a couple of days, Mallory couldn't see that happening. It didn't make sense.

Mallory next considered Georgie. Could Georgie really have been involved in Nate Narkiss's murder? Georgie had demonstrated a legendary attachment to her family home; an attachment so strong that Cora didn't have the heart to tell her to move out even after she'd purchased the Bellavista property. *Was Georgie so threatened by the potential loss of her beloved family home that she'd attacked Nate?* She tried to push away the disturbing idea. *Could Georgie have acquired the fan weapon during the war?*

Mallory's head swirled with confusion, and something else. She was starving. Many hours had passed since dinnertime, and the day had fully dawned. She'd never be able to fall asleep, so she might as well have breakfast.

After eating her fill of Amira's fresh bread, she made up a tray of warmed rolls with jam and tea for Etta. How was Etta taking Nate's murder and Amira and Georgie's detention? She sent a quick text to Cora asking for an update, as it was about an hour since the police had brought Georgie and Amira in for questioning. There was no reply.

Etta responded to her tentative knock on the door of her ground-floor studio with a brusque, "Door's unlocked."

Chaos reigned, with art supplies, brushes and paint tubes scattered all over the table and floor.

"I came by to check on how your cleanup was going and bring you breakfast," said Mallory.

"See for yourself. It'll take me all morning to put everything back in order."

"Let me help," offered Mallory. Etta waved her inside.

Light streamed in through diamond-paned windows framed by linen drapes. The warm white walls, bare wooden floors and French doors that led out onto the back terrace created the perfect backdrop for the exuberant canvases propped up against the walls.

Mallory studied Etta's latest paintings. The massive canvases, large enough to cover entire walls, were swirls of reds, oranges and yellows, with splashes of blue and purple that drew your gaze in and invited you to explore their depths. The brush strokes were broader and much looser than in the detailed portraits for which Etta was known.

"These are gorgeous, Etta. I've always admired your portraits—but these abstracts are amazing. When did you change your painting style?"

"Can't be stuck doing what I've always done."

Mallory began gathering up paint brushes and organizing them into the empty holders hanging from a large pegboard. Thanks to Etta's meticulous labelling, the work went quickly, the two of them working side by side. She was about to mention Georgie and Amira when Etta broke the silence.

"I can't believe Georgie's gotten herself arrested." Etta's hand trembled, and the bag she was holding dropped to the floor.

Mallory crouched down to gather the tubes of paint that tumbled out. "I don't think either of them have been charged, but it's upsetting that Georgie and Amira are being questioned." She handed the bag back to Etta.

"Sorry. I'm more clumsy than usual these days."

"Do you know why Georgie had a weapon in her room?" asked Mallory, continuing to sort through supplies.

"Something she picked up on one of her jaunts abroad is my guess." Etta did not seem bothered by the fact that Georgie possessed such an item. "Have you seen her rooms? Stuffed to the gills, part antiques fair, part flea market. I bet it's a tourist trinket." Etta spoke confidently, but her hands still shook as she put away her supplies.

"I heard a rumor that Georgie worked with the French Resistance. Is that true?"

Etta let out a short laugh. "Impossible. Georgie is eighty-two. She would have been a mere child during the war. Georgie loves to be dramatic. That's not to say she doesn't have a past. A sensational one, if her stories are to be believed. But she's not a killer, and the police are fools if they think that."

"Why do you think Nate was here last night?" asked Mallory. That point had been bothering her.

Etta ran her hands through her short hair. "I don't know. When he came by a few days ago, that was at my invitation. But Cora made it clear she wasn't interested in talking to him so I've no idea why he'd come back unless he wanted to make peace with Cora after that awful council meeting. Or stir things up more."

"Why did you think his plan would be a good option? Cora was so opposed to the idea."

"Because it was our only option," said Etta flatly. "You don't think I haven't considered other partners? I reached out to Jacob Prentiss, who's a big deal heritage restorer in town, but he never called me back. He doesn't need the work, and why would he be interested in our kind of development? Nate was willing to make a deal with us because he wanted Bellavista. I should have known that the house was the one thing that neither Cora nor Georgie was ever going to compromise on. But I had to try something."

She sighed deeply. "And now he's dead and Georgie has gotten herself pulled in for questioning. Well, the police will realize soon enough that they haven't got anything on her, and she'll be back home."

"Georgie's very attached to Bellavista," said Mallory. "At the council meeting, she was distraught when Nate claimed he had an arrangement with Saffron."

"Georgie lives and breathes her family history. She's not making up the tragic stories about her family. They really did happen. I heard that her great-grandfather was one of the original timber barons. Georgie believes the family suffered so much as payback from the spirits of the trees they clear-cut. Make what you will of that."

"How upset was Georgie about possibly having to sell Bellavista? Enough to act hastily and do something she wouldn't normally have?"

Etta shook her head. "Georgie may be dramatic, but she's not violent. I can't imagine her having anything to do with what happened to Nate. I'm sure the police will realize that the fan is nothing more than a curio and that Georgie had nothing to do with Nate's death."

"What about Amira? Do you think she could have anything to do with Nate's death?"

Etta pursed her lips, frowning. "I really can't see her doing anything violent like that." Etta gave Mallory a hard look. "Do you know Amira's background?"

"I know that she and her son were refugees from Syria who were sponsored by Cora's gardening group, and that she was a doctor in Damascus."

"Amira lost her husband in the war. He was a fellow doctor, and when the hospital they worked at was bombed, he was killed. She managed to get across the border into Turkey with their son and stayed in a refugee camp for two years before crossing the sea into Greece. She hasn't been able to retrain here in Canada, so she created work for herself and founded the Kitchen Cooperative, which has been a great success. Despite that, I know that she still grieves the loss of her profession; I suspect that's why she held onto her surgical tools. But for the police to think she used them to kill…I just can't see it!"

"Why hasn't Amira tried to retrain as a doctor? Is it so difficult to do?" asked Mallory.

Etta snorted. "Do you know how many placements there were for foreign surgical specialists last year in Canada? Five. Five in the entire country. Even if Amira won a placement, it would mean being apart from her son for a long time, and she is not able to face that. It was tough enough for her to let Amir go study music in Vancouver."

Etta finished putting away the tubes of paint. "The police are letting the real killer get away while they dither with innocent people. Hopefully, they'll come to their senses soon!"

Mallory hoped she was right. She left Etta to her work and went out into the hallway to check her phone. Cora still hadn't responded. Well, she wasn't going to get anything done waiting around worrying. A long walk by the ocean would clear her head.

Lucas came bounding down the stairs, startling her. She'd forgotten about Lucas. When he saw her, he stopped short and said, "I'm trying to find Cora. There's a bunch of reporters outside. Where'd everybody go?"

"I'm sorry, we forgot to tell you! Everything happened so fast, and I got distracted tidying up after the police search. The police took Amira and Georgie down to the station about an hour ago. Cora went with them."

"Are you kidding me?" Lucas clutched at his curls. "Why do the police suspect them?"

"The police found some suspicious-looking items in their rooms and took them in for questioning. I've texted Cora but she's not answering."

Lucas looked like he wasn't listening. "I gotta go," he said, before dashing downstairs. The back door slammed shut.

Grabbing her jacket, Mallory headed for the door, determined to wade through the crowd of reporters with a "no comment" and go on her walk. As she reached for the handle, the door was thrust open, and in flew someone in a bright yellow jumpsuit and sunglasses, black curls blowing wildly about her face.

"Shut the door!" the newcomer cried. She flung the door closed, threw down her bags and pushed back her aviators. "Why's there a crowd of reporters outside? What's going on?"

Mallory stared in shock. Saffron Kalinsky in the flesh, all five-foot-ten of her.

Hands on hips, Saffron stared right back. "Mallory McKenzie-Chu! What on earth are *you* doing here?"

Chapter 6

> "Finger pointing gets you nowhere."
> – Raquel DeWitt, *The Smart Woman's Guide to Getting it Done.*

Before Mallory could respond, the door flew open again and Cora, Amira and Georgie stumbled inside.

"Shut the door!" shrieked Cora. Mallory could hear reporters calling out as she slammed the door shut.

"Oh, thank goodness, I thought we'd never get through! My goodness, Saffron! We wondered who was in the cab ahead of us. What are you doing here?" Cora exclaimed, embracing her niece. "I'm delighted of course, but we weren't expecting you!"

Saffron hugged her aunt and Amira, and kissed Georgie on the cheek. "Turns out I have a lot of unused vacation, now that I'm working for a European company, so I thought I'd do a stopover before I head to New York." She eyed Mallory. "Looks like a lot has been happening since I left. Why are there reporters outside? What's happened?"

"I've been fingerprinted," announced Georgie, "Cora and Amira too."

"What?" cried Saffron as Mallory looked on, aghast at this new development.

Cora insisted on a cup of tea before she said anything else, so they gathered around the kitchen table. With Georgie's helpful additions, Cora explained everything that had led up to their police station visit, while Saffron peppered her with questions and looked increasingly severe. Amira was still pale and shaken. Etta gave her a searching look when she came into the kitchen, and Amira tried to smile reassuringly.

"Don't worry, it's nothing," Cora was saying, seeing Saffron's frown deepen. "The police got hold of the council meeting footage and heard me say that Nate was a dead man and Georgie threaten to kill him to save Bellavista. They also heard that I had an earlier run-in with Nate, although I don't know how they found out about that."

"What do you mean, it's nothing?" shrieked Saffron. "Someone was murdered on our property and three of you have ended up as the prime suspects!" Saffron turned to Mallory. "Don't you work for Cora? How could you let her agree to a police search?"

At this unexpected attack, Mallory's defenses went up. "How was I supposed to stop them? I only arrived a few days ago. My job is to guide the cooperative through its development application process. I didn't plan to be part of a murder investigation."

"How could we have known you've been in cahoots with Nate?" shot back Cora to Saffron. "Having conversations with him without telling me? I was completely blindsided when he told me!"

Saffron crossed her arms and said, "Look, Etta and I knew you would resist the idea of working with Sand Dollar, but we needed a professional assessment and a partner. Nate's project fits in really well with our expansion plans, and it would be foolish not to take him up on his offer."

"Etta!" cried Georgie, in a tone of betrayal.

"We needed to do something!" Etta said, lowering her chin mulishly. "All we were doing was going in circles, never agreeing on anything; we had to move forward."

Cora's mouth dropped open at this double betrayal. "You and Saffron colluded behind my back? How could you do that? And how does Nate's monstrous luxury resort 'fit in' with our community hub? They—they're absolutely polar opposites!"

Saffron shook her head. "Cora, we weren't 'colluding' — we had a few Zoom calls with Nate. If you would…"

"What? Give up control over my life?" Eyes sparking and face flushing, Cora wasn't backing down. "Walk away from my dream? I was running Bellavista while you were still in grade school. What gives you the right to take meetings behind my back, when I never asked you to? Do you think someone turns seventy and their brain stops working? I know your father asked me to ensure you were taken care of before he died, and I've done that by protecting your share of Bellavista, but there is such a thing as respect, Saffron. You and Etta could have told me what you were planning, and we could have discussed it."

"You don't think we tried?" argued Etta. "When do you listen to us? We're supposed to be a cooperative, but all we've been hearing is what you want, what you're going to do. You don't take into account any of our input, including mine or Amira's. We have ideas too, but it seems what we think doesn't matter. How is this all supposed to work if we make the community even bigger but can't communicate?"

There was a pause, as everyone waited for Cora to lash back. In the silence, the grandfather clock began to chime out the hour, and the chickens clucked for their feed. Cora took a deep breath.

"You're right," she said. "I haven't been listening to you. To any of you. I've been so focused on getting this redevelopment off the ground that I've lost track of who it's for in the first place. Our community needs to come first. I'm sorry, Etta."

Etta looked keenly at her friend, and nodded, accepting the apology.

"I'm sorry as well," added Saffron, to Mallory's surprise. "I should have let you know that I was discussing Bellavista with Nate Narkiss. If I'd been more open about that, you and Georgie might have been less hostile toward him and not be in this predicament."

This was a new Saffron. The Saffron she'd known would have worn her argument down to the nubs before admitting she was in the wrong.

"Did the officers tell you anything more about how Nate died?" asked Mallory.

"They wouldn't tell us anything," said Cora with frustration. "I'm guessing that Nate must have been stabbed as they kept Amira's tools and Georgie's fan for analysis."

"A small wound inflicted must have been minimal in size but lethal in impact," Amira observed. "To bleed so profusely and so quickly, the stab wound must have hit a major artery. Like on the neck or upper arm."

Which Amira would know about because she was a surgeon. Dismissing the thought, Mallory concentrated on what Cora was saying.

"A couple of officers were saying that the person who delivered the blow that knocked Nate out must have been at least five-nine, with good upper body strength, because of where and how hard the blow landed. They're waiting for the official coroner's report to confirm, but that must rule any of us out."

Everyone in the room relaxed for a moment until Mallory spoke. "If Nate was stabbed while unconscious, that could have been done by anybody and they wouldn't have to be five foot nine, right?"

Everyone stared at Mallory. "But I'm no forensics expert," she added hastily. *Should have kept my mouth shut. Better hope that the coroner's report rules out any connection to the Bellavista community.*

Saffron stood. "Well, you must all be completely exhausted after being up all night. I know I am after travelling for twenty-four hours, and I desperately need a shower. I'll see you at dinner."

Collecting her bags in the hallway, Saffron headed for the stairs. Her stomach knotting with a mixture of anxiety and self-consciousness, Mallory ran up after her. How was she supposed to act around Saffron? There was no playbook for this situation.

Saffron paused at the door to the room, taking in that Mallory was already in occupation. "Looks like we'll have to put up with each other for a while. I could get a hotel, but I really need to be on-site. *Someone* has to watch over Cora. Do you think you can handle being roommates again?"

"O-of course. No problem."

"One other thing, Mallory. I came here because Etta wrote to me about the development application and how Cora hired you as the project manager. This is my home and Cora is my family. I'm the one who's looking out for her. I'd advise you to stick to what you do and stay in your lane."

Flinging a towel over her shoulder, Saffron stalked out of the room.

༄

At dinner that evening, Georgie regaled everyone with her account of being interrogated at the police station. After her initial frightened reaction, as well as a long afternoon nap, she viewed the whole experience as another big adventure.

"The police confiscated my Albanico fan," Georgie told them, as platters of fried halloumi salad and maple-glazed salmon were passed around.

"And your nunchuks, bear spray and knuckle rings," added Cora grimly. "It appears that our Georgie has an arsenal in her rooms. Which leads me to ask, why on earth do you have so many lethal weapons in your possession?"

"Gifts, my dear. My... special friends always made sure I was well-armed, although I drew the line at firearms."

"What were you doing to require that level of protection?" asked Saffron. "Were you a spy? Ex-CIA? What?"

Georgie eyed her. "There may come a time when I'm ready to share my memoirs with the world. But not now."

Saffron said nothing, but she looked ready to burst with questions. There was a time when the two of them would have speculated on wilder and wilder scenarios involving Georgie, collapsing into giggles. That camaraderie was gone, replaced by an awkward stiffness. Saffron may have grown in self-awareness since Mallory had last seen her, but that maturity didn't extend to forgiving the past between them.

Mallory had fallen into the habit of helping Amira clear the table and do the dishes. It was still light out when they were finished, so Mallory put on her jacket and headed outside. Sharing a room with Saffron meant that she didn't have a space to decompress after the day, so Mallory was spending more time in the gardens. Her rambles had made her familiar with the property, which helped as she visualized the changes that would be required and how much work would need to be done.

Outside, there was an incongruous sight: five peacocks, their flamboyant tail feathers sweeping the ground, strutted about the lawn, lording it over the flock of frazzled chickens. The rooster that had jousted with Nate Narkiss's shoe was hopping up and down on the roof of the coop, crowing, as Cora and Georgie shooed the peacocks away. Saffron came running out the back door holding a broom.

"Who let the chickens out of the carriage house?" shouted Mallory, joining their efforts. "What are peacocks even doing here?" Mallory waved her arms at the large birds while trying to avoid their sharp beaks. She grabbed a bucket and started brandishing it in front of the peacocks.

"They're escapees from the local petting zoo!" Saffron wielded the broom, trying to disperse the invaders. Her curls blew wildly about her face, and she pushed them out of her eyes.

"They breed like crazy! The park refuses to take responsibility!" cried Cora, her topknot coming loose. "Everyone I call says the peacocks aren't their problem. I called animal control, and they sent someone, but they couldn't capture the birds. The neighbor next door feeds them, so they'll never leave. They're a complete menace!"

Saffron swatted the broom, careful not to hit the birds, trying to scare them away from the coop, which was still wrapped in yellow police tape. The large birds observed her efforts dispassionately. One of them reared back, opening up its tail to its full glory.

"Stop that!" someone yelled.

A man sprinted toward them, puffing from the exertion. It was Pierce Wexford from the council meeting.

"Leave those peacocks alone!"

"Pierce!" hissed Saffron. She confronted the irate man. "I need to get these pests off our lawn. They poop all over the grass and terrorize the chickens."

"Don't you touch my birds. They're not doing anything!"

"They're stealing the chicken's feed and stressing the flock so much they're barely producing," cried Cora.

"I heard you and Nate Narkiss creating a ruckus out here the other day. You've got all sorts of people running in and out at all hours, lights flashing, revving engines and what-not. That's why your chickens are stressed. I heard there was a murder here the other night! Nate Narkiss found dead in your coop!"

"How did you hear about that?" asked Cora, startled. "It's not even on the news yet!"

"I saw the police cars last night and that group of reporters today. I suspected something nefarious was going on!"

"Did the police come and speak to you about Nate Narkiss?" asked Mallory. Pierce had had his own run-in with the land developer at the council meeting.

Pierce pressed his lips together. "I don't have to answer that. I'm here to stop you interfering with these beautiful creatures!"

"Beautiful creatures? They're vermin with wings!" Cora's topknot had completely unraveled by this point.

Pierce sputtered. "The only vermin here is that ridiculous rooster of yours. Having a rooster is against city bylaws. That one – he pointed a bony finger at one of the chickens, who chose that inopportune moment to loudly crow – is a male!"

"Leave Gregory Peck alone!" cried Georgie, flying toward the coop.

"It even has a male name - you can't tell me it's not a rooster!"

"I have a male name, and I'm not male!" said Georgie.

"Oh, really?" sneered Pierce.

Georgie stared him down, lifted her top and flashed her assets to a stunned audience. Mallory clamped a hand over her mouth, not sure if she was going to scream or laugh. Pierce's eyes bugged right out of his head. He turned several shades of red before turning on his heel and stalking off.

"Georgie!" hissed Cora through gritted teeth. "Not. Helpful."

"It stopped Pierce from talking," said Georgie airily. "Anyways, I'm wearing my best brassiere, so what's the problem?"

As Cora bundled the unrepentant exhibitionist toward the house, Saffron fell apart laughing, tears streaming, as did Mallory. When they both recovered, they locked eyes, and memories of how much they used to laugh together, before their falling out, shimmered between them. Saffron abruptly turned back to the chickens, and the moment passed. With a twinge of regret, Mallory helped shoo the last stragglers into the carriage house, temporarily securing the door by pushing the broom through the curved door handles.

"How on earth did they escape?" asked Saffron, wiping perspiration from her forehead. "I suppose they'll have to stay in the carriage house until the police remove the yellow crime-scene tape? When Lucas comes back, I'll ask him to secure the doors." She brushed off her clothing and headed toward the house.

Mallory paused before following Saffron. The back of her neck tingled. *Am I being watched? Is Pierce still loitering about?*

She scanned the bushes bordering the property but couldn't see anything.

Inside, Cora was fuming about their neighbor. "Pierce is delusional!" Cora twisted her mop of hair up and secured it with a clip. "He thinks he's the lord of the manor with peacocks strutting about his grounds."

"Like a Raj of the British Empire," added Georgie.

Saffron's brow furrowed. "Unfortunately, Pierce is right about Gregory Peck. I've been reading up on the city's bylaws, and we're not allowed to keep a rooster. Too many people complain about morning crowing."

"No!" cried Georgie, "I'll fight to the death for him!"

"Let's hope it doesn't come to that, but until we figure out what to do, we have to keep GP out of Pierce's sight."

"We've been keeping him in a small cage in the alcove in the kitchen," said Cora.

Saffron shook her head. "You can't do that — the Kitchen Cooperative could lose its license."

Cora's face fell. "I forgot about that."

"What if we kept Gregory Peck upstairs?" Mallory suggested. "If we put the cage on the verandah, he would be out of sight but still have access to space and fresh air."

"The problem is, when the sun comes up, he can't help but crow, and that's what Pierce complains about," explained Cora.

Mallory thought for a minute. "I could bring him inside at night again. That's what Georgie was doing before, right? There's a little landing outside the door to our room where we could put his cage and that way, he wouldn't see the sun rise and know to crow."

"I suppose that might work for now," said Saffron. "Although I'm not keen on having farmyard creatures indoors."

"Wonderful solution, most ingenious," interjected Georgie. She planted a kiss on Mallory's cheek. "That's all settled. I smell fresh coffee, which means dessert is being served."

Georgie looped her arm through Cora's and headed to the library, where the household had gathered after dinner. Mallory hoped she wasn't going to regret her offer to take charge of the little rooster.

"Is Pierce your immediate neighbor?" she asked Saffron.

"He lives next door in a house he has named Downton."

Mallory laughed out loud, and Saffron managed a reluctant grin.

"As I said, he really does think he's lord of the manor. You should see the mugs the Victoria Heritage Society issued with a picture of Downton on it. Pierce sells them in his store. He made Cora's life difficult when he moved in next door, filing petitions with the city, claiming Cora was bringing down the neighborhood with her urban farming."

She frowned. "Would you believe that Pierce is a die-hard birder? That's why I don't understand his opposition to the chicken coop. The peacocks he adores are useless interlopers to the region while the chickens are useful producers!"

Saffron narrowed her eyes. "I bet Pierce was the one who ratted to the police about Cora's other run-in with Nate." She ran her fingers through her hair, dislodging a couple of errant feathers. "I don't like how the police are focusing on Cora and Georgie. They can't really believe that two frail old women had anything to do with Nate's assault. Or Amira, for that matter."

Cora was strong and lean from years of early morning ocean swims and yoga, and Georgie was a dancing queen in her eighties, but now was not the time to contradict Saffron, especially when the frostiness showed signs of thawing. If Saffron was planning to stick around for the foreseeable future, she needed to stay in her good graces to make this project work.

Chapter 7

> "No news is good news."
> - Raquel DeWitt, *The Smart Woman's Guide to Getting it Done.*

"There's a news conference on Nate's murder at 7 p.m. tonight," announced Cora, as Saffron and Mallory joined the others in the library. "One of the officers mentioned it. If we tune in, we could learn how the investigation is going."

Cora turned on the old TV, and they all gathered to watch. A rumpled-looking Detective Blair appeared on screen.

"We are following up on all leads. The public should be reassured that this does not appear to be a random incident; we believe that Nate Narkiss was specifically targeted. We ask that if any members of the public have information concerning this incident, they please come forward."

A reporter came into the frame. *"With us today is Stan Barber, the director of The Wheelbarrow Foundation, a charitable organization supporting youth in trades."*

A stout man in a flannel shirt and jeans appeared on camera. *"As a founder, Nate put his heart and soul into The Wheelbarrow Foundation. I hope that you'll all join me on May 4th in celebrating Nate's legacy. We want to make this fundraiser our biggest one ever, to honor Nate's memory."*

"What's The Wheelbarrow Foundation?" asked Mallory.

"It's a charitable organization that supports youth entering the trades. May fourth is the annual fundraising gala for the Foundation," said Amira. "Reem's son received a scholarship from Wheelbarrow to start his plumber's training."

"Wheelbarrow is an excellent organization — I'll have to give Nate that," said Cora. "Lucas did his training through Wheelbarrow too."

The reporter appeared back on the screen. Next to her was a short, stocky man with a scruffy beard in a newsboy cap.

"We're here with Brad Jobson, co-owner of Sand Dollar Developments. Mr. Jobson, you must have been shocked to hear of the death of your longtime business partner. We understand you were out of town and only got the news on your return today."

"Nate was my business partner, but first of all he was my best friend," Jobson said, his voice choking.

"I've met him," said Saffron, staring at the screen. "He was on my Zoom call with Nate."

"Nate's development ideas pushed the envelope, so they weren't always popular," said Jobson on camera. "On the night Nate was killed, someone vandalized Nate's office."

Then a sign reading "Sand Dollar Development" appeared on the screen, with a message spray-painted in red: "You'll get what you deserve!"

A close-up of Brad Jobson replaced the defaced sign as he spoke again. "I'll say that right back! I'm offering a $10,000 reward for any information that leads to the arrest and conviction of the person who killed Nate."

Detective Blair appeared again on the screen. "We hope that this generous reward brings in some helpful tips that will lead to the killer."

A flurry of microphones appeared in front of Detective Blair.

"Detective Blair! Have you any suspects?"

"Our investigation is still ongoing," he responded. "All I can say at this stage is that we've identified several persons of interest, and we're continuing to follow up on all leads." Detective Blair nodded and walked off, reporters running after him.

A news anchor with an impressive blowout appeared onscreen to conclude the report. *"While police have not named any persons of interest, it is widely known that Nate Narkiss dealt with several aggressive confrontations at a city council meeting on the night he was killed."*

Mallory's stomach dropped as footage from the council meeting came on screen. A wildly gesticulating Cora yelled, "You're a dead man!" as Nate smirked. Georgie appeared delivering her Scarlett O'Hara "if-I-have-to-kill" line to Nate. The last clip showed Art's red scooter speeding through the hall before slamming on the brakes, inches away from Nate.

"Oh, wonderful," said Saffron sourly. "Nothing like having a giant target on our backs."

☙

The impact from the news report was as immediate as Saffron had feared. First came the calls from local reporters trying to coax statements from the residents.

"No comment!" said Mallory for the umpteenth time before hanging up. She was tempted to turn off her phone but hesitated in case she missed an important call; she was still holding out hope an investor or development partner would contact them. Saffron was having a similarly hard time of it, arguing with someone on her cell phone. Every time Mallory peered out the window from behind the velvet drapes in the library, she could spot one or two reporters loitering out front. It had not even been a day since the news conference, and interest was high. They were all avoiding going out unless absolutely necessary. Amira and Etta were forced to sneak out for an appointment with Lucas's help: he pulled the shared car right up to the back veranda door and they hid under blankets while he drove them out.

Over the next few days, there was even more fallout as friends and acquaintances began distancing themselves.

"I've been dropped by my theatre group!" a devastated Georgie told them. "The drama society said they didn't want to be associated with someone of my notoriety!"

"That group should be thrilled with any publicity," muttered Etta to Mallory. "Last production, I counted five people in the audience and the tickets were free."

Cora was equally distraught when several acquaintances who had expressed interest in buying into the housing cooperative backed out.

"First Flora Plemmens, who I thought was a shoo-in, and now Edith Hashimoto's backing out. What are we going to do?"

The last straw was when Amira reported that orders to the Kitchen Cooperative had dropped significantly and that catering events had been cancelled.

"The customer said they couldn't be sure we would still be operating when her event happened, so she wanted to switch caterers. If business doesn't improve soon, we may not cover our expenses for the season."

While the residents commiserated around the kitchen table, Saffron pulled Mallory into the library and shut the door.

"Mallory, this is all your fault."

"What??" protested Mallory. "How is any of this my fault?"

"You let Cora and Georgie go to that council meeting and publicly threaten Narkiss, which is why the police are focusing on them! And they've got their sights on Amira too!"

"Now hold on a sec, Saffron. Could *you* have stopped those two from attending the meeting? And could *you* have prevented them from speaking up?"

"Well, you can't deny this is a complete mess. We've lost the one investor who could have saved Bellavista, and now everyone is under suspicion for his murder! You need to help me clear everyone's names."

"How am I supposed to do that?"

"Look, I'm not about to wait for the police to figure things out. I bet they're not even bothering to look at anyone else! Why would they, when Bellavista has provided three perfectly good suspects! Like it or not, we have to team up and find someone else to take the police's attention."

Mallory wasn't convinced. *I really don't want to play sleuth with Saffron. It's bad enough she's sticking her nose into my project.* "This is a job for the police. My job is to get the housing cooperative back on track. I thought you told me to stay in my lane. With the development hearing next week, I need to be ready and there's a lot still to do."

"There won't *be* a housing cooperative if we don't clear Cora and Georgie!" argued Saffron. "Who's going to join a housing cooperative where someone was murdered on-site and three of the members are suspects?"

Saffron had a valid point, but despite her own burning questions as to what happened to Nate Narkiss, Mallory's instinct for self-preservation resisted getting involved. Knowing Saffron, the minute things went south, she would be the one getting the blame.

Saffron persisted. "Cora has no idea how tight our margins are, but Etta showed me the accounts. If we don't attract some investors soon, we can say goodbye to the cooperative and this community. It won't survive this big of a setback unless we prove that no one at Bellavista had anything to do with Nate's death."

"But..."

"This project is *your* responsibility, Mallory, so *you* have to help me find out who really killed Nate Narkiss!"

Chapter 8

> "It's all in the details."
> - Raquel DeWitt, *The Smart Woman's Guide to Getting it Done.*

Resistance was futile. In short order, the library was transformed into a war room. Armed with a stack of Post-it notes, a Sharpie, and an easel with a blank canvas borrowed from Etta, they got to work.

"There was a weird incident with a guy on a mobile scooter at the town hall," said Mallory. "He tried to run Nate down. I think his name was Arthur-something...Arthur Papadopoulos? Hold on a minute." Mallory ran up to her room and rummaged through the pocket of her jacket. Back downstairs, she handed Saffron the brochure she had picked up the night of the council meeting.

"**Sand Dollar Development Sucks — Five Reasons to Avoid!**" read Saffron out loud.

1. Drafty windows!
2. Leaking balconies!
3. No soundproofing!
4. Creaking, uneven flooring!
5. Your home will turn into a money pit!

This is what your life will be like if you buy anything from crappy developer Nate Narkiss and Sand Dollar Developments! Don't trust this man with your home! Call A. Papatonis for more information

"Georgie mentioned that Art Papatonis has set up some kind of protest at Sand Dollar's construction site next door," said Mallory. "It sounded like he's been camping out front with signs."

"If Papatonis was mad enough to try to mow Narkiss down in public, he sounds like a perfect candidate for No. 1 suspect. Ok, who's next? Did Narkiss have run-ins with anyone else at the town hall?"

"Narkiss spoke with Metchosin Barnes before the meeting, and it wasn't friendly. From what Cora said, there's history there."

Mallory logged onto her laptop and began a Google search. "I've found something," she said. Saffron came over and peered at the screen showing a shot of a smiling Nate Narkiss and Metchosin Barnes in Vegas. "Victoria Power Couple Ties the Knot," she read aloud. The date was a couple of years earlier.

The door opened and Amira came in with a tray of tea and a plate of freshly baked scones. "I thought you might like some refreshments to start the day. What are you looking at? Oh, Metchosin and Nate Narkiss?"

"They were married a few years ago, and I'm guessing their split wasn't amicable," said Mallory. "I witnessed a tense encounter between Metchosin and Nate, and then she grilled him during the council meeting."

"Now we're getting somewhere!" Saffron wrote Art's name on a second Post-it and stuck it next to the first one on the board, clearly relishing her role as sleuth. As Amira settled herself on the couch next to Mallory, she turned expectantly. "Who's next?"

Cora poked her head around the door. "What are you all doing in here?" She spotted the Post-it notes with "Papatonis —Angry Client?" and "Metchosin Barnes — Angry Ex-Wife?"

"You can't really think that Metchosin had anything to do with Nate's death?" Cora protested. "She's an elected official!"

"So?" responded Saffron. "She wasn't on good terms with him, and there must be a reason for that."

"It's true that Nate wasn't the best husband."

"Aha!" Saffron pulled a chair out for Cora and ushered her into it. "You know the scoop, so do tell!"

"Oh, I feel badly that you suspect Metchosin when she's been so helpful with the housing cooperative."

"You're not doing anything wrong," said Saffron persuasively. "Tell us what you know."

"Well, after Metchosin declared her candidacy, Nate was apparently so jealous of her success that word got around he tried to sabotage her campaign."

"What did he do?"

"Soon after her announcement, rumors spread that Metchosin's platform was hostile to business interests and landowners. An article even appeared in the local paper with a title something like, "Metchosin Barnes's Big Stink." Nate always denied he had anything to do with the smear. But Metchosin suspected that he was behind it, although she couldn't prove it."

"Wow, that's a pretty nasty thing to do to your spouse," commented Mallory.

"Metchosin's no wilting lily; she renamed her campaign the "Stinky Fish" campaign, focusing on her strong business ties. Won by a landslide. But that was it for Nate and her; they broke up shortly after she was elected."

Nate Narkiss sounded like a real prize, thought Mallory. A guy who enjoyed being in control and acted out when things didn't work out the way he wanted.

Still, the case against Metchosin was rather weak.

"What reason would Metchosin have to kill Nate? It seems like all of that was in the past."

"A new election is happening in six months," said Amira. "Reem is running for council, so she knows the other candidates and told me Metchosin is running again. Perhaps Metchosin was worried that Nate was going to do something else to hurt her campaign.

She opposed his development application, so he might have taken his revenge."

"Yes, that's it!" said Saffron, moving the number one ranking to Metchosin.

"That doesn't seem like a very strong motive," said Mallory dubiously. "Especially since Metchosin was savvy enough to turn the smear into a positive. Why would she resort to murder?"

"There must be something else that Nate had on her," said Saffron. "We need to do some digging to find out."

"I don't like where this is going," said Cora, as she got to her feet. "You can't really suspect Metchosin!"

Amira shook her head, her eyes wide and troubled.

Saffron ushered her aunt and Amira gently out the door. "Don't you worry about it," she said soothingly. "We're only speculating. No one's accusing anyone of anything."

Once she had shut the door firmly behind them, Saffron turned to Mallory.

"We need to keep Cora out of this. She's too soft even when her security is under threat. You look into Art Papatonis. See if he's still protesting next door and find out what he had against Nate. I'll follow up with Metchosin."

As she always had when Saffron ran at full throttle, Mallory was scrambling in her wake to keep up. They were both in way over their heads, even if Saffron was confident in the direction the investigation was heading.

᛫ ❦ ᛫

Carrying a covered plate of Amira's freshly baked scones, Mallory walked over to the property next door in search of Art Papatonis. The huge empty lot abutting Bellavista was blocked off from the road by orange webbed temporary fencing and giant signs advertising Sand Dollar Developments and "Future Home of Rock Cliff Resort".

She found Art seated in a folding deck chair on the sidewalk out front, fast asleep with a book on his lap. His red mobile scooter was parked on the street and flanked by two large sandwich boards that read "Sand Dollar Sucks!" and "Ask Me Why!"

Mallory stood uncertainly, chewing her bottom lip as she observed Papatonis. He looked to be in his late seventies, with thick white hair, bushy eyebrows, and an equally lush white mustache. He snorted suddenly, causing Mallory to start and nearly drop the plate. When she righted herself, Papatonis was awake and staring her down with a frown.

"What do you want?" he growled.

"I brought you some treats from next door." Mallory held up the goodies enticingly. "We thought you might be peckish being out here all day."

Papatonis eyebrows rose. "Are those Kitchen Cooperative ginger-apricot scones?" he asked. Mallory handed him the plate and he tore off the waxed paper cover. "Mmmm," he said with a satisfied smile. "These are as good as Mario's were."

His eyes misted over for second before he sent a sharp look at Mallory. "Thank you," he said gruffly. Taking a scone, he offered her the plate. "Have one and sit yourself down a spell. Name's Art. Art Papatonis."

She took a still-warm scone and sat on the curb. "I'm Mallory."

They each took a bite and chewed companionably for a moment.

Mallory broke the silence. "I saw your wild ride at the council meeting. Looks like we both had a point to make with Nate Narkiss, although yours was a mite more dramatic than mine."

Papatonis let out a chuckle that ended in a sigh. "A lot of fuss about a little ol' stunt, but the way the police are going on about it, you'd think I ran him over multiple times. Good thing there was the city webcast on record; showed I never even came close to him."

Mallory started to say something, but Papatonis cut her off.

"If you're about to ask me why, I'll save you the trouble. I wanted to scare him a little, let him feel what it was like to realize you're not in control of your life, that in a blink of a second someone else could change it forever. Sand Dollar Developments did that to my life."

"What did they do to you?"

"Mario and I thought we'd found paradise when we bought a refurbished townhouse by the water, Heritage Acres. He'd always wanted to live by the ocean, so we put all our retirement savings into the purchase. Not a year in, everything started to break down. First the windows wouldn't seal properly — ocean drafts are freezing cold, then the leaks began, first with the balconies and then inside. Sand Dollar promised to fix everything, but they dragged their feet. We were living in a construction zone for years."

"That's really awful," said Mallory. She'd read about the leaky condos of the nineties and how devastating remediation bills were to property owners.

"I've tried to get the condo owners' association to deal with the problems; they keep bringing in Sand Dollar to make the repairs, even when the materials are poor quality, and the work isn't done well. I don't know why the association won't consider hiring another company. Maybe they're all the same. I want to sue, but the association refuses. I think they're scared that if we take Sand Dollar to court, we'll be tied up in legal wrangling for years. The remediation took all our savings. Mario had to live with scaffolding across his beloved view and nonstop construction every day. He died last year, never getting a moment with an unobstructed view. I blame Sand Dollar for the stress, and Nate Narkiss for breaking his promise!"

"I'm so sorry," said Mallory. "It must be awful to have your home turn into a living nightmare. What are you going to do now?"

"Narkiss may be gone, but Sand Dollar is still in business. The Rock Cliff Resort development here is speeding ahead, so I've got to spread the word so folks know not to trust this company." He crossed his arms and sat back in his chair. "My signs and I aren't going anywhere!"

Mallory had a sudden thought. If Papatonis had seen Cora while she was out walking the night Nate was killed, he could validate her alibi.

"Cora was very upset the night of the council meeting and she walked back to Bellavista herself. Tall woman with white hair in a topknot. Did you happen to see her that night?"

"No, I was..." Papatonis bit off what he was going to say. "I didn't see her." He scowled, his friendliness evaporating. "Why all the questions? My business is my business. I don't need to tell you nothing."

Chapter 9

> "Expect others to question your decisions."
> - Raquel DeWitt, *The Smart Woman's Guide to Getting it Done.*

On the way back to the house, Mallory's phone pinged. The text read:

OMG SIS! Chicken Coop Murder is trending on my group What's App!!! I heard about it from a location scout in Victoria!

Mallory's little sister, Gretchen, was in Toronto working on location as a production assistant on a Hollymark movie. With her extensive virtual network, it was no surprise she kept apprised of Victoria news. Another text appeared:

What's going on?? R U ok???
Do M&D know???

Great. All she needed was a full-blown family crisis instigated by her little sister. She quickly texted back:

I'm fine. Nothing to worry about. Not in danger. DON'T TELL MUM AND DAD.

How long would it be before Gretchen spilled the beans? It was unlikely that her parents would hear about the murder otherwise, as the death of a small-town developer was hardly national news. *Should I call Mum and Dad?* Her father would pressure her to come home. Asian parents never fully accepted that their kids grew up into fully functional, autonomous adults, no matter their age. Her mother might understand why she needed to stay for Cora's sake; her father wouldn't. He prioritized family security above all else, and unless his chicks were safely accounted for, he never rested entirely easy. Mallory sighed.

As if on cue, her phone pinged again. A text that read:

Call me.

Oh no. She did not need her big brother bearing down on her. Theo would keep texting or calling until she responded. That dynamic would never change.

She dialed his number.

"Theo McKenzie-Chu," he answered. Theo's salutation never varied, even when he knew exactly who was calling him.

"Did Gretchen text you? I told her, I'm fine. I'm not in any danger."

"A murder happened in the house where you're staying."

"Technically, it happened in the chicken coop, not the house."

"Are you a suspect? Do you need a lawyer?

As an accountant specializing in forensic work, Theo was often hired by law firms, so he had a roster of legal buddies with whom he golfed. With his massive build and numerous tattoos, Theo looked more like a bouncer than an accountant. People were disconcerted to learn that behind the brawn was a razor-sharp mind with a talent for numbers.

"The police took our statements and told us to stay in town. That's it." No need to mention that the police had taken three of them in for questioning.

"You gave a statement to the police without a lawyer present?"

"Theo, it's fine."

"I'm calling someone right now."

"Theo! Come on, I can take care of myself." Theo wouldn't let it go until she said she had legal advice. "I'm seeing a lawyer later today." Becca Gill was technically a lawyer, but not a criminal one.

Theo reluctantly agreed not to call one of his legal pals.

"Did you call Mum and Dad yet?"

Seriously? She was thirty-nine to Theo's forty-two, but that three-year difference would always let him think he could boss her around.

"If I tell them what happened, they'll worry and nag me to come back. I'm perfectly safe and there's nothing to worry about."

"At least text Mum what's happening. Otherwise, Gretchen will get to them first and you know how Dad is. If you don't want him on the next plane out because he thinks you're about to be arraigned on murder charges, call Mum."

He had a point. If anyone could top Georgie in the drama department, it was her little sister, with her dad running a close second. Theo would never not be her older brother, and Walter Chu would never not be an Asian father.

She got Theo off the phone at last by agreeing to contact their parents. She sent her mum a text saying she was fine and not to worry. It was delaying the inevitable, but Mallory needed space and time to think before dealing with the burden of her family's collective anxiety.

☙

"AAAAANND, forward fold!"

Mallory obediently folded her body forward until her outstretched hands touched the cork floor. After briefing Saffron on her encounter with Art Papatonis, Mallory agreed to accompany Saffron on her visit to Metchosin Barnes. What she hadn't counted on was participating in Metchosin's eleven a.m. hot yoga class — and Metchosin herself wasn't even teaching this morning. Perspiration dripped into her eyes, blurring her vision.

I'm upside down and I've sweated out most of my water content ---- how is this good for me?

"I don't know if I can do this much longer," she whispered to Saffron, who didn't appear to hear her, lost in a bubble of Zen as she folded herself into a pose.

Guess this class really is "no sweat" for her.

People often underestimated Saffron's natural athleticism based on what they thought someone of her shape and size could do; Saffron worked hard to dismantle pre-conceptions of plus-sized women. Early in her modeling career, a shot of Saffron in a ballgown hanging by one bent leg from a trapeze ---- Saffron's idea ---- went viral.

Mallory lifted her arms up and attempted to twist in the same direction as the instructor. But the up-and-down motion as the instructor led them through poses was making her dizzy and lightheaded. *How much longer can I hold out?*

"Annnnnd FINAL pose. Let's make our way down to our mats for *savasana*, the corpse pose."

Cringing a little at the unfortunate English translation, Mallory sank to her mat in relief. Her newly purchased yoga gear pinched, and she was soaked through. She glanced over at Saffron, who was resting in repose. Mallory closed her eyes.

A bell chimed deeply, and as the dimmed lights were turned back up, Mallory blinked in confusion. She must have dozed off.

Saffron leaped up from her mat and leaned over. "Time to corner Metchosin," she said under her breath. Mallory struggled to her feet.

They found Kiki ensconced at the front, folding clean towels on the counter.

"Hi guys!" she chirped.

"I forgot you work here," said Mallory.

"Got to pay the bills!" Kiki was cheerfully matter-of-fact. She leaned over and whispered, "I've been dying to speak to Amira. Nate Narkiss is all over social media! Was he really found in the chicken coop?"

Saffron pulled a face. "Unfortunately, yes. And before you ask, we have no idea what he was doing in there or how it happened. And we didn't do it."

"As if I'd think that! Did Forensic Services come out? Wow, I would love to see them in action. I want to hear every detail. I texted Amira yesterday, but she hasn't responded."

"Amira was the one who found Nate," Mallory explained. "She's still shaken by the whole experience."

"Oh, I hope she'll be okay. I heard the police brought Georgie in for questioning and that they found a weapon!"

"Where did you hear that?" asked Mallory, astonished.

"It's all over **Vic in the Know**."

When Mallory and Saffron looked confused, Kiki enlightened them. "It's a blog on everything going on in Victoria. If you want to know anything about anyone who counts in this city, that's where you find your info."

"Good to know," said Mallory, making a mental note to check it out. The blog might have information on who else might have been on the outs with Nate Narkiss.

"Hey, if you guys want to bounce around theories about the murder, text me! I subscribe to all the true crime podcasts: I'm such a crime nerd."

Mallory blinked. She would never have pegged this perky young woman with her hair in a scrunchie and a T-shirt that read "So Cute!" as being a true crime buff. It was a reminder to look beneath the surface. Not everyone was who he or she appeared to be.

"We're looking for Metchosin. She didn't teach the class this morning, so we were wondering where we could find her."

"Mets took the day off." Kiki lowered her voice. "She was pretty upset about Nate. They were supposed to meet for dinner the night he was killed, but he never showed up."

"Really?" said Mallory. "I thought Metchosin and Nate were sworn enemies — that's what it looked like at the council meeting."

"'Meet Nate at Pagliacci's' was on her calendar for six-thirty that night, and I know that they met up a couple of times earlier this month. I have to coordinate her city hall and Bend Studio calendars to make sure there's no overlap. I think she must have had a soft spot for Nate, despite everything."

Interesting. What was Metchosin Barnes doing meeting up with her ex-husband, with whom she was supposedly on such bad terms?

"Do you know if she'll be back tomorrow?" asked Saffron.

"She'll be at her office at city hall today. That's Mets 'taking the day off.' But she won't be back here for a few days. I'm going to see her this afternoon at her office, to drop off some mail for her. Do you want me to pass along a message?"

"We could drop Metchosin's mail off for you. We're going to be in that part of town anyways," said Saffron.

"Really?" Kiki's relief was evident. "I'd really appreciate that. I've got a jam-packed day and I'm not sure how I would fit it in."

"No problem!" Saffron beamed.

ᛒ

Outside the yoga studio, Saffron smiled with satisfaction. "How's that for thinking on my feet? Now we have a reason to go see Metchosin."

Mallory checked her watch. "I don't know if I have the time. I'm supposed to meet with Cora and her lawyer, Becca Gill, about the development application at one."

"Her office is across the street from here. We've plenty of time if we catch a bus to city hall and back."

Mallory wasn't sure what Saffron's plan was going to be once they saw Metchosin. Saffron tended to think on her feet, as she'd just said. At least the visit wouldn't be completely wasted if she could get the councillor to confirm she'd be supporting their application next week.

They caught a bus downtown and Mallory found herself charmed all over again by the quaint local custom —practiced by young and old alike, including teens with headphones — of calling out "Thank you!" to the bus driver when exiting the bus. Their bus driver called back, "Have a nice day!" as Mallory and Saffron disembarked.

As they walked through Centennial Square to the red-bricked city hall, they passed a Celtic band playing on the outdoor stage. The smell of fried onions from a hot dog cart reminded Mallory that it was lunchtime. Hopefully, Saffron had blocked in time for a bite.

Wait, who was that coming out of the archives building? Was that Amira? Mallory turned to see if she could identify the person but had to give up when Saffron strode on ahead.

Metchosin welcomed them into her second-floor office, puffy-eyed and less put together than usual.

"We were at Bend Studio earlier and saw Kiki," said Saffron. "Since we were coming down to this area of town, we offered to drop off your mail."

"Oh, thanks. I appreciate that." Metchosin took the folder and dropped it on her desk without a glance.

"We also wanted to thank you for all that you've done to assist the Bellavista Housing Cooperative," said Mallory. "Our application is coming up before council in a week; we'd really like to know we have your support."

"Ah yes," said Metchosin, shifting in her seat. "As you know, I'm very much in favour of affordable housing options for seniors and renovating existing properties. However, I'm wondering if it's the right time for the Bellavista Housing Cooperative to try to expand. Next year might be a more opportune time."

"I'm sorry, I'm not sure I understand," said Mallory, her shoulders tensing. "Cora has been preparing this application for a while. I thought you were on board with the plans she has for Bellavista."

"Cora has a great vision, and of course, I wish her success in her application. That's why I've helped her through the process, as I would any other citizen. However, there's not much more I can do, other than share the city's guidelines on how to prep for the council meeting."

Mallory and Saffron exchanged looks.

"I hope you're not concerned about the spurious allegations against Cora and Georgie?" demanded Saffron. "You must know that they're complete nonsense. Neither one of them nor any other resident of Bellavista had anything to do with Nate's death."

Metchosin's face flushed. "Look, I want to help Cora. But as a councillor, I have to avoid doing anything that could put me in a conflict of interest, and if I'm further involved, that line could start to get blurry. I hope you understand."

"I see," said Mallory. This was bad. If their strongest supporter on council was waffling, what were the chances their development would get approved by Mayor Petrucci and the other councillors? "I understand that you and Nate Narkiss were married at one time. I'm sorry for your loss. This must be a difficult time for you."

Metchosin acknowledged the condolences with a brief nod. "It's not been an easy time." She stood, indicating that the meeting was over. "I'll get that guidelines document for you." As she walked by her desk, Metchosin brushed up against a folder, which fell to the floor.

Saffron jumped up to assist, gathering the contents together before handing the folder back to Metchosin.

"Thank you. I won't be a minute."

After receiving the printout from Metchosin, they said goodbye and left.

Outside city hall, Saffron turned to Mallory.

"I saw a receipt made out to Metchosin for a HUGE amount! Two guesses who it was from, and both names begin with the letter "N"!"

Chapter 10

> "Sometimes a little nugget of information can become a goldmine."
> - Raquel DeWitt, *The Smart Woman's Guide to Getting it Done.*

"Saffron, you can't just look at someone's personal papers!"

"Can I help it if that invoice fell on the floor face-up? It's not as if I rifled through the file. Anyways, don't you think it suspicious that Metchosin paid Nate $100,000? Why would she do that?"

Mallory gave up and let Saffron speculate to her heart's content on the short bus ride back.

"A donation to The Wheelbarrow Foundation?" theorized Saffron.

"Wouldn't the receipt have been from the Foundation and not Nate?" Mallory scrolled through her phone. "I don't see anything about a donation on her re-election campaign website, and that's the kind of sum a politician would publicize for the goodwill."

Saffron's eyes lit up. "Could it have been a bribe so that Nate wouldn't pull a stunt and interfere with her campaign again?"

"I don't know," said Mallory slowly. That sounded farfetched, given that Metchosin had handled the previous attempted smear with aplomb. "Maybe they owned a property together and Metchosin bought Nate out?"

"Have you seen Victoria's housing market? That sum wouldn't pay for half a studio. They divorced over three years ago and the date on the receipt was April 24, which was...three days ago."

Saffron grabbed Mallory's arm. "That was the night Nate was killed! When Metchosin was supposed to have met him for dinner! What if she did meet him and that's when the transaction happened, but she's pretending the meeting didn't take place to avoid having to explain the payment?"

"An unexplained deposit that size in Nate's accounts will attract police attention," reasoned Mallory. "If Metchosin wrote a cheque or e-transferred the funds to Nate, the police will find that record."

Saffron frowned. "We can't ignore a lead like this. Metchosin dropping her support for the cooperative shows how damaging these allegations are hanging over Cora and Georgie."

Better not push the point. Once Saffron got hold of an idea, it was impossible to move her from it.

By the time they reached Fort Street it was past noon, and Mallory couldn't ignore how hungry she was. Saffron suggested they grab some stuffed rolls from the Daily Bun before her appointment. "Una Park bought out the previous owner, and she's been doing some great fusion fare."

In the café's small, brightly painted interior, decorated with the owner's own artwork, appetizing wafts of cinnamon, caramelized sugar and savory spices enticed their noses.

"Hey, Una," said Saffron to the café's owner.

"I thought you were back in London! What can I get for you?" Una asked, wielding her tongs with an intricately tattooed arm.

Mallory's mouth watered as she checked out the chalkboard menu promoting that day's specials:

"I'll try a 'BTS Delight' — I love bulgogi beef."

Saffron selected a tuna casserole bun called the "Ahoy Matey." Una placed the rolls into separate paper bags. "They're fresh out of the oven so I'll leave the tops unfolded. Anything else?"

As Saffron dithered between a cinnamon roll and an oatmeal chocolate chip cookie the size of a small plate, Mallory looked around the café, taking in the funky décor. Her eye caught the words "Sand Dollar" in the window, and she went over to check out the small decal that read: "Property managed by Sand Dollar Real Estate Ltd."

"Does Sand Dollar Real Estate Ltd. have any connection to Sand Dollar Developments?" she asked, as Una rang in their order.

"It's the commercial leasing arm of Sand Dollar Developments. They manage most of the retail businesses in this area. The whole block has been talking about what happened to Nate; we're all shocked. I can't believe he was found in your chicken coop!"

"Did you know Nate well?" asked Saffron.

"I met with him once or twice when I first leased this place, but I deal mostly with his partner, Brad Jobson. Brad's a regular customer and when I saw him the other day, he looked terrible, really broken up about Nate. He was up island in Campbell River on a weeklong fishing trip when it happened, and he didn't hear about it until he came back to town."

And held the news conference that messed everything up for us, thought Mallory. Well, that ruled out Brad Jobson as a suspect, if he was out on a fishing boat five hours from Victoria.

"Metchosin's been finalizing a deal with Brad to expand her business into the space next to the studio for a smoothie bar. At first, I was worried about the competition, but Metchosin assured me that she'd focus on blended health drinks, not tea or coffee. Before Metchosin signed the lease, she checked our menus for overlap. I really appreciated that."

Metchosin came across as much more conscientious in business than Nate. They really did make an odd couple.

"Pierce from The Seasoned Connoisseur was furious that the retail space went to Metchosin," continued Una. "He's right next door to it. I've been telling Pierce to open an online shop and store his goods in that massive house of his in Rockland. He's always talking about how much space he has. I think he likes being in the center of the action too much to leave."

"Pierce Wexford from the heritage society?" asked Mallory. "He lives right next to Bellavista, and he was at the council meeting where Nate presented his development application."

"You've seen him in action then. Pierce filed so many complaints with the business association when The Bend opened. He was constantly running down to Sand Dollar's office, complaining about the heat and the dampness and all the damage it was doing to his antiques. He really had it in for Nate."

☙

"Let's drop by to see Pierce since we're here," said Saffron as they left the Daily Bun, teas and treats in hand. "You've still got fifteen minutes before your appointment."

"What for?" asked Mallory.

"Pierce didn't get along with Nate and felt slighted by missing out on the retail space. He might have had it in for Nate, especially if he felt publicly humiliated by him."

"I don't know about that. What are you going to ask him?"

"Something will come to me," said Saffron confidently.

That was exactly what Mallory feared; Saffron's tendency to wing everything and jump in without checking where she was going to land. With some trepidation, she followed Saffron across the street to Pierce's store.

Painted on the window in an appropriately antique-looking font were the words, "The Seasoned Connoisseur Est. 1986" and below, "Pierce H. Wexford, prop." The door chimed as they entered the store. Inside, the air had the sharp tang of lemon polish and a slight mustiness. Pierce looked up as they came in. His toothy smile changed into a scowl as he realized who they were.

"If this is about the peacocks, I don't have time to hear it."

"Not at all," said Saffron. "We're here to... look at some antiques." Saffron stopped, her eyes widening as something occurred to her.

"In fact, do you have any antique swords or knives? Anything sharp or pointy?"

Pierce looked torn between wanting to throw them out of the store and making a potential sale. "I can show you a set of nineteenth century letter openers that were once owned by Sir James Douglas's wife's second cousin. Exquisite detailing and truly one-of-a-kind."

While Saffron pretended to be interested in Victorian desk accessories, Mallory scanned the store. Lots of side tables, a couple of desks and chairs, and massive armoires that people used to snatch up to store their equally massive televisions, but nothing that resembled a potential weapon, at least to Mallory's untrained eyes.

"So..." Saffron was saying as she wandered through the store, picking up random objects. "Is this for opening letters too? Look at that point! Would it make a good weapon?"

At Pierce's befuddled look, Mallory jumped in. A bit of flattery might help. "You made some excellent points at the council meeting. The heritage society is lucky to have someone with your leadership so dedicated to preserving Victoria's landmarks."

Pierce visibly thawed. "So much of Victoria's history is in its rich architecture. If we allow heritage buildings to be demolished willy-nilly, we lose an irreplaceable history."

"So true, so true," said Saffron, picking up the thread. "And your well-known business acumen must also be a great benefit to the society. I heard the society turned a small profit last year from the sales of your heritage house mug collection."

"My little project has been moderately successful," said Pierce, trying to look modest and failing entirely. "We're issuing a second design this spring and plan to do a different heritage house each year. Hopefully, the series will be snatched up by discerning collectors."

"I'm sure you'll agree that a grand house like Bellavista Manor is worth preserving," said Mallory. "We hope that we can count on you and the society to support our development application next week."

"There's preservation and then there's running a poultry farm," Pierce sniffed. "I can't say I'm very happy about having a commune right next door to my home. Cora wanted forty chickens at one time, can you believe it? I shut that down very quickly."

"I can assure you that we will be abiding by restoration guidelines and that any new development on the property will be tasteful and appropriate. If you'll let me send you a copy of the plans..."

Pierce was still on his soapbox. "People think that the heritage society is living in the past, but if we forget the past, what does that do to our future? Nate Narkiss couldn't see that. He tore down a superb example of an Italianate villa to put up a flashy new concrete development. Everything always had to be bigger and newer with him."

Pierce bringing up Nate gave Mallory an opening.

"You must have been shocked to hear about Nate's death so soon after the two of you got into that dispute at the council meeting."

"Not as upset as Cora and Georgie, I'm sure," said Pierce, his eyes narrowing. "Since it happened right on their property."

Oops. That didn't land as expected. Mallory hurriedly changed the subject.

"Una at the Daily Bun mentioned that you were hoping to expand your business into the retail space next door. I'm sorry to hear that you didn't get the lease. I can imagine that you're concerned about the steam from the yoga studio affecting your inventory."

Pierce scowled. "I don't see why Bend Studio got the space when I had seniority as the longest-running business on the block. I was very surprised when Nate told me that Metchosin would get the lease. She must have used her clout with the board of directors at Cedar Grove to obtain a membership for Nate."

"What's that?" asked Saffron. "Metchosin got Nate into Cedar Grove? That's a super exclusive golf club," she explained to Mallory.

"Memberships are by invitation only and the dues are over $20,000 a year. I know because Cora leads protests over water waste at the golf club."

"Nate was completely obsessed with becoming a member at Cedar Grove, for the business connections and social clout," said Pierce. "He was bragging at the council meeting that he had been accepted. Without Metchosin's endorsement, there was no chance he would have been invited to join. Every article I've read about him repeats the story of that silly bet he won by eating ramen every meal for a whole year. To save money to buy the first property he developed. From ramen to Cedar Grove Golf Club, that's a remarkable ascent."

"It sounds like you didn't like Nate all that much," commented Saffron.

Pierce's mouth closed in a tight line. "I had no personal issues with Nate. It was all business between the two of us. It's a different story for Metchosin, though. One can understand if she's less than devastated to hear that Nate is no more. I heard that she was still paying him alimony all these years later. She must be relieved that she doesn't have to deal with him with her re-election campaign coming up."

Could that be why Metchosin paid $100,000 to Nate the night he was killed? Was it an alimony payout? Mallory wondered. Behind Pierce's snobbery, there lurked an unpleasant strain of jealousy and resentment at Nate's success, as well as a whiff of misogyny toward Metchosin. Metchosin's puffy eyes were evidence of her distress about her ex's death. Could it have all been an act?

"Pierce, you live right next door to Bellavista. Did you see Cora out walking that night or hear anything unusual?" Mallory asked.

"The police asked me the same thing, but I wasn't at home that evening and didn't see anything."

"Where were you?" asked Saffron.

Pierce drew himself up haughtily. "I don't see how that's any of your business. Please excuse me, I need to get back to work."

Before either of them could say another word, Pierce hustled them out of the store.

Chapter 11

> **"Not everyone is who they say they are."**
> - Raquel DeWitt, *The Smart Woman's Guide to Getting it Done.*

"Did you catch what Pierce said about Metchosin still paying alimony to Nate?" Mallory asked Saffron after Pierce had shut the store door behind them. "Do you think that's what the large payout was about?"

"Could be. I didn't expect Pierce to be so gossipy about Metchosin. That tidbit about Metchosin sponsoring Nate into Cedar Grove is intriguing. Why would she do that when she wasn't on good terms with him? I'm beginning to wonder if Nate had something over Metchosin."

"You mean blackmail? Do you think that's what the payout to Nate was about?" Mallory didn't like the idea even if it fit the facts. Cora would be extremely upset if it were true, given how much she admired the councillor.

Cora.

Mallory suddenly drew her breath in sharply. "My appointment with Cora and Becca Gill! I forgot all about it! What time is it?"

"It's about a quarter past one and Becca's office is right near here. What's Cora meeting with Becca about?"

"Becca's firm is advising us on the development process. Today we're discussing the lease structure for the new units being developed at Bellavista. She'll also be coordinating the development and construction team, once we source them, and professionals we need, like engineers, architects and surveyors. It's a massive undertaking with a lot of moving parts and people to deal with, so we'll be relying upon her. Becca's also been working closely with planning staff at city hall on zoning and getting our development permit application completed. She's been really essential."

"Why didn't Cora include me in this meeting?" asked Saffron, looking put out.

"We scheduled it before we knew you were coming. Cora didn't know you'd be in town."

"Well, I'm here now and I'm coming too," said Saffron. "I need to know what's going on. I don't like being sidelined." She started to march down the street, not checking to see if Mallory was following.

Mallory let out a heavy sigh. *Here we go again* — Saffron barreling through without regard for anyone else, taking over when no one asked her. If she'd known she'd have to deal with Saffron again, she would never have taken on the Bellavista project.

༄

Becca's office was housed in an early-twentieth-century brick building with no elevator. The flight of stairs leading up to her office was so worn down that each stair tread sported a defined dip in the center.

In the foyer, a woman with straight brown hair clipped severely on each side spoke into a headset. She looked up when they entered and gestured with a smile toward the small reception area where Cora was already seated. With high ceilings, exposed brickwork and colorful kilim rugs, Gill and Company had a charmingly vintage vibe.

"Hello!" called Cora. "You're right on time. Saffron, I wasn't expecting you to join us, but what a pleasant surprise."

Saffron managed to look less ruffled at her aunt's affectionate tone.

"Alright, I think I have everything I need. Yes, Mrs. Foster, thank you." The receptionist disconnected the call and said to them, "Ms. Gill shouldn't be much longer."

The receptionist spoke softly into her headset. Not a minute later the door to the right of the reception area opened.

"I'm sorry that I couldn't be more help, officers," Becca was saying as she showed Detectives Blair and Grover out. "Please let me know if I can be of further assistance."

The two officers stopped short when they saw Cora, Saffron and Mallory.

"Ms. Sherman, Ms. Chu --- er--- McKenzie-Chu, er, good afternoon," mumbled Detective Blair. "We didn't expect to run into you here."

"We've an appointment," said Cora with a lift of her chin. "Ms. Gill is handling our development application. By the way, this is my niece, Saffron Kalinsky."

"I see," said Detective Blair. He chewed his lip for a moment. "We were planning on coming by Bellavista later, as we've a few more questions for Ms. Hoskins."

"Etta? Whatever for?" asked Cora, her voice rising. "We told you everything we know and you've turned our home inside out. What else is there to ask?"

Detective Blair bristled at her tone. "That's for us to decide. Please keep in mind that this is an ongoing police investigation."

"You'll be pleased to know we've completed our inspection of the chicken coop," said Detective Grover. "Your chickens can come home to roost!"

"Detective Blair, have you looked into Metchosin Barnes's relationship with her ex-husband?" interjected Saffron. "From what we've been hearing, they weren't on good terms at all. In fact, we came across some info..."

Detective Blair cut her off. "If you have information or tips to share, we would be happy to hear them down at the station.

Otherwise, I strongly suggest that you stick to your own business and leave the investigating to us."

Detective Blair shot them all a look of distrust before huffing out of the office, Detective Grover following after with an apologetic look over his shoulder.

"Fine," Saffron muttered to herself. "We'll figure it out ourselves."

"Figure what out, dear?" asked Cora, but Saffron strode into Becca's office and didn't answer.

Becca ushered them into her office and took her seat behind a mid-sized wooden desk with leather inlay shaped like an inverted rainbow.

"That's a very unusual desk," commented Mallory. "I've never seen one like it."

Becca smiled. "It's originally a blackjack table from an old casino. I found it at The Seasoned Connoisseur and thought it would make a great office desk. See, I can spread my paperwork around and still have plenty of space. I have my computer on a different table, but the set-up works."

Becca went to her printer to collect some documents.

"Were Detectives Blair and Grover here to talk about Nate Narkiss?" asked Saffron.

Becca put the paperwork down and took her seat behind the desk. "They wanted to know if I knew of anyone who might want to do him harm. I told them I have no idea."

"Did you know Nate well?" asked Mallory, curious as to the connection between the poised young lawyer and the skeevy land developer.

"We ran into each other a couple of times in Saanich, as Nate was doing a development there and my grandfather's company was working on a development next to it. Anyway, let me show you the paperwork I've prepared."

Becca clearly wanted to drop the topic, so they moved on.

☙

Once Becca had walked them through the leasing set-up, she turned to the actual development work.

"If you're going to replicate some of the design elements in Bellavista into the new units, you couldn't do better than to go with Jacob Prentiss. He's built a name for himself in restoring heritage homes and incorporating contemporary elements in a way that works with the original design."

"Why not recommend your grandfather's company?" asked Cora. "Gill Construction? It has such a solid reputation."

"That would put me in a conflict of interest," said Becca. "I don't want that, as I'm really enjoying working on this project. Besides, Grandpa Bas thinks very highly of J.P.'s work."

"I've heard of Jacob Prentiss," said Mallory. After speaking to Etta, she'd done some research on Prentiss and other developers specializing in historic restorations. "But doesn't he focus on high-end single-family properties? I haven't seen him involved in a multi-unit conversion project like this one. Etta mentioned trying to get in touch with him and never hearing back."

"I still think it's worth connecting with him to see what he can do. A side of his business focuses on providing on-the-job training on historic restorations for local youth entering the trades, so there may be cost savings for you. Their highly specialized skills are in demand worldwide."

"Very similar to The Wheelbarrow Foundation," remarked Mallory. "Is there any connection?"

"Um, yes," Becca shifted in her seat. "I believe that there may have been a joint program of some kind. Have I shown you the plans I discussed with the city's planning staff? Since we're preserving the main house and converting the stables and tennis courts into new units, the project qualifies for funding under a couple of municipal and provincial programs. The planning staff was very enthusiastic that thirty percent of the new units will be a low-cost option. Affordable housing is a critical issue for Victoria these days, as it is everywhere."

"Thirty percent?" asked Cora, frowning. "I wanted to make all of the new units affordable."

"That's not practical," objected Saffron. "You know the project can't afford that and still be sustainable."

"The percentage should be higher," insisted Cora. "At least eighty percent."

"Cora," Saffron responded with a bit of annoyance, "I'm not going to agree to anything more than forty percent – that's as high as we can go unless we're able to drum up more investors or funding. We need to be able to cover our basic costs!"

"I'm working on it. I've a few calls lined up this afternoon with potential investors."

"Have any of them confirmed their interest?" asked Mallory. She feared that the suspicion lingering over the residents had permanently scared off investors.

"Not yet, but I'm optimistic."

Saffron shook her head. "See Becca, this is what we're dealing with. Investors are backing out because they don't want to be associated with a property that has an ongoing criminal investigation. It doesn't help that the police are treating Cora, Amira and Georgie as persons of interest. No amount of optimism is going to resolve that black cloud."

"The police can't really believe that those three would have had anything to do with Nate Narkiss's death?" asked Becca.

"We're positive they don't have a case, but for some reason, they've zoned in on Bellavista residents," explained Mallory. "Someone as high profile as Nate Narkiss must have had enemies; there must be other people the police could be looking into."

Becca worried her bottom lip with her teeth, then got up, saying, "Excuse me for a minute," and left her office, closing the door behind her.

Saffron's eyes widened. "What's that all about?" she asked.

"Something's troubling her, and she's figuring out whether she wants to tell us or not."

"You got all that from a little lip nibble?"

"Didn't you notice how she redirected your questions away from her relationship with Nate? And I saw the expression on her face when Detective Blair said we needed to stay out of the investigation. I think Becca knows something."

The door opened again, and Becca came back in and closed the door behind her. When she sat back down, she handed Saffron a business card.

"Here's the name of a criminal lawyer I know who's very experienced. I hope he can be of help."

☙

"Ok you two, what was that all about?" demanded Cora once they were outside. "All those questions about Nate Narkiss. Becca was clearly uncomfortable."

"We need to suss out any connections for clues as to who might have wanted to harm Nate," explained Saffron, "to take the focus off you three. You can't worry about ruffling people's feathers if you don't want to remain prime suspects."

"Oh pish. The police will realize very soon that none of us is involved. Nate was a sleazy businessman whose dicey deals caught up with him. Becca has given us a lot to work on before next week's hearing, including reaching out to Jacob Prentiss again and seeing if the revised lease terms will appeal to new investors. I want to focus on Bellavista's future, not on who might have had it in for Nate Narkiss."

Mallory silently agreed with Cora. Leave it to the professionals to solve Nate's murder and get to work on the property redevelopment. With the hearing date fast approaching, they needed to take action now.

"What if we hosted an open house at Bellavista?" she asked. "I could contact people who've expressed interest in the cooperative and invite them to tour the property. We could blow up the plans and display them to show what the redevelopment will be like. There would also be an opportunity to canvas on-site input from attendees on what they're hoping to see at Bellavista and their preferred features for their homes and community space."

"I love that idea!" cried Cora. "I'll send you the names of additional people I was thinking might be interested. Amira can offer Kitchen Cooperative's products to highlight the benefits of having homegrown produce on hand. Do you think we could get Jacob Prentiss to attend?"

"It's worth a try," said Mallory, feeling her excitement grow. Quickly calculating how long it would take to get the message out and the event organized, she suggested Saturday, which would give them two days to plan.

"Hold on a minute." Saffron frowned. "How can we host an open house when Bellavista is still a crime scene? This isn't going to work."

Mallory's spirit deflated. How could she forget the yellow crime-scene tape plastered all over the place — it wasn't the selling feature they needed. Her eyes lit up with a new idea.

"We'll host a virtual open house! If we do a video walk-through, we can edit out the yellow tape and avoid problem areas. The video is bound to attract interest —even if it's prurient interest due to Nate— and once we post it, we can track interest through the number of viewings. I helped the DeWitts with their Seventy-Two Questions house tour interview with Vogue, so I know what to do. Guests won't get to sample the Kitchen Cooperative's products, but we can show Amira in action and also tour the gardens and greenhouse. I think this could work."

"Even better!" beamed Cora. "And less work for us."

Saffron still looked unconvinced, but progress had been made. This was where Mallory thrived, working in her wheelhouse, drawing upon her strengths. Not playing at detective.

Chapter 12

> **"Put your best foot forward."**
> - Raquel DeWitt, *The Smart Woman's Guide to Getting it Done.*

"Do I look alright?" asked Cora, as she stood on the front steps of Bellavista, fidgeting with the shawl draped over her paisley-printed maxi-dress so it didn't block the mic pinned to her front. "Can you hear me alright?"

Worried about the impending hearing date, Cora had convinced Mallory to shoot the video tour the next day. Mallory had agreed, figuring that the low production values could be offset by editing. She had asked Kiki to shoot the tour on her iPhone, since that was the best they could come up with on such short notice. Georgie fluttered around Cora, wielding an arsenal of cosmetic tools. The selection of Cora as the main presenter had created some initial tension with Bellavista's resident thespian, but Georgie appeared content to be make-up-artist-in- chief.

"You look gorgeous, Cora!" said Kiki, giving her a thumbs up as she pointed the iPhone at her. "You're coming through loud and clear!"

"Ok, Cora, I'm going to count you in," said Mallory. "We're going live in five, four, three...."

"Good afternoon! My name is Cora Abigail Sherman and I'd like to welcome you to a virtual tour of Bellavista Manor, the site of the new Bellavista Housing Cooperative!"

Cora smiled widely at the camera. "Designed by the great Samuel Maclure in 1923, Bellavista is a marvelous representation of the British Arts and Crafts style popular at that time. You can see that we've maintained the original timber-frame design and color scheme."

As Cora gestured toward the white timbers, Kiki panned the camera upward.

"Oh, yikes!" Kiki's hand flew to her mouth. "There's a raccoon on the roof! I caught it coming out of the top gable!"

"We'll cut that out later -- focus on Cora!" Mallory motioned for Kiki to keep filming Cora, who was already heading through the front door.

"Let me introduce you to our home..." As Cora glided down the hallway, providing carefully rehearsed snippets of information about the house's history, Mallory let herself relax.

In front of the fireplace, Cora pointed out the original delftware tiles that adorned the surround as flames flickered invitingly. Clouds of smoke billowed out, causing Cora to double over, coughing.

As Lucas flew in waving a fire extinguisher, Kiki swiftly pivoted the camera toward Cora, who was waving her hands, trying to clear the air.

"Let me show you the kitchen!" Cora practically sprinted down the hallway, Kiki running behind. The overhead lights flickered and went out one by one as they passed, plunging the scene into darkness.

What the heck is going on?? Quickly checking that Lucas had the hearth under control, Mallory ran after them.

"Cora," she cried, "Stop filming! We need to regroup!"

Heedless of Mallory's direction, Cora was already onto the next segment, a cooking demonstration with Amira. Cora raced through the introduction, her pitch going higher as she sped up.

"At Bellavista, we love to learn! Our communal gathering space provides a place for residents to host parties and take cooking classes! Amira's going to share the secret behind her famous sourdough rolls!"

As Kiki zoomed in, Amira removed a large mixing bowl from the oven and placed it on the counter.

"This is our sourdough starter. I call her "Jane Dough," Amira quipped, lifting the tea towel. The fermenting mixture let out a huge burp, spraying chunks of dough into the air. Glasses plastered in dough Cora flung her arms wildly. "Help! I can't see!"

Grabbing tea towels out of a drawer Mallory rushed over to Cora. Before she could stop the filming, Kiki darted through the open French doors, clutching the phone camera in front as she ran down the path.

"Look at the amazing view! Isn't it amazing!" Kiki rambled. "We have an amazing greenhouse! Oh look, let's go see what's down here!"

Mallory helped Cora remove her glasses and rinsed them in the sink. "Why's Kiki still filming? We've time to start over and post the video later tonight."

Flushing, Cora looked nervously at Georgie, who was attempting to extract dough from Cora's hair. Georgie lifted her chin and said, "We wanted to film the tour live."

"What do you mean 'live'?" Mallory's mouth fell open in shock. "You mean, this is a livestream? We're broadcasting *live*?"

She couldn't believe that they'd done that without consulting her.

"It was the best way to get as many eyes as possible on short notice," insisted Georgie. "Over two hundred people pre-registered to view the tour — you wouldn't believe the interest on *Vic in the Know*!"

"No, no, no, no, no!" Mallory sprinted through the veranda doors after Kiki. She found her down by the tennis court filming Saffron.

"This tennis court will be transformed into multi-unit, multi-level modern townhomes," Saffron was saying as she gestured toward an enlarged development plan. "As you can see, we've designed the space to integrate seamlessly with the landscape and existing orchard. By centering the buildings around an open courtyard, we'll have access to nature while extending residents' living space."

Thank goodness Saffron's so good at this, Mallory thought, pausing to catch her breath. *Maybe we can salvage this.*

With professional ease, Saffron continued a walk-through of the tennis court redevelopment before ending up in front of the stables. "These nineteenth-century constructions will soon be transformed into a communal gathering space, complete with facilities for cooking, exercising and more!"

Saffron glanced up at Kiki. "Are you filming me from the right-hand side? That's not my best look! Can you take me from this angle?"

Saffron doesn't know we're live! Mallory realized, frantically waving to her to stop, but she was reaching for the sliding barn door, saying, "Let me give you a quick preview before the transformation."

As the massive barndoor slid open, what looked like hundreds of rats swarmed out, skittering over Saffron's sneakers before fanning out into the grass. Mallory froze in horror. "AAAGGGGGGHHHH" shrieked Saffron, beside herself with terror.

Snapping out of her shock, Mallory raced over and with Saffron's help, managed to slam the barn door shut. Shaking, Mallory yelled, "Kiki! Stop filming!" A stunned Kiki sprang to life, jabbing at her phone.

"Kiki! Why did you do a livestream?" Mallory's whole body shuddered. She couldn't tell if it was from anger or the shock of coming face to face with her worst phobia.

"I didn't know you didn't know!" Kiki looked stricken. "Georgie told me to set up the livestream on *Vic in the Know*, so I did!"

"What!" Saffron's flushed face grew redder. "Are you kidding me?" She grabbed Kiki's phone and scrolled through. "How many people are watching this? Ack, over four hundred views! Look at the comments!" She handed Kiki back her phone and clutched her head.

Mallory willed her horrified brain to think. There was no way to remedy this, not when the video was going to be shared a million times. Video!

"Kiki! Does the livestream stop once it's over or does it stay up? Pull it down!"

Kiki bent her head over her phone, her fingers flying.

"How did this happen?" asked Saffron, shock giving way to anger. "Mallory, why didn't you oversee the set-up? Gosh, what a disaster!"

Before Mallory could defend herself, someone called her name. Cora came hurrying towards them, hair still wet from the dough incident.

"Please, we need you back at the house! The police are here and they're questioning Etta!"

☙

As Mallory had dealt with the police officers before, they quickly agreed she'd go with Cora while Kiki and Saffron did damage control about the rodent invasion and video. Rushing back to the house, Mallory and Cora found Amira standing outside the library. She put a finger to her lips when she saw them. As unobtrusively as possible, they slipped into the room, where Detective Blair was talking to a truculent-looking Etta while Detective Grover took notes.

"I don't see why you need to ask me anything more, Detective," Etta was saying. "I said everything I had to say in my statement."

Detective Blair pulled out a sheet of folded blue notepaper from a manila envelope.

"Ms. Hoskins, is this your signature?"

She looked at the sheet, eyebrows raised. "Yes. I sent that note to Nate Narkiss last week asking him to meet with me. I said in my statement that Nate showed up at Bellavista on the twenty-third at my invitation."

"There's no date on this note," pointed out Detective Blair, tapping it with a pudgy finger. "And no postmarked envelope, plus the note doesn't suggest a specific date or time to meet. How do we know that you didn't give this to Nate to get him to come here the night he was killed?"

"I didn't!" Etta sat up straighter, her eyes widening in alarm. "If you had the envelope, you'd see that I mailed it to him weeks ago!"

"Did you send the note by registered mail?" When she didn't respond, he said, "I thought not."

Detective Blair carefully tucked the note back into an envelope before acknowledging Cora and Mallory's presence for the first time. "I'm beginning to think that there's more going on here than what we've been told," he remarked. "First, Ms. Sherman and Ms. Vandervoss each have very public confrontations with Mr. Narkiss at the city council meeting. That night, he's found with head wounds and stab wounds in your chicken coop, and we find not one, but two sets of potential weapons on your premises. And now we have this conveniently undated note inviting Mr. Narkiss to visit Bellavista."

"That's ridiculous!" protested Cora. "We had no reason to harm him!"

"So you say."

"Have you verified whether either instrument could have wounded Nate Narkiss?" inquired Mallory.

Detective Blair's mustache bristled. "The lab is still working on the analysis," he admitted. "But I have to say, we'll be keeping our eyes on all of you. You're still considered to be persons of interest in this matter."

He stood. "Ms. Hoskins, thank you for your time. If we need to ask you more questions, we'll let you know."

He nodded to Detective Grover, who bounded to his feet, and the two officers left. Cora darted over to the couch and squeezed Etta's arm as Amira slipped in to sit on Etta's other side.

"Detective Blair thinks I lured Nate here!" said Etta, a waver in her voice. Her hand trembled as she clutched her cane.

"Nonsense," said Cora firmly. "Your note proves nothing. This so-called evidence is purely circumstantial!"

Mallory wished she could share Cora's confidence that the police had no case against them; Etta's undated note gave the police a very neat answer to the question of what brought Nate to Bellavista that fateful night.

Amira shared her pessimism. "Even circumstantial evidence can be made into a case," she said, her voice shaking. "What if the police believe they've solved Nate's murder? What if they think we were in a — what do you call it — a conspiracy? How can we fight against that?"

At that moment, Saffron and Kiki came into the library. "Lucas is calling the exterminator. We managed to get the livestream to stop, but the video's still up," said Saffron. "Even if we pull it down, who knows how many people took screenshots or forwarded copies? The internet really does live forever." She flung herself down into an armchair. "What did the police want?"

As Mallory filled them in, Saffron groaned. "As if things couldn't get any worse. Should we be thankful that at least no one's been charged yet with anything?"

"This is utter nonsense," said Cora forcefully. "If the police really thought any of us was involved, they would have arrested us by now. We can't waste our time worrying about what the police are doing. We have to focus on the hearing next week and drumming up potential investors."

"How can we pretend that everything's fine?" asked Saffron incredulously. "This investigation is still active and now practically the entire household is implicated!"

"Well, what do you suggest?" snapped Cora. She leaned back, rubbing her temples distractedly. "Sorry, I don't know what else to do."

"This is getting out of hand," said Mallory. "It's time we saw a lawyer."

Chapter 13

> *"Know when to ask for help."*
> *- Raquel DeWitt, **The Smart Woman's Guide to Getting it Done.***

"I'll call Theo and see if he can recommend anyone," Mallory said. The second police visit in as many days had thoroughly unnerved her. She should have listened to Theo and pushed harder for Cora to contact a lawyer as soon as the police started questioning them.

"I agree," said Saffron, to Mallory's relief. "We need advice before we do anything further."

Etta nodded. "I could tell that Detective Blair didn't believe me about the note!"

"I am not yet a permanent resident," added Amira, "so I have worried about what it would mean if the police charged me. I cannot risk that."

Of course. Amira's legal status in Canada could be jeopardized if she were involved in a criminal investigation. All the more reason to talk to a lawyer.

"I've got the business card Becca Gill gave us," said Saffron, rummaging through her handbag, "but I'm happy to go with Theo's referral." Handing the card over to Mallory, Saffron noted the name on the card. "Simon Green. I went to middle school with a Simon Green. Wonder if it's him?"

Mallory went out into the hallway, closing the door for privacy, and pulled out her phone to text her brother. A minute later, her phone rang.

"Theo McKenzie-Chu. Everything okay, Mallory?"

Hearing her brother's familiar gruff tone immediately comforted Mallory, and some of the tension she'd been holding in released.

"Do you know someone in the criminal law field we can talk to, for general information," she added hurriedly.

Theo's growl came through loud and clear. "Are you in trouble? Did the police charge anyone?"

"No, but I don't like where they're going with their line of questioning." Mallory admitted, relieved to be sharing her fears with someone not directly involved. "The police are zoning in on the conflicts between the land developer who was killed and the Bellavista residents. I'm worried they're not considering any other suspects."

"Let the police do their job and stay out of it, Mallory."

She let out a sigh. "When are you going to accept that I can look after myself? Look, Cora's real estate lawyer recommended a Simon Green for criminal law. Could you look into him or recommend someone else?"

Theo perked up. "Simon Green? If it's the same Simon Green I played rugby with at U of T, he's a good guy. Yeah, could be him since he was a law student from Victoria. What firm is he with?"

Mallory read out the name, and Theo was silent for a moment. "Ok, I Googled the firm and yes, it's him. Call Simon right away, okay? And be careful." Theo hung up. Mallory's throat felt parched; she'd neglected to drink anything all morning. Heading into the kitchen to get a glass of water, she was about to push the door open when raised voices came through the door.

"You must tell Cora soon! You cannot keep this from her!" That was Amira, followed by someone murmuring in response. Making a show of clearing her throat, Mallory entered the kitchen to find Etta seated at the table with Georgie, who was checking her manicure while Amira put a tray in the oven.

"I really need a glass of water," said Mallory brightly, feeling the tension in the atmosphere. What was that all about? Who's the one with the secret? "Looks like you're getting lunch ready. Can I help with anything?"

Amira managed an unconvincing smile. "Would you let everyone know that I'll have tea ready soon?"

Back in the library, Mallory searched for the firm's website on her phone and showed Saffron Simon's head shot, featuring a man with thick, brown hair and an engaging smile. Saffron smiled. "Well how about that, it's little Simon Green! He's still got that cowlick." Saffron took the business card back. "I'll give him a call and see if he remembers me," she said, heading out.

"How come you're seeing so many lawyers?" asked Kiki, confused. "Isn't one enough?"

"They each have their own area of expertise," explained Mallory. "Like a surgeon versus a GP versus a heart specialist. Becca Gill deals with real estate matters, Simon Green focuses on criminal law."

"Huh, I should know this if I'm going to become a criminologist," said Kiki. "Listen, I'm feeling really badly about the livestream. Now you guys are in more trouble with the police. How can I help?"

She'd already forgotten about the livestream debacle. "Can you see about getting the video pulled down? I hate the idea that it's up there."

"I'll do whatever it takes," said Kiki. She got up, looping her satchel over her shoulder. "I'll text you as soon as it comes down."

Lucas popped his head around the door. "Cora, okay if I take the truck out for a while?" he asked. "I need to…to run some errands."

"Could you pick up some supplies while you're out?" asked Cora. "We're low on some staples; I left a list on the kitchen counter."

"Sure." He ducked his head out.

Cora watched him leave, a furrow on her brow. "I'm worried about Lucas. He seems very distracted and hasn't been keeping up with maintenance tasks. This whole situation has been so disruptive."

Saffron came back in with a satisfied smile. "Simon can meet with us in half an hour, at 1:30 p.m. Where's Lucas going? I saw him putting a couple of duffel bags in the truck."

"He's running errands," said Cora. She got to her feet and sniffed the air. "I can tell that Amira's heating up savory pastries. Let's get you some lunch before your meeting."

☙

The meeting with Simon Green put their minds at rest; they were to direct all further requests from the police for interviews through him. He explained that he could represent all four of the residents so long as they agreed and there was no conflict of interest. If anything changed, they would need to consider getting separate representation.

"I don't think the police have a solid case against Cora, Amira, Etta or Georgie," he reassured them. "But call me if they try to interview anyone again."

"Little Simon Green grew up!" said Saffron, grinning as they left Simon's office together. "Ha, I'm still taller than him."

"He didn't seem to mind," said Mallory. It had been transparently clear that the cute attorney harbored a major crush on Saffron Kalinsky. However, unlike the Saffron of old, she hadn't gone into total flirtation mode and had stayed focus on the purpose of the meeting. *A bit of growth there? I know nothing about Saffron's personal life, whether she's seeing anyone.* A pang went through her. The ease with which they'd fallen back into their old banter made her forget that they weren't part of each other's lives.

As Saffron pulled up to Bellavista, they saw two police cars, their siren lights flashing, parked in front of the house. Saffron parked and they raced to the house. Once inside, they found Cora and Amira standing in the hallway, both very upset.

"What's going on?" cried Mallory.

"The police are looking for Lucas," Amira told them in a shaky voice. "We told them he left more than an hour ago in the truck."

"Why do the police want Lucas?" asked Saffron.

Cora wailed, "They think he killed Nate!"

☙

"The police say they've got evidence that Lucas is dealing in illegal drugs!" cried Cora. She paused to blow her nose, tears spilling down her cheeks. "They suspect he was making a sale to Nate and the drug deal went wrong that night. I can't believe it."

"What? I'm calling Simon right now," said Saffron, pulling out her phone.

"Did you ever suspect Lucas was involved in drugs?" asked Mallory with concern.

"No!" Cora was adamant. "I had no clue! It doesn't make sense! Lucas is such a hard worker and dedicated to Bellavista. You've seen how much he does around here."

"I never had any sense of it," admitted Amira, her eyebrows drawing together in puzzlement. "People can be very clever at hiding drug use. With the news reports about the opioid crisis, we should not be surprised about it affecting people we know."

"How did the police discover that Lucas was dealing?" asked Mallory. "It never came up the other two times they were here."

"An anonymous tip," sniffed Cora, pulling out another tissue. "They traced the supply to a feed distributor up in Nanaimo who smuggled the drugs through the docks and repackaged them as chicken feed. I suppose that's why Lucas went up island so often. He was picking up supplies and drugs at the same time."

Amira shook her head sorrowfully. "Lucas was so careful with our chickens, making sure that they always had a special organic feed. He went to Nanaimo so many times, but I did not think to ask why."

Saffron ended her call and turned to her friends. "Simon says he'll be here in five minutes."

Detectives Blair and Grover came into the library, a couple of officers behind them wearing gloves and carrying large plastic bags. A grim-faced Detective Blair told them, "We found some heroin hidden upstairs behind the ceiling tiles and under loose floorboards in Lucas's room."

"We also found a large stash in the chicken coop, hidden inside the feedbags," added Detective Grover. He turned to Cora. "Ms. Sherman, it looks like Lucas cleared out in a hurry with most of his belongings. Any idea where he might have gone?"

Cora shook her head. "I'm sorry, I don't know his friends. He told me his mother lives up island near Ladysmith, but I don't know her address."

"We need to find him. He could be in danger if gangs are involved, which is likely. The Nanaimo gangs wouldn't take kindly to someone barging into their territory. We also have to consider him a person of interest in Nate Narkiss's death."

"Do you really think that Lucas killed Nate over drugs?" asked Mallory.

Detective Blair shrugged. "Nate could have disturbed Lucas while he was stashing the drugs inside the coop. Or Nate could have been buying drugs from Lucas and the deal went wrong. Hard to say."

At that moment, the doorbell rang, and Saffron ran to let Simon Green in. Detective Blair appeared to know Simon, addressing him with grudging respect and giving him the search warrant. Having thoroughly scoured the property for the rest of Lucas's drug stash, the police conferred quietly with Simon before leaving.

Simon came back to the waiting group. "It looks like Lucas is now the prime suspect in Nate Narkiss's death. While the police are not yet prepared to say the rest of you are no longer persons of interest, their investigation appears to be going in that direction."

Saffron nodded and said, "It's terrible if Lucas is trafficking in drugs and if he was responsible for Nate's death. At the same time, I'm hugely relieved that the focus is off Cora and everyone else."

Cora wiped her eyes. She hadn't stopped tearing up since she'd heard the news. "I can't see Lucas being violent, even if drugs were involved."

The drug smuggling explained Lucas's obsession with taking care of the chickens and their coop; their care was a great cover. What didn't make sense was that Nate died due to a drug deal gone wrong. Nothing that they'd found out so far had even suggested that drugs were an issue for Nate. While drug addicts could hide their addictions from even loved ones, how was it possible that neither Metchosin nor Becca was aware of Nate's drug use and that it hadn't come up as a factor in the police investigation? Unless they weren't sharing that information. Or Nate found out about Lucas's drug trading and decided to confront him? That was a stretch. For Mallory, something wasn't adding up.

Exhausted by the day's events, Mallory escaped upstairs. Dinner had been a replay of the entire day and she was fighting off the beginnings of headache. Saffron had slipped out before dinner and she hoped Saffron, always a night owl, stayed up long enough to let her fall asleep. As she collapsed onto her bed, her phone pinged. Her mother was answering the text Mallory had sent earlier. The text read:

CALL US!

Her mother answered after the first ring. "Gretchen told us about the murder at Bellavista! Are you okay?"

"Mum, I'm fine, really. It's been stressful dealing with the police investigation but none of us is in any danger." Except in danger of being charged with murder, she thought.

"Mallory!" It was her dad, Walter, on the extension. Now she had anxious parents in stereo. "We'll get you on a flight out of Victoria tomorrow."

Did no one in her life think she could book her own flight? Not to mention make her own decisions? Mallory gritted her teeth and said, "I'm not leaving. The police are investigating and everything's under control."

"They've caught the murderer?" asked Walter hopefully.

"No, but..."

"No? What are you talking about; you can't stay there!"

Why didn't her family trust her ability to assess the situation for herself? The injustice of it boiled up, but it was pointless to argue. Only one factor could outweigh her parents' need to assert control over a situation in which they had none. Time to play her ace card.

"I'm under contract to deliver this project, so I can't leave until after the council hearing at the earliest. I promised Cora that I would see the development application through."

The McKenzie-Chu family's generational work ethic won out; Mallory should stay to finish her job. After adroitly diverting the conversation away from the police investigation by asking about her mother's latest paper for her Psychology 201 class, Mallory asked her father, "How's Bob?" For several weeks, Walter McKenzie-Chu had been engaged in a battle of wits to guard his beloved bird feeder against a wily neighborhood squirrel he'd nicknamed Bob.

"I tried a deterrent using distilled garlic water that I read about on the Google, but it didn't work," said her father. Fiona was the more internet-savvy of her parents, but Walter had recently become enthralled by "the Google" and DIY videos on YouTube. "So I've suspended the feeder using a *horizontal* wire instead of a vertical one so he can't climb up or down! I've great hopes for this one. Oh, your mother wants to speak to you."

Fiona came back on the line. "Mallory, Raquel DeWitt called asking for your current address. I hope it was alright to give her your address in Victoria. I thought it might have to do with some final payment."

By the time Mallory ended the call, her headache was pounding in her temples. Drat — she'd need to take something for it, or she'd never get to sleep. Her family was much more concerned than she had expected, even her usually unflappable mother. Mind you, this was their first encounter with an actual murder. She took a quick shower, letting the hot water ease the tension in her shoulders. Thankfully, the plumbing held up. When she emerged, Saffron's bed was still unoccupied.

Mallory tucked herself into bed, hoping to distract herself with the book she had purchased for the flight out. It turned out to be a poor choice of reading material; a suspense novel set in a creepy old mansion where the inhabitants kept turning on each other. Mallory gave up after two chapters, unable to focus or care about the outcome.

Her phone pinged again. She really should think about automatically shutting it down in the evening. It was a text from Kiki letting her know that she'd managed to get the video pulled down from the *Vic in the Know* blog. Kiki added, "Over three hundred comments and they weren't all negative!"

Mallory adjusted the phone settings so she wouldn't be interrupted until the next morning. As she tried once again to court sleep, her thoughts flitted between the open house shenanigans, the two police visits, and now Lucas under suspicion. Not to mention that roof tiles kept tumbling down out of nowhere. It was all too much, and her brain was having a very difficult time coping. After another five minutes of tossing and turning, Mallory gave up and got out of bed.

The jangle of a doorknob cut through her mental jumble as she shuffled downstairs to make a cup of tea. She paused, nerves on edge, listening. It was rare to find anyone downstairs after nine o'clock and it was now close to 11 p.m. Maybe it was Saffron returning from wherever she'd gone? Mallory looked down the hallway toward the front door, but no one came in. Spooked, Mallory hurried toward the kitchen.

As she waited for her tea to heat up in the microwave, Mallory tried not to obsess over every squeak or gurgle the old house made. A shadow passed in front of the kitchen window. Was that a tree branch? Or was someone out there?

The kitchen door opened, making Mallory shriek. "Oh my gosh, Saffron! You almost gave me a heart attack!"

"You're still up? You're not going to drink that, are you? I'll put the kettle on."

Soon they were sitting at the worn kitchen table with mugs of decaf Earl Grey and a plate of Amira's sesame seed cookies. It felt like old times as Saffron told Mallory about her evening.

"I called Simon to ask what to do if Lucas showed up here, and he suggested we meet for dinner."

"Oh, really?" Simon must really be smitten. "Where'd you go?"

"Down by the Inner Harbor. There's a restaurant by the water made from a converted shipping container. They serve great fish and chips, and this amazing Thai curry coconut fish stew."

"What did Simon have to say?"

"He suggested we change the locks in case Lucas tries to return. Cora won't like that idea, but I think we should do it."

After clearing up the tea things, Saffron went to take a shower while Mallory headed back to bed. Changing the locks made sense. Lucas may have been part of the Bellavista household, but did any of them really know him that well? Mallory wasn't concerned for her safety; Nate had been the target. All the same, she didn't fall asleep until Saffron returned.

Chapter 14

> "Sometimes you've got to get your hands dirty."
> - Raquel DeWitt, *The Smart Woman's Guide to Getting it Done.*

Once Mallory got an idea in her head, it was difficult for her to let go of it until she was able to do something about it. It was as if her brain was a dog and the idea was a squirrel her brain was chasing — in fact, whenever Mallory got distracted as a child when she was supposed to be doing homework or a chore, her mother would call it Mallory "going squirrelly." Mallory herself called it "shiny object" syndrome; if something sparkly caught her attention, she couldn't help looking. The same thing happened at work, but in that controlled environment Mallory was much better able to minimize distractions and focus on the task at hand, especially with Raquel's hyper-regimented schedule. In Mallory's own personal life, things were a bit less organized. Make that a *lot* less organized. Mallory was chronically late to appointments or forgot them altogether. She was always missing bill payment deadlines, despite meaning to set up automatic payments. Full of good intentions, for some reason, she had great difficulty setting up effective personal systems; this was a source of great frustration.

Luckily, where work was concerned, Mallory had the ability to fully commit to a project and hyper-focus until it was done. With the police apparently satisfied that Lucas was the main suspect now in Nate's death, Mallory turned her attention to offsetting the effects of the livestream and preparing for the hearing that was in a week's time.

There was plenty to do in the Bellavista household. The locks had been changed, the other residents overruling Cora's objection, and while the old house still creaked and gurgled at night, sleep came easier. Kiki proved very useful, showing herself adept at replacing lightbulbs, mucking out the carriage house after the chickens' residency, and helping Mallory take photos of the property for promotional materials.

Mallory also got to know the members of the Kitchen Cooperative better. As the Kitchen ramped up to their summer production levels, Mallory helped harvest produce from the gardens and greenhouse and sat on the patio with Reem and Bisharoo shelling peas. With the warmer weather, Etta would join them to work on a new canvas while Cora, ever productive, mended torn linens for reuse or crafts. Most of the time, Saffron was on the phone running her business, but she popped up now and then to give input on the co-op's development. They'd settled into a comfortable rapport, a huge improvement from when Saffron had first arrived on the scene. Had they managed to put the past behind them? She didn't give it much thought, grateful that Saffron seemed to be respecting her role as project manager.

As Raquel DeWitt's house manager, Mallory had firsthand knowledge of how Raquel would plan random encounters with people of influence and means — running into them at the hair salon, bumping into an acquaintance at a gallery opening, finding herself limbering up next to someone at a community run — to build up a roster of social contacts for her next promotional tour or charitable event. It was time to put those tactics to good use.

First, she placed yet another call to Jacob Prentiss. After looking into other developers without success, she was pinning her hopes on Prentiss as the one who could best deliver on what the co-op wanted. So far, her efforts to contact him had not met with any response.

Next, Mallory consolidated a list of confirmed contacts who had shown interest in the co-op. Among them, Cora, Etta, Amira and Georgie had an extensive social network; it was time to reach out to see if any of their friends and contacts were interested in the new Bellavista development. Finding Cora in Amira's sitting room, where they were watching an old episode of *Star Trek: The Next Generation*, their nightly habit as Amira had become a rabid fan, Mallory asked how she could get hold of the APHIDS, Cora's gardening group.

"Check Government House tomorrow, as it's our regular gardening day," said Cora, looking up from her crochet project. "I'm not able to join them; you could take my place, but I warn you, they start very early."

"I'm going to pitch the Bellavista Housing Cooperative and see if I can get them to sign up," said Mallory.

Amira burst out laughing at something on the screen. "Oh, Dr. Beverly, you really are an amazing woman!" she said admiringly.

"I've tried several times," said Cora to Mallory with a sigh. "Be prepared to be turned down. My friends are fairly set in their ways and not interested in change."

♋

All the same, it was worth a try. Waking at the crack of dawn the next day, however, was a struggle. She tiptoed through the mess of Saffron's belongings scattered around the floor, leaving Saffron snoring in her bed, oblivious to the world. Mallory didn't want to miss catching the APHIDs first thing. On the short walk to Government House, she breathed in the cool, misty air as she rehearsed her pitch.

"Hey, there!" called a voice. It was Art Papatonis, still parked in his lawn chair in front of the construction fencing next door with a book, his signs on full display. "Where are you off to so early?"

"I'm going to offer my gardening services at Government House," Mallory answered cheerfully. "How goes the protest?"

Papatonis grunted with satisfaction. "Had the chance to enlighten some potential investors who came to check out the site. Oak Bay types looking for a luxurious retirement. They backed away after I set out Sand Dollar's dismal track record."

"Do you think you could direct them our way?" asked Mallory, only partially joking.

"Send me your promotional materials," answered Papatonis. "If Narkiss and Sand Dollar Developments are out of the picture, I'm more than happy to promote Ms. Sherman's co-op. Here's my cell number and email."

"Thanks!" said Mallory, surprised at his affability. "You seem in better spirits these days."

"Looks like I might finally have a buyer for my condo. Not the price I wanted, but it's going off the market and I can move on."

"That's great news."

"Enjoy your walk. It's been years since I've explored those gardens."

"You should check them out," said Mallory. She wiggled her fingers. "Maybe get a little dirt on your hands?"

Papatonis chuckled and waved her off.

Volunteers were already hard at work in the garden beds of Government House as she entered the gates. An imposing stone edifice with large gabled windows and a modern steel roof, the residence of the King's representative had extensive grounds that were open to the public from sunrise to sundown. Mallory had spent many a lazy Saturday as a student with a blanket and book on the manicured lawns. Passing a stand of towering redwoods and a waterfall flanked by a rustic Japanese lantern and a flowering cherry tree, Mallory found two of Cora's group, Agatha and Doreen, deadheading roses in the Italianate rose garden. The women raised their heads and waved when they saw her, having heard from Cora to expect her.

"I've come to help," said Mallory. "Cora couldn't make it this morning."

"Wonderful," said Agatha, "We could use another pair of hands. Edith's at the dentist so we're down one today."

A few minutes later, Mallory was lugging topsoil in an ancient wheelbarrow. Her back ached, but she gamely kept up with the women as they worked their way through the flower beds. Mallory wished she'd brought a bottle of water; even that early in the day the sun beat down and there was little shade where she was working.

"Break time," called Agatha an hour later, to Mallory's relief. "Not too shabby," Agatha added with a smile, "keeping up with a bunch of octogenarians."

Finding a flat-topped boulder, Mallory sank down, wiping the sweat from her face. Gratefully, she accepted a chilled bottle of iced tea, taking a large swig, and sitting back to enjoy the views of the Olympic Peninsula and Cascade Mountains, framed by a wide stretch of sparkling sea. The gentle buzz of honeybees serenaded her as she looked out over the scene. The craggy slope to the rear of the house had been developed into an attractive rockery, with purple lobelias and trailing moss nestled between winding gravel paths and flagstone steps, offset by tall-stemmed alliums, their spherical heads bobbing in the breeze. It was a gorgeous spot with a unique vantage point.

She took the break as an opportunity to talk up the co-op's development plans. Agatha and Doreen listened to her spiel politely, after assuring her that they weren't put off by recent incidents at Bellavista.

"I don't know if I'm ready to give up my privacy," said Agatha frankly. "I've always lived on my own and I don't want to have to deal with other people all the time."

Doreen nodded in agreement. "I raised five children and never had a place of my own, so I'm relishing being in my little studio. I get up in the morning and no one tells me what to do or what to eat or where I have to be. It's wonderful!"

Mallory tried again. "Living at Bellavista won't take your privacy or independence away. If anything, being part of a larger, supportive community will ensure you can live independently much longer. With varied meal plans plus a self-catering suite, you have the best of both worlds. There's also no pressure to get together with the other residents, except for a monthly maintenance meeting. And you'd have access to many amenities, including the residents' garden, activity center, not to mention on-site fresh produce. Family would be able to visit and stay in the guest residences, and the co-op is planning to implement a driver service for medical appointments and shopping trips."

Doreen looked thoughtful. "My children live in another city, and I rarely get to see them. Having a guest suite would mean they could come for longer visits. Living on my own, I do worry about anything happening to me and no one noticing."

"I'd miss my condo community too much," said Agatha. "There are young professionals, families with little children, seniors like me. Why would I go live with a bunch of old people when I'm eighty-five years young?"

Fair point. Mallory hadn't considered that Bellavista was not that different from Nate's Rock Cliff Resort, catering exclusively to an aging population and possibly isolating them into a seniors' bubble. What if they expanded the criteria for some of the new units to include multi-generational living?

At risk of letting her mind wander off topic, Mallory tucked Agatha's comment away for later, but couldn't hide her disappointment. Agatha reached over and touched her arm, saying, "Why don't you put my name down anyways? I can always take it off again if I decide not to join. If it helps Cora's application before council, I'm happy to do it."

"Me too," said Doreen. "And I'll give joining the co-op some more thought. You're going to have some excellent amenities."

"I was hoping to have a chat with Edith too," Mallory said happily. "Is there a way I could get in touch with her?"

Agatha grimaced. "Edith has a cell phone, but she rarely remembers to put it on and never responds to texts." Agatha thought for a moment. "It's Thursday. That means tonight's bingo night for Edith at the Quadra Community Center. That is likely the best way to reach her. Edith's grandson, Seth, volunteers as the bingo caller, so she always makes sure to attend. He's so helpful to his grandmother, even after his injury, which he got working for that wretched Nate Narkiss."

Mallory's ears perked up at the mention of Nate Narkiss. "What happened to Seth?"

"When Seth was getting his trade ticket, he worked for Sand Dollar Developments," said Doreen, "and he complained about the working conditions. Said the work sites weren't safe. As soon as Seth got his certification, he quit, but not before he was badly injured. Edith was very upset about it because Seth couldn't work in construction after that."

"That's awful," said Mallory. Did Seth hold a grudge against Sand Dollar and Nate Narkiss for his career-ending injury?

Agatha sniffed. "Nate Narkiss has always been shady. He got his start when the first leaky condos were making the news. My mother's condo was one of those affected. Sand Dollar came in promising that they could fix anything well within our budget, but they did shoddy work. The costs kept going up and up and up…and we were paying out more and more, until the owner's association had enough and got a second opinion. We learned that half of the work was unnecessary and poorly done. We found out recently that Sand Dollar had a plant on their board, a buddy of Nate's, and he made sure the association voted to give work to Sand Dollar. Blatant conflict of interest! It took all my savings to remediate my mother's condo and then I had to sell it at a loss. We were told not to bother trying to sue. Now I've learned that the same person has been buying up other condos at another location, Heritage Acres, with the plan to fix them and resell them at a profit!"

"That's so unethical!" said Mallory. Something Agatha said twigged a memory for Mallory, but she lost the thread, distracted by someone coughing nearby. Branches rustled. Was someone there?

"Probably a deer," said Doreen, noticing Mallory's glance at the bushes. "They've taken over the Garry Oak Grove at the bottom of the gardens." She sighed. "No matter what we do, they always come back to eat the roses."

Mallory said goodbye to the two women and left the gardens. Papatonis wasn't in his lawn chair, though his scooter was parked in its usual spot when she passed by. She'd better not forget to send him that promotional information. She tapped a reminder into her phone. When she got back to the house, the alarm sounded, and she printed out the promotional brochures she'd put together and returned to Papatonis's spot. Ruling out leaving the brochures on the lawn chair where they would blow away, she checked the scooter's paniers. A side one was unbuckled, so she lifted the top to put in the brochure. Something red caught her eye. A can of spray paint? Was Art the anonymous vandal of Sand Dollar's sign*s*? It seemed likely, but it was none of her business. She tucked the brochure in and returned to Bellavista.

With Agatha and Doreen now on the list of prospective co-op members, Mallory set her sights on recruiting Edith and the bingo hall attendees. And maybe slipping in some questions about her grandson's experience with Sand Dollar Developments...if it came up in conversation. But she met with unexpected resistance from Saffron when she proposed her plan to attend the bingo hall that evening.

"We need to look for big-time investors," said Saffron. "Not small fry like Cora's gardening buddies."

"I'm working on the big investors too, but not having any luck," said Mallory with a sigh. "The more we can show council that there's genuine interest in this kind of housing development, the more likely they'll approve our plans."

In the end, Saffron decided to go, because, as she said, "I've nothing else to do."

Saffron talked Georgie into joining them, and the two went through Georgie's well-stocked closet looking for appropriate apparel. When they both emerged sometime later, Saffron was decked out in a long-sleeved, very loud floral chiffon shirt with stretch pants and platform wedges, and Georgie was wearing a stretch leotard, leggings and Uggs topped by a leopard-print puffy vest. They were both sporting sun visors.

"You look like you're about to go on a cruise. For swinging seniors," said Mallory.

"Don't mock your elders." Georgie's head tilted to one side as she assessed Mallory. "You could use glamming up yourself. Give me five minutes and you won't recognize yourself."

Mallory looked down at her uniform of striped, long-sleeved cotton top, cardigan and jeans. "Thanks, I'm good."

"But you could be better," said Georgie frankly. Mallory made a face and Georgie laughed. "I've got something that will jazz you up. Look!"

Georgie opened an enormous tote bag and pulled out an assortment of items. "Daubers!"

"What are those?" asked Mallory.

"They're for stamping your bingo card! And these are our good-luck charms. They're essential. I have one for each of us!"

Saffron's dauber was green, and Mallory's was blue. Georgie's was gold glitter. Georgie handed Mallory a troll doll with blue hair, which she tucked into her tote bag.

Checking her wristwatch, Mallory announced, "We should get going. Bingo starts in fifteen minutes, and we may have to find parking."

They did need to find parking, as the lot was full, and they had to park way up the street. At the entrance to the community center, a bored-looking teen sat behind a folding table playing on his phone.

"We'd like three bingo cards, please." Mallory pointed to the stack of bingo cards on the table.

The teen didn't bother to look up from his game. "They're $12 for six."

"We only want three."

"$12 for six," he repeated.

She pulled out a twenty and the teen counted out change.

"It's foursquare tonight," he called after them.

Inside the hall, a game was already underway. Mallory spoke to a few volunteers, who agreed to let her use one of the tables at the back to set up her promotional display. As the three of them looked for seats, they were met with a few glares. The room had about twenty occupants sitting in rows in front of folding tables. Scanning the room, she spotted Edith Hashimoto seated near the front, wearing a visor like Saffron's and Georgie's, with an impressive array of daubers and dolls in front of her. The handsome young man in flannel up front spinning the bingo globe, she figured, must be Edith's grandson, Seth.

She motioned to Saffron and Georgie to take the second-row seats while she slid into the seat beside Edith.

"Hi, Edith," she whispered, and was immediately shushed by other players.

Edith turned and whispered, "Hi Mallory. You can't sit there. That's Cindy's special seat." She went back to concentrating on her card, dauber at the ready.

"N8!" Seth called out.

Mallory moved one seat over, hoping she wasn't sitting in someone else's "special seat." She placed her blue dauber and troll doll in front of her on the table. The room was tensely silent, the only sound being Seth's voice calling out the numbers and the occasional thump as bingo players simultaneously stamped their squares. No one said a word. She was perplexed by the silence; she'd been expecting a merry group event with people socializing as the calls went out.

"E10!" called out Seth. He flashed a grin. Mallory guessed he was very popular with the audience. Most of the players had a row of colored daubers in front of them as well as a collection of good luck charms. She spotted other troll dolls, a few "My Little Pony" dolls, some Beanie Babies and a surprising number of Buddhas and miniature statues of the Virgin Mary.

"B3!"

She leaned over to Edith. "Is that your grandson Seth up front?"

"SHHHH!" hissed the room. Mallory retreated to her seat.

"L17!"

"BINGO!!!!!"

She turned to see Georgie jumping up and down, beside herself with excitement, an equally delirious Saffron jumping next to her. Seth came down from the front and checked out Georgie's card. "I'm sorry, ma'am, but you only have four squares in a row."

"I know! I got all four!"

"We're playing foursquare tonight – you need to get all four rows along the outer edges."

It took a while for Seth to explain the logistics to Georgie, and when she started arguing, the crowd began to get restless. Reading the mood of the room, Mallory shoved their daubers and dolls into her tote bag and herded a protesting Saffron and Georgie toward the back.

As Saffron and Georgie comparison-tasted the cookies on offer at the refreshment table, Mallory observed the crowd. The tightly packed hall held at least fifty people, most of them at or past retirement. The perfect target audience.

After the final call was made and the winner declared, participants gathered up their belongings and made a beeline for the refreshment table. Mallory stood beside the enlarged redevelopment plans, trying to catch the eye of anyone curious enough to check out her brochures. They were few and far between.

She spotted Edith and Seth heading her way.

"Hi Edith! Did you have a good time?" asked Mallory.

"I always enjoy myself," said Edith smiling. "Even more when I win. Mallory, this is my grandson, Seth."

Seth reached out his hand. "Seth Hashimoto," he said, shaking her hand. "Sorry that your friend didn't win." He nodded in Georgie's direction.

"She'll get over it. You do this often?"

"Every week. Wouldn't miss it because I get to spend time with my *Obaasan*." Seth gave his petite grandmother a squeeze. Edith beamed.

"What have you got here?" asked Seth, taking in the brochures.

"That's what I wanted to talk to Edith about. Edith, has Cora mentioned that Bellavista is now running as a housing cooperative and is looking to expand? Are you at all interested in one of our new units?"

"I'm happy on my own, thank you," said Edith. "I love my little one-bedroom near Cook Street village. I'm so close to the ocean and the shops."

"*Obaasan*, take a look at these units." Seth checked out the posted plans. "You'd have access to the gardens and be within walking distance of Government House."

"The location is wonderful," agreed Edith, "but I don't think I'm ready for a retirement home. I'm only eighty-seven."

Georgie wandered by at that moment. "Mallory, my dear," she said, "Do you happen to have a pen and some masking tape?"

"Bellavista is more than a retirement home," continued Mallory, after Georgie had been supplied from her capacious tote bag. "It's an intentional community with supportive facilities. You get to experience privacy and independence but also friendship and support at close hand when you need them. We're looking to install some electric vehicle chargers and have an on-site vehicle for common use. Even if you don't drive, you could sign up for a driver to take you to appointments and shopping."

"That sounds fantastic, don't you think so?" asked Seth. "*Obaasan*, I'll take a brochure and we can talk about it."

When Edith agreed, a spark of hope lit up inside Mallory. Seth led his grandmother over to the refreshments, where Saffron was talking to an older couple in matching outfits at her table. Maybe they'd stir up some real interest in the cooperative.

"Hey, I recognize you!" the wife said to Saffron.

Saffron perked up. "Yes, that was me, in that perfume ad that aired a couple of years ago. I get recognized sometimes from that."

"I don't know about a perfume ad, but I definitely saw you on that YouTube video about the house tour! Is this the same property? That was hilarious! The exploding dough! The peacocks!"

Saffron's smile faltered. "Those peacocks are something else, aren't they? Did you catch my spiel about the community center? Let me tell you about the improvements we're making."

"Is Jacob Prentiss involved?" asked the husband. "He does terrific restoration work."

"No, not Prentiss, but we're looking for contractors to work with us on the redevelopment."

"Pah! This project is way behind where it should be if you haven't got a contractor yet." The man dropped the brochure back on the table and walked away. Saffron caught Mallory's eye and shrugged. Over at the other end of the table, it looked like Georgie was having much more success, talking animatedly with someone while a line-up started to form behind them.

Seth came over to Mallory and spoke in a lowered voice. "I saw on the news that the police are looking for Lucas Turner in connection to Nate Narkiss's murder. I didn't want to say anything in front of *Obaasan*, but I remember Lucas from my trades training with Sand Dollar. He didn't strike me as the aggressive type."

"We're all shocked as well," she said. "Do you mind if I ask you some questions about working with Sand Dollar Development?"

"Sure, what do you want to know?" asked Seth.

"I heard you were injured on the job and had to change careers."

"Yeah, I apprenticed as an electrician with Sand Dollar Developments about a year ago. It wasn't the best experience. Some of the guys didn't bother to wear steel-toed boots or hard hats or even safety goggles. No one monitored compliance with safety procedures. They put the signs up, you know, so if anyone inspected the site it would all look good? But there was pressure from the older guys to act tough and not wear the gear. I got ragged on if I wanted to do things the right way. I've heard that residential building work sites can be like that, but I've never seen someone trying that kind of stuff on a commercial site."

"Did you work with Nate Narkiss directly?"

"With Brad Jobson more than Nate. I knew Nate by sight, but he was the business guy, the guy making the deals, right? He was on the site I was at maybe once, twice, and that was it. Brad ran operations at the site. I reported to him and to the site manager."

"And how was Brad to work with?"

Seth frowned. "He liked showing he was the boss. The worst part was that he cut corners on jobs. Brought in low-grade materials. It started to grate on some of the guys… they take pride in doing a decent job— we're skilled tradespeople, right? Brad didn't respect that; he tried to squeeze the most money out of a project and he didn't care if the work was done well. When I started with him, Nate and Brad were doing up old buildings. Ever heard of "reno-victions"?"

Seth used air quotes around the term and she nodded. She had heard of the strategy by landlords to evict tenants on the basis that they needed to do major renovations, then upgrade the units out of the price range of the original tenants.

"Nate and Brad specialized in those. And condo remediation—you know, the leaking condos and problems with building envelopes? I got tired of the unsafe conditions, though, and quit after I got injured."

"Did you ever hear about or see any drug use on work sites?"

"No way!" Seth shook his head adamantly. "One time someone showed up high when Nate was on-site, and Nate fired him. I remember that time because he wasn't on-site that often. Nate made it clear to the crew that he had zero tolerance for drugs on-site and would fire anyone who came to work high."

"What about Brad? Does he apply the same standard?"

Seth squinted his eyes in thought. "I heard from some other guys that Brad turned a blind eye to that kind of stuff. I got out of that situation as soon as I could. Sorry, I don't know anything more."

"You've been really helpful; thanks so much. What do you do now? I heard you left construction."

Seth smiled. "Crazy as it sounds, that injury was the best thing that ever happened to me. Worker's Comp set me up with a career assessment coach and I got retrained in alarm and security systems. I get to use my electrician's training but spend less time on my feet. I like the work, the benefits, and best of all, my girlfriend doesn't worry anymore about me coming home injured."

"It sounds like you landed in a good place," said Mallory.

Seth grinned. "I landed in a *great* place."

☙

On the ride back, Mallory shared with Saffron the details of her conversation with Seth and his confirmation of Nate's aversion to drug use.

"I'm sure that the police got it wrong about Lucas and Nate," insisted Mallory as she drove back into town. "Nate hated drugs; he wouldn't have been dealing with Lucas. I think Lucas must know who assaulted Nate and that's why he's been acting weird and took off."

"That's my theory too," said Georgie, nodding sagely from the back seat. "People were most interested when I shared it tonight."

"What?" cried Mallory aghast. "Why were you talking about the investigation? The last thing we want is people still associating the co-op with Nate's murder!"

"Why do you think Georgie had so many people lined up to talk to her?" asked Saffron as she scrolled through her phone. "Didn't you see the hand-written notice she posted on the wall: 'My Night with a Murderer'?"

Mallory groaned. "Georgie! Lucas hasn't even been charged with anything!"

"You have other things to worry about," said Saffron, looking up from her phone. "Cora texted me. It appears you have a visitor."

Chapter 15

> *"Expect the unexpected."*
> *- Raquel DeWitt, The Smart Woman's Guide to Getting it Done.*

"Surprise!"

An astonished Mallory found herself enfolded in an exuberant hug on the front steps of Bellavista.

"Raquel! W-what are you doing here?"

Raquel beamed her bright-red-lipstick smile. "The twins are away at volleyball camp, and I'm between book tours, so I decided to take a trip and come see you! Look at this darling place!"

"If you'd told me you were coming, I could have made arrangements," said Mallory nervously. Was Raquel planning to stay at Bellavista?

"Not to worry! I'm staying with my cousin, Hope. She has this fabulous condo, right on the waterfront."

Mallory's shoulders relaxed in relief. But they tensed back up when Raquel added, "Would you give me a ride to her place? I forgot to ask the cab to wait for me."

Raquel had arrived with five huge pieces of luggage and the assumption that Mallory would be able to drop everything to cater to her immediate needs. On the car ride to her cousin's condo in the Laurel Point Inn, Raquel booked spa appointments for the next day and insisted, despite Mallory's protests, that Mallory join her.

"Since you left, we hardly get to see each other and next month, I'll be touring," pouted Raquel as they pulled up in front of the condo.

"When will we ever get this opportunity to do spontaneous things together?"

"What about Hope? Won't she want to go to the spa?" asked Mallory desperately. She really didn't have time to indulge in spa treatments.

"Oh, she's coming too! I've arranged for pedicures by the thermal pools! I'm doing all the wellness things this trip before the book tour." Raquel let out a dramatic sigh, adjusting the silk scarf draped around her neck. "I can't say I'm excited to be travelling again, especially when you won't be at home taking care of everything."

"I'm sure Phyllicia is taking great care of you all," said Mallory.

"Oh, she's wonderful, but she's not you," said Raquel. "I think Phyllicia would be much happier in her old position as housekeeper rather than concierge. Now, what do you think about coming back to work for me?"

Mallory blinked. That was unexpected. "We agreed that you didn't need me any longer because the twins were leaving for school, remember? What's changed?"

"It's not the same! You know what I need to have with me when travelling, my comforts at the hotels, even the books I like loaded onto my reader! I miss you and want you to come back to work with me."

"It's not that simple," said Mallory, taken aback. "I've started my own business and I've got obligations to other people now. I never expected to be asked back."

"Well, what do you think?" Raquel demanded. "Now that I've brought it up. Will you give it some thought? Please?"

A frazzled Mallory drove back to Bellavista. She parked the car and sat for a moment, staring into space. What a day, starting with physical labor at dawn and ending with her chauffeuring her old boss around town in the middle of the night. Her to-do list had gotten a whole lot longer, and now she had to take two precious hours out of her packed schedule to spend "quality time" with Raquel. She let out a loud groan, banged on the steering wheel and stamped her feet in frustration. Spent from her hissy fit, she slumped back in the seat. When was she going to learn to say no?

That was the uncomfortably astute observation made by her mother on a call the next morning.

"You've got your own business now," said Fiona, after hearing Mallory grouse about Raquel's arrival. "Raquel has never been good about respecting your boundaries. I'm afraid you're going to have to enforce them yourself. Even if that means disappointing the marvelous Ms. DeWitt."

"I know," said Mallory. Her mother was right, but it smarted that she had to point it out to her daughter.

"Hold on, your father wants to speak to you."

Walter came on the line. "What's your old boss doing out there? If she bothers you, tell her to mind her own business." Walter McKenzie-Chu was not the soul of diplomacy when it came to anyone causing grief to his family.

"How's Bob?" she asked, not wanting to rehash the whole issue again.

"I thought I'd figured out the *perfect* Bob-proof contraption with that horizontal wire, but do you what the little devil did? We had a snowfall last night and the wire got encrusted with frozen snow. I looked out the kitchen window and saw Bob, upside down, crossing the wire fist over fist, like one of those soldiers in basic training! The frozen snow helped his grip! I couldn't believe it."

Mallory laughed. She wasn't missing spring in Montreal, with its freak snowstorms. "Next time, get it on video!"

"I sure will! You take care, and don't let DeWitt walk all over you."

Easier said than done. At least her family had stopped pressuring her to return home. That had to count as progress.

Her phone pinged. Raquel had sent a text suggesting they meet for breakfast before their spa appointment at eleven. Her old boss was losing no chance to take up all her available time. In an uncharacteristic flash of rebellion, Mallory sent a text declining, and, in the thrill of that small victory, booked the morning entirely for herself. With all that had been going on, she hadn't had time to wander through the city and check out her favorite places. She'd made great progress in signing up potential members to the cooperative the last two days and lining up repair work to be done. Her to-do list could wait for a few more hours.

ଓ

The day shone bright and clear as she took a very pleasant stroll from Bellavista, down Rockland Avenue toward the downtown core. On Fort Street, she passed The Seasoned Connoisseur, where Pierce was arguing out front with a driver who had the audacity to park a huge van in his commercial parking space. She popped into The Daily Bun to say a quick hello to Una and grab a cinnamon roll. As she munched on her breakfast, relishing her solo adventure, she passed new storefronts, restaurants and a few high-rises, unexpected in a town that generally favored low-rise development.

One of her favorite bookstores, Russell Books, had moved to a larger space across the street from its original location. Mallory was browsing the career section when she backed into a staffer restocking a shelf.

"Oh, hi Mallory!"

It was Kiki, working at yet another job.

"Kiki, do you even sleep? How many jobs do you have?"

"I'm saving up for school and a place of my own, so I take whatever's available. I'm here one morning a week, helping to restock."

Mallory looked around the bookstore, known for its excellent selection of new and used books and knowledgeable staff. "I've always wanted to work in a bookstore."

"It's great fun. And the employee discount is not too shabby." As Kiki went back to restocking, Mallory asked impulsively. "Kiki, when's your break? Are you free to join me for tea?"

Twenty minutes later, Kiki and Mallory were seated in a booth at the Dutch Bakery & Diner, across the street from Russell Books. Seeing Kiki eyeing the sandwich platters passing by, Mallory tactfully ordered croquettes with a salad, and invited Kiki to select something from the menu; Kiki happily chose the daily special of tuna on rye with a side of pickles. While waiting for their orders to arrive, Mallory asked, "Kiki, you mentioned you're really into true crime, right?"

"Yeah, I've applied to get my criminology diploma. I've read all the true crime books at Russell's." She leaned forward and lowered her voice. "Why, does this have to do with Nate's murder?"

Mallory wanted someone else's objective opinion on her concerns, and who better than a self-confessed true crime expert? In giving Kiki a rundown of the case against the Bellavista residents, she had a momentary qualm, but Kiki seemed unfazed. In an instant, she transformed from a bubbly K-pop star look-alike into a laser-focused investigator.

"Right," said Kiki, spearing a pickle with her fork, "the police need to establish the three prongs for proving guilt: motive, means and opportunity."

Mallory nodded.

"I'm not seeing the evidence or motive." Kiki waved the pickle for emphasis. "You're worried because you think Etta's hiding something, and that Amira's been encouraging her to confess. I think you need to ask them what's going on. Or, now that Saffron's here, see if she can talk to them?"

"Those are fair points."

"In addition," began Kiki, then paused to take a bite of pickle. "Wow, these are super good! In addition, how do these women even benefit from Nate's death? On the face of it, Nate Narkiss posed a threat to their cooperative, but the real threat is that Saffron could decide to sell her share of Bellavista to him or that Cora could buckle and agree to sell. What would killing Nate get them? A delay? But not for long. There'd always be another buyer."

Mallory nodded slowly, absorbing Kiki's point.

"Unless they killed him by accident," said Kiki, "and we can rule that out because all three would have had to work together to bring Nate down. He was a big guy. I can't see that they're involved. The police don't have a case, in my opinion."

Well, this was embarrassing. When Kiki spelled everything out, it was obvious there wasn't a strong motive for any of the women to get rid of Nate. The police would come to that realization too.

"Simon Green said much the same thing when we met," admitted Mallory, "but I thought that's what all criminal defense lawyers say to make their clients feel better."

"On the other hand," said Kiki, moving onto her sandwich, "I can totally see Georgie doing it if it was a crime of passion."

Mallory blinked at that.

"Lucas being the culprit is a real possibility, and that bums me out," said Kiki. "I'm in and out of Bellavista practically every day and I never suspected drugs. I'll need to improve my observation skills if I want to be a criminologist."

"None of us suspected Lucas," said Mallory. "I still don't feel right about him being responsible for Nate's death. It feels so...random."

"Back to the original question, then," said Kiki, tapping the Formica tabletop for emphasis. "Who benefits? Who benefits from Nate Narkiss being dead?"

"Nate doesn't have any dependents or family," said Mallory slowly. "At least, Metchosin didn't mention any family and I haven't found anything about family in my online searches. I read somewhere that Nate left his entire estate to The Wheelbarrow Foundation."

"What about Nate's businesses—who gets those?" asked Kiki, taking a bite of her sandwich. "Wow, this is super delicious too! Why have I never eaten here before?"

"According to an article I read online, Nate and his business partner, Brad Jobson, own Sand Dollar Developments together and were best friends," Mallory told Kiki. "Recently, Nate made moves to work with Jacob Prentiss and Landmark Developments, the big heritage renovations firm. Pierce told me that's why Nate was so eager to join the golf club; he wanted the social clout so he could move in the same circles as Prentiss."

"I got the sense from something Metchosin once said that Nate might have played dirty in his business dealings." Kiki frowned. "Maybe Nate ticked someone off? Snatched a deal away from someone or angered a competitor?"

"That's a more likely scenario," agreed Mallory. "I'll search around the *Vic in the Know* blog and see if I unearth any recent gossip about Nate. Thanks, Kiki. It really helped to hear your perspective. Now, if you can teach me how to balance out my two jobs, I'll be fine."

Kiki finished her sandwich and wiped her hands with her napkin. "Two jobs? Now you're sounding like me. Who are you working for besides Cora?"

Mallory filled Kiki in on the demands posed by Raquel and her endless wellness treatments.

"Ooh. I loved *The Smart Woman's Guide to Getting It Done*," cried Kiki. "Sometimes I hear Raquel's voice in my head when I'm struggling with a task, like she's my personal coach."

"I know that voice well," said Mallory dryly. "Let's just say, Raquel's secret to getting it done is to delegate it to me! I'm worn out trying to round up investors for the cooperative without running around after her. How do you balance all your many gigs and keep them straight?"

"I'm married to my phone and the voice memo app. If I don't have an alarm going off telling me where to be, I'm lost."

"Me too. I have alarms going off telling me when to go to bed!"

"I also have a secret weapon." Kiki reached down for her bag and pulled out a hardcover journal. "See this? It's a bullet journal." She showed Mallory the dotted pages where she'd marked down the month and the days of the week by number down the edge of the page. "I tried regular agendas, but there was never enough space and I can only do so much on my phone. I start a month on the left page and then use the right page for to dos, notes and random thoughts. I can keep adding pages as needed. Then when that month is over, I turn to another page to start the next month."

"That's brilliant," said Mallory. Her desk drawer at home was filled with half-used agendas, diaries and journals, every type of time management and organization system under the sun. She'd have to give bullet journals a try.

"But why do you have to accommodate Raquel when you don't work for her?" Kiki said, a puzzled look on her face.

The million-dollar question. Mallory put down her cup. "It's complicated. Raquel was my first boss, and we were a team for a very long time. She knows that I've got another job, but I think she's so used to relying on me to arrange things she can't break the habit. I'm hoping that her cousin Hope will occupy her time while she's here."

Kiki's eyes brightened. "If Hope is Hope DeWitt, then she's on some of the same boards as Metchosin. I bet Hope has great connections. You should ask Raquel if her cousin knows anyone who'd be interested in investing in the co-op development."

"I'm not sure…" The idea left Mallory uncomfortable. While Raquel had always been generous, getting Mallory passes to events for her family or restaurant reservations for special occasions, Mallory had never thought to use Raquel's connections for advancing her business.

After Kiki left to finish her shift, Mallory headed to the library. In the public computer lab, she spent the next hour reading blog entries, newspaper articles and the Landmark Developments website, and taking extensive notes. The *Vic in the Know* site had plenty of items on Jacob Prentiss, mostly benign fluff pieces about Prentiss's philanthropic activities and new restoration projects. However, there was one entry dated a month earlier tagged #PrentissisaPhony that stood out; the post insinuated that Prentiss paid off city officials to look the other way when his developments skirted building code requirements. Interesting.

She took a break from research to make another call to Prentiss's office. This time the receptionist admitted he was out golfing and wouldn't be back. Mallory didn't want to give up on Prentiss, but at what point would calls to his office start to look like stalking?

Mallory steadily worked through the materials until her alarm went off. She glanced at her phone. Gaaaah! Barely enough time to get to the spa appointment! Grabbing her bag, she rushed out, berating herself for yet again failing to plan for travel time.

Just then, a ping announced a text. Raquel.

Hope can't make it, so I invited your friend Saffron to take her place.

She'll pick you up if you text where you are!

A string of unfamiliar epithets ran through her head. What in the blazing saddles was Raquel up to now?

Chapter 16

> **"Every now and then, it's good to take a break."**
> **- Raquel DeWitt,** *The Smart Woman's Guide to Getting it Done.*

Nestled among Douglas firs and fragrant cedar, the newly constructed hotel and spa took full advantage of the spectacular views over Cordova Bay. In the hushed, sand-hued lobby, Mallory and Saffron signed in for their appointments. The calming, west coast palette extended into the changing room, where driftwood shelving adorned cedar-lined walls and heated stone flooring warmed their feet. Under the invigorating blast of the deluxe shower, Mallory made liberal use of the organic bath products, emerging in a cloud of eucalyptus and citrus. She was snuggling into a plush, warm robe when Saffron poked her head over the changing room door.

"Looks like Raquel signed you up for a hot stone massage and a seaweed wrap. You're getting the full West Coast experience. You're in Room 3."

"What treatments are you getting?"

"Full body massage and then a facial!" Saffron's face lit up with a blissed-out expression. "She booked joint pedicures for us afterwards down by the thermal pools on the deck. I can't wait!"

Mallory slipped on a pair of complimentary woven-straw flip-flops and headed for Room 3. Despite her annoyance with Raquel pre-empting her day, she found she was looking forward to her treatments. Her shoulders were stiff from her gardening work out at

Government House, not to mention the tension she'd been holding for the last few days. The unexpected pampering had put Saffron in a great mood. Why not luxuriate in Raquel's generosity and enjoy herself?

In Room 3, Mallory found a sturdy-looking therapist smoothing down the massage table covers and layering terrycloth towels on top.

"Welcome!" said the therapist brightly. "Are you Mallory? I'm Chevonne. I'll be giving you both of your treatments today."

"Hi," said Mallory. I've never done a hot stone massage before, so let me know what I need to do to get ready."

"Oh, you're going to love this treatment. You'll be *amazingly relaxed*. We'll have to carry you out of here!" Chevonne had a booming laugh. "Now shimmy out of that robe, pop onto the table face-down on your tummy and we'll get started."

Mallory did as she was told, slipping between the towels before Chevonne rapped on the door with a cheery, "Yoo-hoo? Are you ready?"

"Yes," answered Mallory. She breathed through her mouth. Was her nose supposed to be squished like that against the massage table?

"Oh, dear!" cried Chevonne. Something clicked near Mallory's head. "I forgot to attach the headrest. Scoot over to this end of the table and put your face into this."

Mallory "scooted" over. The headpiece made lying face-down much more comfortable. She took in a relieved breath through her nose, let it out and felt her body sink into the mattress.

BAM! Mallory's whole body jerked awake at the thundering sound of rocks being poured into a steel bowl.

"Oh, sorry!" trilled Chevonne, "I'm getting the stones ready. Here we go! Get ready to be relaxed."

Mallory closed her eyes again and tried to relax, waiting for the treatment to begin.

Chevonne gently placed a hot stone at the base of Mallory's spine and added stones one by one in a row. The heat from the stones made Mallory feel as if she was melting into the table. Chevonne placed more hot stones along Mallory's shoulder blades and down her arms. Mallory's jaw went slack.

CRASH! Mallory jolted awake.

"Oh, clumsy me!" cried Chevonne. She had dropped stones onto the wood floor. Chevonne bent down and began picking them. Clunk, clunk, went the stones as they dropped into the bowl. Mallory's jaw clenched. Clunk. Clunk. Clunk.

"I have some fresh stones ready to go," said Chevonne. "This time, please scoot down under the towel and when you're ready, flip yourself over."

For the second time, she "scooted" down and rolled her body over. All that twisting and turning made her feel like a trussed turkey on a spit. Her sinuses appreciated the change, though. A warm, damp cloth dropped gently over her closed eyes. She took another deep breath. In and out. Relax, she told herself. Breathe.

Mallory jerked awake. "Ack!" The fresh stones were blisteringly hot.

"I must have left them in the heater too long!" cried Chevonne in distress; "My fingers are like Teflon. I can never tell how hot the stones are. Oh, look at your poor arms! Here, let me put some aloe vera on those burns."

By the time her treatments were finished, Mallory looked like an unraveled, naked Egyptian mummy and smelled like something left out on the beach. Red welts covered her arms and torso from the stones, and she had developed an itch from whatever was in the seaweed wrap.

A passing spa guest recoiled as Mallory lurched out of Room 3. Looking for the sign to the thermal pools, she stumbled down the hallway past the sauna. The door opened as a guest came out and a vaguely familiar voice floated up through the open door.

"I bet Metchosin was livid when Nate moved on to Becca Gill! That's why they were always at each other's throats!"

Curiosity got the better of her. As she navigated her way inside the sauna, a cloud of steam rose from the hot rocks, blocking her view.

"Excuse me. Sorry!" She tried to avoid landing on any of the other patrons as she found an empty spot on the bench and sat, leaning back against the heated wood. When her eyes adjusted, she could make out three forms sitting on the bench across from her. Which one of them had dropped that tantalizing bit of gossip?

No one spoke as the heat continued to rise. Mallory broke out into a sweat. The other three women were naked except for discreetly placed towels. She didn't have a towel with her so unless she was prepared to go completely *au naturel*, she was stuck baking in her robe. The impression of being a trussed turkey returned with a vengeance.

As the heat grew unbearable, one of them said, "I thought Becca only dated Nate for a couple of months?"

"It wasn't how long she dated him; it was when. There might have been crossover, shall we say? No wonder Metchosin was ticked off about paying alimony."

"Why didn't she expose him?"

"Too humiliated, I guess. But then Becca broke up with him recently, did you hear? I suppose his charm wore thin."

"Shhhh!" hissed the third guest. She pointed to the sign on the wall that read "Silence Please."

Everyone lapsed back into silence. Mallory waited a while longer, but the two gossips appeared to have been properly chastened. Unable to bear the heat any longer, Mallory gave up and left, hurrying out to the thermal pools.

ঞ

"Mallory, over here!" Saffron waved from her seat on the sun-filled deck.

Mallory plopped onto the padded armchair next to Saffron. A smiling pedicurist invited her to put her feet into a steaming tub. Bliss…this was the relaxation she'd been waiting for. She took in the views of the waterfront, sun glinting off the smooth stretch of water in the sheltered bay and breathed deeply.

"Where've you been?" asked Saffron, "Our pedicures started a while ago. Mine's already done, so I asked if I could get a manicure too and they fitted me in. Raquel went to check out lunch options."

Mallory filled her in on the sauna room gossip.

"Interesting," said Saffron. She tried to reach into the pocket of her bathrobe, to the alarm of the manicurist, who was still filing her nails. "Mallory, see if you can reach into my pocket and get my phone."

"I thought we weren't supposed to bring phones into the spa."

Saffron gave her a look. "As if. You know my password."

"You're still using the same password from school? Are you asking to get hacked?"

"I changed it! It has a different number at the end. Try "39."

Muttering under her breath, Mallory typed in Saffron's old password and added "39." "Ok, I'm in. Wait, are you using your actual *age* as part of your password?"

"Never mind that. Google 'Nate Narkiss' and 'Becca Gill,'" instructed Saffron.

Mallory scrolled through the hits. "Bingo!" She found a photo of Nate and Becca at the previous year's Wheelbarrow Foundation Gala.

Saffron craned her neck to look, her hands still captive to the manicurist. "What do you know? Okay, now try 'Nate Narkiss' and 'Jacob Prentiss.'"

The search pulled up a recent article about Nate's anticipated merger with Landmark Developments. There was an accompanying photo showed a smiling Nate on a golf course standing next to a large, grey-haired man with a barrel chest.

Saffron leaned over to look. "That's Jacob Prentiss. I recognize him from local magazine articles. Looks like Nate was shopping for a new partner."

"Nate Narkiss and Jacob Prentiss are revolutionizing Victoria one heritage property at a time," Mallory read aloud. "This article is dated from about six months ago. It says that Prentiss's firm was behind the renovations at Butchart Gardens."

Butchart Gardens was one of Victoria's most popular tourist attractions. A former rock quarry, it had been converted by the owners into a sunken garden wonderland that continued to attract visitors from all over the world.

"I'll see if there's an article about Nate's other business ventures." Mallory's fingers flew across the small screen.

"This article is dated about eight years back. That would be before he married Metchosin. "Brad Jobson and Nate Narkiss are poised to revolutionize development in Victoria," Mallory read out loud.

"Who knew Victoria was such a hotbed of revolution?" quipped Saffron.

"Shhh... Let me read. It says here that Brad and Nate met as kids and became lifelong friends, getting their start in flipping properties together. The article mentions the ramen wager Pierce told us about. Hmmm. According to this, Nate and Brad were planning to merge their two companies, Sand Dollar Enterprises and Sand Dollar Development into a mega full-service development and land management company called NextGen Developments. Never heard of it." Mallory looked up at Saffron. "I wonder if Brad and Nate didn't end up merging their companies and Nate decided to go into business with Jacob Prentiss instead?"

"Brad has been the model of the grieving friend and dedicated business partner. But if there was a breakdown in the partnership, leaving Brad out of the Prentiss deal, that would lead to a lot of bad feelings," said Saffron.

Then she sat back, frowning. "I still think Lucas is the real culprit. But there's a backstory to Nate's relationship with his ex-business partner and his ex-wife. Not to mention Becca dating Nate! Who's been telling us the truth and who's been spinning a tall tale? I'd go back to Metchosin. Something smells fishy and it's not her name."

෮ଓ

The demands of Mallory's growing to-do list, however, took precedence the next morning over further investigation.

"I've gone through Lucas's list," Cora began, when Mallory came downstairs for breakfast. "And tagged the tasks we can manage ourselves." Cora's brow puckered. "With Lucas gone, I'm beginning to see how much he did. I'd like to replace the lightbulbs with more energy-efficient ones. Would you be able to help me with that?"

"Sure. Do you want to do that after breakfast?"

"I'm in the middle of clearing out the second-floor, which will take me a while, so I thought we could do the lights later this afternoon."

"Okay, great. I'm working on getting a contractor in to help us with the larger repair jobs on the list. I'll make some calls this morning, and hopefully we can have someone in soon." Mallory did have "get a contractor" on her list of to-dos but had become completely absorbed last night in researching the numerous ties between Prentiss, Metchosin, Nate, Becca and Brad. It was time to get the co-op project back on track.

As Cora headed upstairs, Mallory's phone rang. It was Raquel. What now?

"Mallory! Can you come pick me up? I'm at Bolen Books, and I'm supposed to meet my cousin Hope at the Empress in fifteen minutes!"

And how is this my problem? But Raquel had hung up. Not for the first time, Mallory marveled at how the world's foremost self-help author was incapable of doing anything for herself. Should she send an Uber? Raquel probably didn't know how Uber worked. Resigned to spending the next half hour chauffeuring her former boss around, Mallory went to ask if she could borrow the car yet again.

Chapter 17

> "Play by the rules. Or don't."
> - Raquel DeWitt, *The Smart Woman's Guide to Getting it Done.*

High tea at the iconic Empress Hotel was legendary for several reasons. First, for the hushed elegance of its turn-of-the-century setting and second, for the staggering $89 per person cost before tax or gratuities. As Mallory escorted Raquel to where her cousin Hope was seated, she looked with interest at the potted palms, tasteful, upholstered-seating arrangements and plush carpet. Hope turned out to be an older replica of Raquel, from her silver-grey bob to the reading glasses dangling from a chain of sea-glass. She greeted Raquel with a warm hug and an exuberant kiss on the cheek.

"Welcome, welcome! Mallory, I've heard so much about you from Raquel! So glad to meet you! So glad!"

Mallory smiled politely. "Pleased to meet you. Raquel, you'll get a ride back with Hope?"

"Where are you off to? You're joining us today." Raquel waved her hand at the third armchair, gesturing for Mallory to take a seat.

"Yes!" echoed Hope. "Please sit! Sit!"

Mallory squelched her qualms about not getting back to her to-do list right away and took a seat in a plush armchair. Old habits were hard to break. Could she get away with having a quick cup of tea and a chat, then make her excuses? Mallory gulped as she did a mental calculation of her budget.

"High tea for three," said Hope to the hovering waitstaff. "My treat," she told Raquel and Mallory. "My treat. So don't even try to fight me for the bill."

Mallory hid her grin as she imagined these two immaculate women arm-wrestling over the bill. What would they think if they saw her relatives almost coming to blows at dim sum as they fought for the privilege of slapping down their credit cards? Her own mother once threw out her back after a wrangle over a lunch bill with one of her husband's sisters.

Out of habit, Mallory picked up the teapot when it arrived and started pouring the fragrant tea, admiring the porcelain cups with their delicate blue, pink and gold pattern. When Hope finished regaling Raquel with the latest family gossip, Raquel took up a topic that surprised Mallory.

"Hope, we need your advice on how to reach Jacob Prentiss, the developer. Mallory's working on a development project for a cooperative and she's been having trouble reaching him."

Mallory blinked, surprisingly touched that Raquel understood what her job was, let alone was willing to petition her cousin Hope for help.

"Not returning your calls?" said Hope, arching an eyebrow. "He's a hard man to pin down. I've been trying for weeks to get in touch about the art gallery's summer fundraiser. If you want to find him, he's at Cedar Grove, the golf club. He likes playing a round in the afternoon. Hmmm, you'll never get in unless you go with a member. They're such sticklers for the rules at Cedar Grove." Hope rolled her eyes. "Luckily, I happen to be one. I'll set up a tee time for us— this afternoon — and we'll track J.P. down."

"Oh, thank you, thank you!" cried Mallory gratefully. "That's wonderful, wonderful." She blushed as she unconsciously mimicked Hope's habit of repeating words. Fortunately, her new benefactor didn't seem to notice, or perhaps she was used to receiving effusive thanks.

Hope wasn't finished griping about the clubhouse rules. "Would you believe, their dress code is from the 1950s and won't allow women to wear collarless or sleeveless tops? When I first joined, I wrote to the governing committee pointing out the many top women golfers who wear sleeveless tops during championship tours, but do you think they took any notice? I'm not about to suffer through a hot flash without proper ventilation, so I pop a cardigan over my tank top and no one's the wiser. None the wiser."

A server glided up with a tiered plate stand and for a moment, everyone was preoccupied with making their selections.

"Now tell me more about this cooperative and why you need J.P.," said Hope, as she helped herself to a miniature quiche.

Mallory briefly outlined Bellavista's development plan for Hope.

"I may know some folks who would be interested in investing in a community like Bellavista," said Hope thoughtfully. "Let me put out some feelers and see what I can do."

As Mallory bit into a tiny scone topped with a dollop of Devonshire cream and strawberry jam, she felt optimistic about the project for the first time in a while. Maybe meeting Hope was the break the co-op needed.

☙

Raquel declined to join them on the grounds that a root canal would be more enjoyable than such a "mind-numbingly dull sport." Under Hope's patronage, Mallory was quickly kitted out with a set of clubs and a spare pair of golf shoes, and soon found herself whizzing down the freeway in a golf cart. The weather was picture-postcard perfect, with clear skies and a gentle breeze from the ocean that surrounded the exclusive golf course on all three sides of the peninsula. Mt. Baker's snow-covered peak floated over the horizon. For diehard golfers, Cedar Grove was paradise.

"J.P. will already be well into the course at this hour, so we'll scoot around to find him," said Hope as she whipped around a turn.

"Are we allowed to skip holes?" asked Mallory, clutching the side rail with one hand and her hat with the other.

"Who's going to stop us?" Hope scanned the horizon, her eyes squinting under her visor. "There! He's on the fifth hole!" Hope pulled up to the trio of golfers. "Halloo!" she trilled, as she leaped out of the golf cart. Mallory followed her as she approached a powerfully built man about to tee off.

"Hope! I wasn't expecting you," he said, straightening up and greeting her with a wary expression. "This isn't your regular day. I'm sure someone told me that you golf on Tuesdays."

"I like to mix it up a little." Hope gestured to Mallory. "J.P., this is Mallory McKenzie-Chu. She's working for Cora Sherman on her cooperative development at Bellavista. Bellavista Manor, you know."

"Ah, yes." J.P. surveyed Mallory, his gaze assessing under his thick, grey brows. "I apologize, Ms. McKenzie-Chu, I've been out of town until today and haven't had an opportunity to return your calls."

"Well, how convenient that you've both ended up at the same place!" said Hope with a sly smile. "I see you're a group of three. May we join you? I'll sit out but Mallory can play through."

"What? Oh no, I'd much rather watch," said Mallory hastily. She doubted her three under par score in miniature golf would impress this crowd.

"Actually, I was about to bow out myself," said J.P. quickly, "I remembered that I have a meeting this afternoon so I should get back to the office."

Judging by their looks of astonishment, this was unwelcome news to the other players. *Hmm, is it possible that Hope is a pro at golf?* wondered Mallory, hiding her smile.

"Well, in that case, hop in. I'll give you a ride back to the clubhouse!" said Hope. Before he could object, Hope hustled J.P. into the golf cart and soon the three of them were off again.

"Mallory, you're on!" said Hope. This was as captive an audience as she could wish for. Mallory launched into the pitch she'd prepared, highlighting the heritage value of Bellavista and the advantages of investing in the cooperative's project.

Before she'd said a dozen words, J.P. held up his hand. "You don't need to convince me that Bellavista is a rare gem worth saving. My 'bread and butter' is refurbishing heritage properties, and there's no shortage of them. But why should I invest in this development?"

"Bellavista is more than an opportunity to preserve the past — it's the opportunity to develop the future of housing in Victoria."

"What do you mean by that?"

"Co-housing projects combine architectural preservation with the benefits of a supportive and integrated community. At Bellavista, the bones of the model are already there. The main house would act as the heart of the community and the converted stables and other satellite buildings would provide both additional housing and communal space. Bellavista could become a showcase for everything Landmark Developments does best with heritage properties, as well as an opportunity to innovate beyond restoration work."

J.P. said nothing, so Mallory persevered. They'd reach the clubhouse in a few minutes, and she needed to make the most of her time. "I read your recent interview in Boulevard Magazine about how you're having trouble attracting skilled tradespeople to your projects. Lots of students want actual work experience before graduating. The Bellavista project could attract new apprentices in carpentry, electrical, plumbing and interior design – they get to work on a multi-phase heritage property conversion and at the end of the project you get a ready-made workforce skilled enough to take on new commercial projects."

J.P. pursed his lips. "It's an intriguing premise. But if you're not selling at the luxury price point, where's the money to support the conversions and additional renovations coming from? I heard that Cora has struggled to get financing for the main house renovations—who's going to pay for improvements to the rest of the property?"

Mallory was prepared for that question. "If we are able to complete the main house repairs and renovations, those units could be marketed and sold as part of the co-housing project, creating revenue to support the rest of the renovations and development."

The golf cart skidded to a halt in front of the clubhouse. Her time was almost up. "Your website mentions the work you've done with Habitat for Humanity to create affordable housing, so this project aligns with the type of projects you've supported before."

J.P. chuckled. "I'm a strong supporter of affordable housing, but I'm sorry if you think I'm prepared to single-handedly finance the project. That's not on the table." His face grew serious. "I don't cut corners or compromise on heritage projects, no matter what some lousy blogger alleges. This project will be expensive, and you can't expect Landmark Developments to cover shortfalls."

Mallory said, "Not at all. I've made a list of provincial and municipal programs that offer grants to support heritage conversions. I'm sure you're familiar with those grants through your current client projects. Did you know that funding is now available to support co-housing initiatives and apprenticeship programs? I think Bellavista would qualify. I'm happy to send you the preliminary numbers."

Mallory held her breath, hoping she'd said enough on the short ride to pique J.P.'s interest.

He said, "I'd like my associate to hear this. Come by my office tomorrow at 10 and bring your numbers with you."

"Thank you so much!" cried Mallory, fighting the urge to pull out a fist pump. *Yes!*

J.P. unfolded his huge frame and stepped out of the cart. "It was a pleasure to meet you, Mallory. And to see you too, Hope."

Hope grinned wickedly, darting out of the driver's seat to clasp J.P.'s arm. "Don't think I'm letting you get away from me just yet. Not just yet. We've some business to discuss as well. Mallory, would you care to join us in the clubhouse for a drink?"

At that moment, Mallory's phone buzzed in her pocket. *Cora!* "Oh no, thanks very much. I'll need to get back." Mallory hastily said goodbye and pulled out her phone to check her messages.

To her dismay there were a couple of texts from Cora and then an entire thread from Saffron. She'd forgotten to let Cora know where she was. Mallory dialed Saffron.

"Where are you?" demanded Saffron as soon as they were connected. "I've been trying to get hold of you all afternoon!"

"I was out with Raquel's cousin, Hope. Wait until I tell you what..."

Saffron cut her off. "No time for that. Meet me in Emergency at Royal Jubilee Hospital. Cora's had an accident!"

Chapter 18

> "Life wants to teach you something. Let it."
> - Raquel DeWitt, *The Smart Woman's Guide to Getting it Done.*

Arriving at Royal Jubilee Hospital, Mallory rushed into the Emergency ward, where she found a worryingly pale Cora seated in the waiting area while Saffron paced next to her.

"Cora, what happened? Are you okay?"

Cora waved her hand. "Pfft, everyone's making such a fuss. I'm fine."

"No, you're anything but fine," countered Saffron, her face flushed. "She took a nasty tumble down a ladder. We're waiting to get x-rays because she might have broken her ankle."

"How did it happen?" asked Mallory.

"It happened because you weren't there to help her like you said you would be!" Saffron was fuming. "You didn't even call to let Cora know where you were or when you were coming back."

"Hush, Saffron, it's not Mallory's fault. I decided to get a head start on the lightbulbs and lost my footing, that's all."

A wave of guilt and shame washed over Mallory. "I should have been there to help or at least called. I'm so sorry, Cora. I meant to text you when Hope offered to take me to see Jacob Prentiss, but I forgot."

"Did you get to meet Jacob Prentiss?" asked Cora excitedly. "What did he say?"

As Saffron scowled, Mallory filled Cora in on her five-minute golf cart pitch. "I have a meeting with J.P. tomorrow morning to go through the financials. He hasn't committed to anything but he's willing to hear us out."

Cora sat back, a broad smile on her face. "You know that I don't hold with patronizing such a huge waste of property and resources as that golf course, but you did a good thing, Mallory. With J.P. on board, we have a real chance before council. Well done!"

Saffron wasn't as forgiving. When Cora finished the admission process and was finally wheeled away by a nurse to take x-rays, she rounded on Mallory.

"All you had to do was call Cora to let her know you'd be late and to wait for you. Or answer your phone. Why did you make her worry?"

"I know I messed up," said Mallory contritely. Saffron had every right to be upset at what had happened to her aunt. "I honestly forgot. But I take full responsibility for what happened to Cora. It won't happen again."

"The minute your old boss snapped her fingers, you dropped Cora. How can we trust you?"

That stung. Mallory strived to be responsible and conscientious. She didn't know why the passage of time seemed to have little meaning for her or why she would fully intend to do something —like text Cora —and immediately forget to do it. Her inability to assess how long it really took to complete a task was an endless source of frustration and self-recrimination. Embarrassment flooded her being.

Saffron wasn't done. "You haven't changed, Mallory. You promise to be there for your friends, but then you bail on them!"

Mallory's chest constricted at the unfairness. *She* was the one who bailed on her friends? But she couldn't muster the words to push back, not when she was feeling so guilty about neglecting Cora. Turning, she stumbled down the hallway towards the elevator.

As the doors closed, she let her tears fall. Cora was counting on her. The whole cooperative was counting on her. And she'd let them all down.

☙

Outside the hospital, Mallory found an empty coffee shop and slumped into a seat, needing some headspace away from everything. Her phone pinged. It was Gretchen on What's App, sending a brief "Hey there" with accompanying photos, goofing around with the crew from her Hollymark set, wearing reindeer antlers and carrying baskets of holly. Mallory smiled, but then her emotions overwhelmed her, and her tears spilled over, blurring her vision. Why was she such a screw-up? Seeing her little sister made her long to be with her family. She opened the FaceTime App.

"Mallory?" Fiona's voice was a question as she took in her daughter's woeful expression. "Everything okay?"

Her mother listened without interruption as Mallory poured out everything. Mallory paused to blow her nose. Between sniffles she said, "I've really only had one job my whole life, and now I'm messing up my one chance for a fresh start. Why can't I get it together?"

Fiona frowned. "Wait a minute. You're not responsible for Cora's decision to get up on that ladder. The others at the house could have helped her. Where was Saffron? Why does everything rest on your shoulders?"

"Because I'm the project manager. I'm the one they hired…"

"To get the project through the city's development process. Somehow, you've turned that role into becoming Bellavista's PR person, marketing person, fundraiser, and now handyman. Your boundaries are blurring, and you're acting way beyond the scope of the job. No wonder you're overwhelmed."

"I should be able to handle this, Mum."

"I think you're setting unrealistic expectations on yourself. That's a recipe for failure. Figure out what you're supposed to be doing and draw the line. Cora and the others mean well but if you're going to continue to offer up yourself for their every need, of course they're going to take you up on that, and you'll end up right back here, over your head and feeling as if you're not getting anything done."

Her mother's wisdom resonated. She had to be the one to set the boundaries, to define her role.

Mallory took a deep breath. "What should I do about Saffron? I don't know how we're going to keep working together, when I feel like I'm on eggshells all the time."

"Hmmm. Sounds like you and Saffron may have some history that's getting in the way."

Mallory winced. Their failed grad trip. It was time to hash it all out, hurt feelings and all.

"Thanks, Mum. I really needed one of your pep talks today."

Fiona smiled. "You've got this."

༺ ༻

After washing her face in the coffee shop washroom and applying some lipstick for courage, Mallory returned to the waiting room. Saffron looked up warily as she approached.

Mallory took a deep breath. "Can we talk?" She gestured to the row of seats and they both sat down.

"Look, I love being on the Bellavista Project. I really believe in what Cora is trying to create and I want to be part of this. This afternoon has taught me that I need to clarify what my role is on this project and set clear expectations."

Saffron said nothing, listening.

Mallory continued. "As project manager, I should have contacted Cora about where I was this afternoon, and I'm truly sorry about that. However, I'm being pulled in all sorts of directions and I'm finding it hard to stay on track. I think going forward, if there are tasks related to the upkeep and repair of the house, I'll defer to you and the others. My focus will stay on the application process. I'll discuss this with Cora when she's feeling better, but I wanted to clear this with you."

Saffron nodded slowly. "Okay, that seems reasonable."

"We need to talk about something else that's affecting how we interact with each other. Our Hawaii trip."

Saffron scoffed, all the hurt from twenty years ago flashing across her face. "What do you mean, 'our' Hawaii trip? You didn't go on it, remember?"

"And you're still mad about that."

"Heck, yes!" said Saffron, crossing her arms. "I spent half of our last semester talking about it, planning it, booking it and then you cancelled at the last minute without warning. It was supposed to be our big grad trip and then you bailed!"

"Wait a minute." Mallory held up a hand. "Are you really blaming me for bailing? You booked the tickets before I even confirmed that I was going!"

"That's not true! We talked about it all the time, how much you wanted to go to Hawaii to visit your relatives."

"I did want to go, but it wasn't the right time for me. I told you that."

"What are you talking about?"

"I couldn't really afford it, not with university tuition going up."

"Mallory! I would have covered for you on the trip, you know that."

Mallory shook her head. "I knew you would say that. If I was going to go at all, I wanted to pay my own way and when that wasn't possible, I prioritized my education."

"I don't understand how you could let a silly thing like…"

"It wasn't a silly thing." Mallory sighed. "Back then you never had to worry about money, Saffron. I didn't resent you for that, but I did try to tell you I needed to save for college. You wouldn't listen when I suggested we try a local trip instead, like Tofino or the Oregon Coast. You went ahead and booked everything without checking with me if I could afford it, and then you expected me to be fine with it all. That's not all. When you invited Josh to join us, how did you think I would react?"

"I don't get what the problem was – you liked Josh but then you acted all weird about him coming!"

"Sure, I liked Josh, but I really didn't want to play third wheel for the whole trip! I knew what was going to happen. The same thing that happened anytime a new guy appeared on the scene. You acted like I didn't exist. Or worse, like I was an inconvenience. Who wants to feel like that on vacation?"

There was a moment of silence. "I'm sorry," Saffron said, looking contrite. "I should have paid more attention to what you were saying. Josh wanted to go surfing, so I didn't think about how you'd feel if he came along."

"That was pretty obvious," said Mallory. "Anyways, to come completely clean, that wasn't the only reason I didn't go, although it was a major factor. I just felt weird going to Hawaii when my parents were always talking about taking us back to see my dad's family and where they met. The more I thought about it the more it didn't seem right for me to go without them."

"I wish you'd told me that," said Saffron. "I would have understood. If it's any consolation, I had a crappy time without you. All Josh wanted to do was "catch the waves", so I spent the whole time sitting on the beach waiting for him. We didn't do any of the things I'd planned to do with you. No scooter rides around town. No trek up Diamond Head. I was bored out of my mind."

"That makes me feel a *little* bit better," admitted Mallory.

"Hey!" Saffron mock-punched her arm. "Okay, I may have deserved that. It was selfish of me not checking to see whether my plans worked for you and assuming because I wanted the trip, you would too."

"And I should have said straight out that I couldn't afford the trip and that I didn't want Josh to come, instead of letting you down at the last minute. I don't know if I could have explained about my family, as that part of it didn't really become clear until later."

"Did your family ever get to Hawaii?" asked Saffron.

Mallory smiled. "Our whole family went together for the first time ten years ago and we've been back a few times since then."

"That's great." Saffron gave Mallory a long look. "Are we good now?"

Mallory nodded. "Yeah, we're good."

Impulsively, Saffron reached out to hug her friend. "I'm glad we hashed this all out."

"Me, too," said Mallory. "Now if we can get Cora home in one piece, that would be the icing on my cupcake."

Unfortunately, the x-rays showed that Cora's ankle had suffered a break and she wasn't going home anytime soon. As Mallory and Saffron waited to see if Cora would be able to have emergency surgery, Amira and Etta appeared.

"I thought you were going to wait at home!" said Saffron in surprise. "We don't know how long we'll be."

"Etta has something to tell you." Said Amira. "It can't wait."

Chapter 19

> **"Follow the money."**
> **– Raquel DeWitt,** *The Smart Woman's Guide to Getting it Done.*

"I have Parkinson's," announced Etta baldly. "Amira knows; she noticed that I've started to lose my balance. She's been taking me to see a specialist and get treatment. It's only a matter of time before I'm in a wheelchair. That's why I pushed for a deal with Nate Narkiss — I wanted the renovations to be done before I needed them."

"Why didn't you tell us?" cried Saffron.

"I didn't want Cora to worry. I saw that she was taking too much on, and now look at what's happened." Etta's eyes welled up with tears.

"I'm so sorry, Etta," said Mallory. How could she have missed the signs that Etta was unwell? Etta's cane, the hand tremors, Etta dropping things. Even the change in Etta's painting style from the detailed portraits she had produced all her life to the wide-brush abstracts. It all made sense now.

"It's better to let everyone know," said Amira gently. "We can all support you."

"I don't want to need support!" said Etta roughly. "I don't want to lose my independence. But I'm realizing that I must accept that things are different for me. I *will* need support; I can't hide from that or pretend I can do everything myself."

"I'm glad you told us!" Saffron reached out to hug her old friend. "Now we can plan so much better, knowing what you'll need in the future."

"I need to tell Cora." Etta looked as if she was bracing herself. "She's not going to be happy that I hid this from her."

"We'll talk to her together," said Saffron encouragingly.

By tacit agreement, Mallory and Amira discreetly left the room so that Etta could have a private chat with Cora once she was back from her assessment. In the hospital cafe, over paper cups of lukewarm coffee, Mallory told Amira about her meeting with J.P.

Amira's eyes brightened with enthusiasm. "You can show J.P. that Bellavista can be a place where everyone can be together. People who are overlooked, older, isolated— why should these people be alone in a boring place? In ordinary housing you have your house or your apartment, but you are not connected to others unless you live with family. At Bellavista, there is private space and independence, yes? But also, you have the opportunity to be with others for meals and conversation and to work together in the gardens. You can be alone, but you do not have to be. Time and space for self, time and space with others."

"It's a great concept," said Mallory. "Creating a community that lives and works together while allowing for independence and privacy is a lovely idea." She took a sip. Her own need for space and solitude ran deep. "But there must be some conflict when people are so enmeshed in each other's lives and living spaces."

"That is expected! We are human beings, yes? It is the human condition, to be in conflict." A shadow fell over Amira's expressive face, and Mallory remembered that, of course, Amira had lived through the very worst kind of human conflict. The moment passed, and Amira continued, "We have been fortunate; we are all good friends. It is true, if new people come in, it may not work so well. We do not know. But I think that if we are clear on what we value and what is important for the community, it can work. We can only try."

"What were the ideas you were going to share about the cooperative? I'm sorry, I forgot to follow up with you," said Mallory. Yet another thing she'd forgotten.

"I read one of Cora's clippings about Bellavista that described a sparkling water bottling company that operated on the property," said Amira. "Georgie remembers finding crates of old bottles in the basement. Then I thought, what if there was special zoning on the property to allow for the business? In my hometown, it was very common for people to run businesses in their homes. I asked Metchosin how to find out and she sent me to the city archives. The people there were very helpful!"

"And did you find anything about special zoning?" asked Mallory. "Is this for the Kitchen Cooperative?"

"Yes! The City of Victoria Archives sent me a copy of the records today. I can send you the email. Bellavista is still zoned as commercial! This means the Kitchen Cooperative can expand and we can develop work/live units. Metchosin told me that they are becoming very popular, especially for young professionals and people starting their own businesses."

Mallory listened to Amira with growing excitement. A whole new avenue of opportunity had opened for the cooperative. While senior housing could be the primary focus, the cooperative could also develop and market work/live units and multi-generational housing.

"I can see this really appealing to a lot of people," said Mallory, "Even some of Cora's friends told me they didn't want to live in a retirement complex. If Bellavista was a multi-generational community with retired and working people, even families with children, the atmosphere would be very different. Amira, this is wonderful!"

Impulsively, Mallory said, "Amira, will you come with me to the meeting with J.P. tomorrow? Cora won't be able to come now, and

I'm sure you can articulate much better than me the benefits of living in a communal situation."

Amira looked thrilled by the invitation. "Thank you! Yes, I would very much like to join you."

☙

In J.P.'s office, Mallory and Amira were introduced to his associate, Dax Derwent, tall and slender in a sharp-looking, silver-grey damask pantsuit Mallory instantly coveted, although it was completely out of her wheelhouse.

"Dax, this is Mallory McKenzie-Chu and Amira Hassan. Dax is my go-to numbers person. If your project has a chance of succeeding, they'll know right away. If it's destined to fail, they'll know that too."

Dax handed out glossy business cards, grey with white embossed print — "Dax Derwent, Lead Developer (they/their)" — and leaned back against the wall with their arms crossed as J.P. ran through the cooperative's pitch with impressive recall. When J.P. stopped, Dax looked out from under angled auburn bangs and peppered them with questions.

"You've tagged some funding possibilities – that's a good start – but who's the target market for this kind of development? How many retirees are going to want to pay top dollar to run an urban farm or live communally?"

Mallory had come prepared. "The social research backs us up. People are craving communities where they can connect with their neighbors and make strong social connections. Physical and social activities like working in the gardens and greenhouses can really add to quality of life." She pulled out the article she had found in a publication aimed at senior citizens and handed it over.

"There's tons of research," she continued, "showing that people, especially baby boomers, want more and more to be able to age in place. If the infrastructure and community support is built in, that becomes possible. Think of the appeal of living in a customized neighborhood attuned to your needs."

Amira spoke up then. "The Vandervoss family received special commercial zoning for the property when they first built Bellavista. For several decades, they operated a sparkling water company. I've confirmed that the commercial zoning is still in place."

"Which means that you could market some units as work/live homes," said Dax, their green eyes lighting up. "That's an interesting feature to consider. If people can run their businesses out of these units, their value increases, and you may have a lot more interest. But it may not be enough to make this venture profitable if you're marketing to retirees."

Agatha's comment coming to mind, Mallory added, "We don't have to limit the co-op to seniors' housing, although that would be its primary focus. What if we created a multi-generational mixed-use property? In Japan, it's common to run senior centers along with daycares; both generations benefit from their interaction. Some of the best urban designs make creative use of sightlines for privacy and central courtyards to create connection. They've been proven to have an enormous impact on the well-being of residents. Bellavista could become a model for other heritage projects in Victoria."

She stopped talking, flushed with the effort of communicating how strongly she felt about Bellavista's potential.

"What do you think, Dax?" J.P. swiveled toward his associate. Dax pursed their lips, shaking their head.

"I hate to say it, because there are many great features to this development, but I think it's too risky, J.P. Even with the third-party funding sources, which are not guaranteed, a multi-phase project of this size and scope would be a drain on our main business resources. There's no guarantee anyone is going to buy into this model."

J.P. sat back, tapping his fingers thoughtfully before slapping the desk and making everyone jump. "Alright, you've both convinced me to reconsider the project."

When Dax started to object, J.P. held up a hand, saying, "You know I value your opinion highly, Dax, but I'd like to consider this project further. It could be the start of a whole new line of business for us. Let's look at the development plans and the property, then run some preliminary estimates. Would you set up a tour for us?"

Mallory nodded. "Whenever you like! Thank you so much!"

J.P. waved her thanks away. "Let's meet tomorrow. We'll give you our answer in a couple of days, but I'm not promising anything. Dax here is not completely on board, so I need to take their opinion and that of the rest of my team into account. The project must make sense on all fronts, especially the numbers."

Despite that caveat, they floated out of Jacob Prentiss's office on a cloud of hope and optimism. Outside, Mallory pulled Amira into a hug. "Great job, Amira! The work/live zoning really got their attention!"

"I am so happy!" said Amira, beaming. "I can't wait to tell everyone!"

Chapter 20

> "Gather your team."
> – Raquel DeWitt, *The Smart Woman's Guide to Getting it Done.*

As Amira had a meeting with the Kitchen Cooperative, they headed back to Bellavista. Eager to share the news of J.P.'s interest, they facetimed Cora at the hospital as soon as they arrived. While Amira joined her crew, Mallory searched for Saffron, but she wasn't in the house. Half an hour later, though, a text pinged. She was parked out front and could Mallory join her?

Mallory flung open the passenger door. "Where've you been? I've got news!"

"Come on, get in! Wait until you see what I have for us."

A few minutes later, Saffron pulled up in front of Breaking Good, a smash therapy room in the warehouse district near Chinatown. The sign outside read, "Cheaper than Therapy – Go Ahead and Break Something!" They were soon decked out in overalls, hard hats, gloves and goggles and ready for their safety tutorial.

"Welcome, guys!" The friendly host greeted them. "Choose your weapon, keep your safety goggles on, and get smashing!"

Saffron chose a baseball bat. Mallory went for a sledgehammer. Soon the room was filled with the sound of exploding glass and crockery as the two friends gleefully smashed everything from old TVs and electronic goods to furniture and ceramics, all to a thumping soundtrack. Mallory swung the sledgehammer with abandon, letting out all the pent-up frustration and anxiety that had been simmering for weeks. *Take that, police investigation!* An ancient Commodore monitor smashed to the ground. *That's for all my free time going to chauffeuring Raquel around.* A mirror exploded into a thousand pieces. *This is for me having to please everyone all the time.* As item after item fell victim to the wrath of the sledgehammer, the weight on her shoulders slipped away. She stopped thinking about anything at all and surrendered to the sheer enjoyment of the experience. It was glorious. By the time they were done, they were laughing so hard they could barely stand up. All around them was chaos and destruction and they couldn't stop beaming.

"That was incredible!" said Mallory as they walked out an hour later, sweaty and pumped up with adrenaline. "I feel fantastic!"

Saffron grinned. "The best way for me to celebrate my fortieth birthday! I'm starving now – let's get some dim sum!"

☙

Victoria's picturesque Chinatown — the oldest in North America — consisted of a single street block marked by the impressive Gates of Harmonious Interest and lined with small souvenir shops, teahouses, groceries and restaurants. They headed for Dynasty Dumpling, a tiny, family-run restaurant that specialized in house-made dumplings and hand-pulled noodles. Mallory apologized the whole way for forgetting Saffron's birthday.

"Why would you remember it?" asked Saffron in surprise. "It's not like we've been regularly marking the occasion."

All the same, it was embarrassing how often she forgot special occasions and birthdays of family and friends, even with calendar reminders and prompts. She'd see the reminder pop up, make a mental note to send a birthday greeting or pick up a gift and promptly forget. Out of sight, out of mind. She still got her own family's birthdays mixed up.

In the restaurant's front window, glistening barbecued ducks and barbecued pork loins hung from hooks. Behind the front counter and cash register, freshly baked goods were displayed in trays. It reminded Mallory of a restaurant her family used to visit near where she grew up. Her mouth watered at the sight of coconut honey buns, steamed sponge cakes and cream-filled rolls. The small restaurant had self-seating, so they found a booth in the back and took in the specials written up on the chalkboard.

"Food first, then we can talk "shop"," said Saffron. "Hmmm, duck noodle soup for me, I think."

Mallory squinted at the chalkboard, debating her choices. "They have a good selection of vegetarian pot-stickers. If I order a bunch, will you share them with me?"

"I never say no to pot-stickers."

Saffron ripped off the top of the paper-wrapped chopsticks, slipped out and snapped the connected sticks and deftly folded the wrapper into a chopstick rest. "Ta da!" she said with a laugh. "I still remember what you taught me!"

The waitress came up to take their order. It was Kiki yet again.

"Hi guys!" she said with a big smile. "Great to see you!"

"You work here too?" asked Mallory. "I've counted four other jobs already!"

Kiki shrugged. "Got to pay the bills, right? Five part-time jobs equal one full-time one. What can I get for you today?"

She hadn't clued in on how hard Kiki had to work to make a basic living. How embarrassing. They gave Kiki their orders and asked for a pot of jasmine tea. Kiki leaned in and whispered conspiratorially, "Let me know if you need to run any theories by me. I'm game." Straightening up, she told them, "You know, Nate used to come in here all the time. He always wanted the same booth, with a girlfriend or a business associate. He was a decent tipper, but his buddy Brad was a terrible tipper, and mean too."

"What a jerk," said Saffron, who was known to be vocal about people who didn't tip well not deserving to eat out.

Once Kiki had brought back their meals and drinks in record time, Mallory picked up a dumpling with her chopsticks, dipped it in black vinegar and took a bite. Crisp skin and juicy filling, exactly the way she liked them. "Saffron, tell me what you've been up to. And then I have news to share too."

Saffron had been meeting with Metchosin at city hall to find out about grant programs and co-housing opportunities.

"Metchosin really knows her stuff and has the connections. She helped me register in the available grant programs, so we're getting closer to making this co-housing project a reality."

"That's great news. I'm glad she's supporting the development." Mallory wondered if Metchosin's change of heart had anything to do with Lucas being named a person of interest, replacing the co-op members in the investigation.

When Saffron heard about their visit to Jacob Prentiss, she was thrilled.

"That's amazing! If Jacob Prentiss invests with the next phase of the project, that will make all the difference!"

They talked excitedly about the project, and just as they were finishing their lunch, Detectives Blair and Grover walked into the restaurant.

"Don't look now," hissed Saffron, rolling her eyes.

"Be nice," murmured Mallory.

Saffron turned her scowl into an aggressive smile that was hardly an improvement. Spotting the two friends, the officers approached their table.

"Ms. Kalinsky, Ms. Chu, um, McKenzie-Chu," said Detective Blair formally, "We were about to pay you a visit. We can talk to you now if that's alright."

Saffron gestured for the two officers to join them. At the sound of their voices, Kiki's head whipped around, and she hurried over with two chairs that the two men pulled up to the booth.

"Do you have news about Lucas?" asked Saffron, as they got settled.

"Unfortunately, not." Detective Blair pursed his lips.

"What was it you wanted to tell us?" prompted Mallory. "Did you rule out Georgie's fan as the murder weapon?"

"About that." Detective Blair cleared his throat. "Yes, as a matter of fact, we did. It appears, um, the coroner has determined — that the stab wound was not caused by the Albanico fan. It turns out that the fan is an imitation, a prop device commonly used in sword-swallowing acts. Miss Vandervoss confirmed that a friend of hers from her circus days gave it to her."

Circus days? Mallory and Saffron exchanged startled looks. Before they could absorb this titillating insight into Georgie's past, Detective Blair had moved on.

"Due to the roughness of the edges of the wound, it was determined that the wound wasn't caused by a blade or surgical instrument, so that rules out Ms. Hassan's surgical tools as well. The coroner has concluded...well, she has concluded that the wound was created by a lethal peck... administered by a bird."

They both looked at Detective Blair blankly.

"A rooster, in fact."

"You can't be serious," said Saffron. "Gregory Peck killed Nate Narkiss?"

"Who?" Detective Blair looked confused.

"The rooster's name is Gregory Peck," murmured Detective Grover to his colleague. "The situation is not without precedent," Grover explained to Mallory and Saffron. "There was a report a few years ago from Australia about a homeowner who kept chickens, and one of the birds turned on her and pecked her varicose vein. It was a vulnerable spot and the homeowner bled to death before she could call for help. She was found dead in her own driveway. It was a real tragedy. The coroner believes that Nate Narkiss had a similar medical condition that contributed to his hemorrhaging while he lay in the coop unconscious."

"That's unbelievable," muttered Mallory.

"We are going to have to bring the rooster in…"

"For questioning?" cried Kiki, who was still hovering nearby. Detective Grover tried unsuccessfully to hide his grin.

"For *analysis*," finished Detective Blair acidly. "If the rooster was the…culprit, then his beak will match the puncture wounds and there may be other…evidence on him."

"What evidence?" asked Saffron. "It's been a week, and any one of the other chickens could have pecked Nate. GP wasn't even supposed to be in there. How can you tell that he was the one that killed Nate?"

Detective Blair was not about to be challenged. "The coroner has completed her analysis and confirmed that the size and location of the wounds on Nate's body are consistent with a poultry beak, specifically, one belonging to a male chicken, e.g. a rooster. So, Ms. Kalinsky, unless you are a certified coroner and can give a second opinion, we're going to go with Dr. Horobet's findings. We will be sending a car up to fetch the rooster later today."

"Are my aunt and her friends still considered persons of interest?" demanded Saffron. "You can't think that we deliberately set our pet rooster on Nate with the intention to kill him? That's a pretty wild conjecture."

Detective Blair admitted, "At this point, with our interest in Lucas Turner, who remains at large, and the coroner's report, we do not consider Ms. Sherman, Ms. Vandervoss, Ms. Hoskins or Ms. Hassan to be persons of interest any longer."

Mallory and Saffron exchanged looks of relief.

"However," the detective continued, "while the evidence suggests that Nate Narkiss died due to hemorrhaging caused by a rooster peck, someone harmed Nate Narkiss and he died as a result; we intend to find out who that was."

"Do you still think it was murder?" asked Mallory. "Do you think Lucas is responsible?"

"Mr. Turner continues to be a person of interest," Detective Blair answered gravely.

Then he rose from the booth, indicating the briefing was over, and Detective Grover, who had been animatedly conversing with Kiki, hastily left his seat.

The detective shared one parting thought. "If this case really is about drugs, then dangerous people could be involved. If Mr. Turner gets in touch with you, please let us know at once." He scowled at them from under his thick brows. "Don't try to deal with him yourselves."

Chapter 21

> "Don't assume you know everything about someone."
> – Raquel DeWitt, *The Smart Woman's Guide to Getting it Done.*

"Gregory Peck did what??"

Back at Bellavista, Saffron broke the news about Gregory Peck to the disbelieving residents. Etta openly scoffed at the idea that the rooster was responsible but looked relieved that the police no longer considered any of them prime suspects. Amira immediately headed to the library and started Googling "lethal roosters" on her laptop.

"Georgie, why have you never told us about your time in the circus?" demanded Saffron. She had ranted the entire car ride back about the unnecessary stress Georgie's deception had caused. "You should have told the police the fan was a prop right away!"

"I didn't know the fan wasn't real," said Georgie airily. "My dear friend Hector, a world-famous sword-swallower, entrusted the fan to me. The fan was a key component of his act. How was I to know that it was a fake?"

"How did you end up in the circus?" asked Mallory, fascinated by this glimpse into Georgie's past.

"I joined Hector's troupe after I was robbed of all my worldly possessions on a train while travelling to the south of Spain to pursue my passion for flamenco. I was alone on the platform at Cadiz, sobbing, when the Los Muchachos Circus Troupe started unloading from the train. The kind circus folk took pity on me and invited me to join them."

"What did you do in the circus?" Saffron was drawn into Georgie's story despite her annoyance with the storyteller.

"I discovered I had a talent for bending myself into the most interesting positions. I became a contortionist. It is a skill that has unexpectedly come in handy during my life."

No one knew what to say to that.

But Georgie continued on, breaking the silence by objecting strenuously to Gregory Peck being handed over to the police.

"They cannot take my dear boy!" she exclaimed. "They will have to pry my cold dead fingers off his body!"

"I think we've reached our quota for cold dead bodies," responded Saffron dryly. "Come on, help me put GP's feed together and make sure he has everything he needs. I'm not sure how long they're going to keep him at the station. I'll give Simon a call too about this latest update."

Saffron led Georgie away, the latter running on about blankets and squeaky toys. Still trying to digest the news that Georgie used to be a circus performer and that Nate Narkiss had been killed by the rooster, Mallory joined Amira at the library table, where she was reading an online article.

"A domestic rooster attacked a seventy-six-year-old woman in Australia," Amira read aloud, "and pecked her leg, causing significant hemorrhaging and death. This is from CNN's website. The story received global attention about the risks of keeping domestic poultry. I do not believe it, but it is true."

"It says that the victim had a number of pre-existing conditions, including diabetes, varicose veins and hypertension," said Mallory, reading over Amira's shoulder. "Nate was a relatively young man — how could he have hemorrhaged from a mere bird peck?"

"Perhaps due to the way he was lying, or the specific vein that was hit," suggested Amira. "Or he may have had hypertension –

high blood pressure. It is a common enough condition without any symptoms. I would not have imagined that a bird's beak could kill, but you see from the Australia case that it is possible."

"Truly a one-in-a-million way to die," agreed Mallory.

Saffron came back into the room. "Did you find anything?"

"We found the Australia story that Detective Grover mentioned," said Mallory. "A woman did indeed die from a rooster peck. A direct hit on a varicose vein."

Saffron plopped down on the sofa. "There you have it. If the police are satisfied Nate's death was caused by a rooster peck and not by human hands, I'm not going to question it! That's what Simon recommends we do as well. Keep our heads down and stay out of it."

"Don't you want to find out what happened?" asked Mallory. "Someone hit Nate hard enough to knock him out and then dragged him into the chicken coop — it's manslaughter, which is still a serious charge. And Lucas is still missing and the police think he did it."

"It's clear what happened," responded Saffron. "Lucas was involved with drugs and took off because the police were closing in. We don't know Nate's history or if he bought drugs from Nate, but if Lucas was his dealer, they could have had a dispute. If Lucas didn't assault Nate, then someone else found Nate annoying enough to punch. That could be anyone. I'm more than happy to leave that puzzle to the police. So long as they don't think any of us had anything to do with it."

"That doesn't make sense, though," said Mallory, frowning. "Seth told me that Nate hated drugs and fired a guy caught using at the work site. I meant to tell Detective Blair at the restaurant but got distracted by the news about Gregory Peck. It doesn't seem logical that Nate would go from hating drugs to being a user."

"Why not?" Saffron wasn't about to back down from her theory. "I know many former smokers who are radically anti-tobacco. It could work the other way too. Or maybe Nate's public aversion was a way to hide a personal drug-use problem. I'm relieved we don't have to worry any more that someone is out there dispatching random bodies in our chicken coop. Let it go. Besides, isn't the development hearing in a few days? I can't wait until that's done so I can go back to London."

Mallory wasn't as ready as Saffron to let the matter go. Saffron had a point, though. She already had enough to deal with.

※

Brainstorming ideas for turning around Bellavista's public image took up a lot of mental energy. What was it that celebrities did after a public scandal? They ran after positive press, often in the form of some public demonstration, like participating in a charity race, or making a large donation to a children's hospital. Scrolling through the *Vic in the Know* blog, Mallory landed on a recent article about the Wheelbarrow Foundation and its upcoming gala.

"Wheelbarrow's Director, Stan Barber, reports that while ticket sales are going strong for the upcoming gala on May 4, their caterer is experiencing staff shortages, and they haven't been able to replace their florist. He fears that without sufficient volunteer support, the gala may not be able to go ahead."

Running downstairs to the kitchen, Mallory found Amira and Georgie preparing lunch.

"I've an idea," she said, pulling up a chair to the table.

"Do you want a sandwich?" asked Georgie. "We're making vegetable hummus wraps."

She'd forgotten to eat breakfast again, and now it was close to noon. Her stomach growling, Mallory accepted a wrap.

"Have some tea," Amira offered, placing a cup of Earl Grey in front of her. "What is your big idea?" she asked.

"Remember at the news conference the director of the Wheelbarrow Foundation said that they'd be going ahead with their annual fundraising gala? I just read that the Foundation's been having difficulty with their caterer and with finding enough volunteers. What if Bellavista offered to provide floral arrangements and some of the catering through the Kitchen Cooperative? We could manage to do it at cost, and the positive publicity and association with the foundation would be great for the housing cooperative."

"Hmm…I don't know," mused Etta. "Do we want the co-op to be associated with the Wheelbarrow Foundation? Doesn't that draw attention back to what happened here?"

"We can't stop people from talking about Bellavista and the fact that Nate was killed on the property," answered Mallory, "but we can show that we're unfazed by the gossip because we had nothing to do with it. If Wheelbarrow accepts our help, then that would show everyone that there's nothing to the allegations. After all, no one's been charged with anything."

"Do you really think that would work?" asked Saffron, who had come in while Mallory was outlining her idea. "Donating centerpieces and appetizers isn't going to drown out the gossip about Bellavista residents being questioned by the police or our handyman being a person of interest, is it?" Saffron helped herself to a wrap.

"Maybe not," said Mallory, "but it would give people something else to focus on, something more positive. We'd be rescuing the gala."

Saffron looked thoughtful. Then she nodded. "Let's do it. Positive PR to take over the negative PR, it's done all the time. Ok, what do we do?"

Saffron was on board with her idea; why did that make her so happy? "I'm going to reach out to Wheelbarrow's director today and make the offer," said Mallory. "I'll find out what the logistics are in terms of number of tables, number of expected guests and total cost. Saffron and Georgie, you can figure out the floral arrangements and other decorations. Amira, can you talk to the Kitchen Cooperative and see what you have in stock that could be used as appetizers? Don't make anything yet, though. We need to confirm first."

"They usually hold a charity auction at the gala," said Etta. "I could donate a couple of my paintings."

Amira added, "the Kitchen Cooperative could also offer to host a private meal. That was very popular at the high school fundraiser last fall."

"Great ideas!" said Mallory. She had a team, everyone pitching in and pulling together. "I should get going if I want to catch Stan Barber. Is it okay if I borrow the car? Let's meet up again this afternoon for a check-in."

Before she forgot, Mallory put a reminder in her phone for the afternoon meeting before scrambling out the door.

Chapter 22

> "It never hurts to ask."
> – Raquel DeWitt, *The Smart Woman's Guide to Getting it Done.*

While it was a risk showing up without an appointment at The Wheelbarrow Foundation, Mallory's successful ambush of J.P. on the golf course proved that people had a much harder time saying no to someone in person than over the phone or by email. The foundation's head office was in a striking chrome-and-glass building on the waterfront near Fisherman's Wharf. As she walked by the bustling wharf, with its open-air restaurants and tourist hordes, Mallory admired the rows of brightly colored float homes bedecked with spring blooms and the working fishing boats selling their fresh catch of the day.

The building directory showed that Stan Barber's office was on the top floor. Hearing raised voices coming from the office, Mallory loitered uncertainly in the hallway.

"I'm going to make sure everyone knows what you did!" shouted a voice, muffled by the door. "You'll be ruined if it's the last thing I do!"

"If that's a threat, you better make it count!" answered another. "If Nate knew what you've been up to, he never would have trusted you!"

The voices grew fainter, as if they were moving farther away. A door slammed, followed by the thud of angry stomps down a staircase. Then there was silence. Should she knock now or come back later? Before she could decide, the door to the office flew open and a man in a flannel shirt and jeans came storming out. Seeing Mallory, he stopped short, looking flustered.

"Hello!" said Mallory, recognizing him from the news conference. "It's Stan Barber, right? Do you have a minute?"

"Sorry, if it's about making a donation, could you leave a message?" he asked distractedly. "I'm in the middle of organizing the annual gala."

"I'm actually here to help with that," said Mallory, flashing her most winsome smile. Stan looked up at her with desperate, hope-filled eyes.

"You serious? Come in!" he said. From the building's exterior, Mallory had expected the director would be in a corner office with floor-to-ceiling views of the harbor. Stan's office turned out to be a modest-sized space with basic office furniture located in the back of the building overlooking the parking lot. Stan gestured to a wooden chair and Mallory took a seat.

"You with the volunteers?" he asked, as he moved to sit behind his desk. "What kind of help are we talking about here?"

"I'm with the Bellavista Housing Cooperative," Mallory began. "We heard that your caterer and events manager both took ill at the same time, so we thought we would ask if we could contribute."

"Bellavista...why does that name sound familiar?" mused Stan.

Mallory gulped. "It's where Nate Narkiss..." she began awkwardly.

"Right." Stan rocked back in his chair. After a moment he said, "Okay if I say this is kind of weird?"

"Might as well be upfront about it," Mallory agreed. "As I said, we're offering to help. We'd be happy to donate centerpieces and appetizer trays for the gala. As a show of support at this time."

"Well," said Stan, taking out a handkerchief and mopping his brow. "Weird as it may be, I'm gonna accept, as we don't have other options. Thanks. What do you need from me to get started? You know the gala's in two days, right?"

"If you could share the number of tables and guests, I can have the team start prepping now."

Stan stood and offered his hand to Mallory. "Thanks again," he said, giving her hand a hearty shake. "I'll be frank— you've saved me. I didn't know what I was gonna do with the two of them sick. The volunteers are calling every five minutes asking for instructions, and I don't know what to tell them! What do I know about decorating? Give me some joists to install, I can do that!"

"I may be able to help with the setup," said Mallory. More positive PR for the cooperative. "I used to organize charity events."

"Really?" Stan couldn't hide his relief. He rubbed his hand over his balding head. "This is the first gala I've ever managed. Nate saw that I enjoyed helping the new trainees, so when I retired last year, he asked me to step in as director for Wheelbarrow. But you know, I don't really know what I'm doing."

The director was unexpectedly frank. Stan handed over an enormous planning binder and the list of volunteers with an air of relief. After promising to take charge of the volunteers the next morning, Mallory left as Stan fielded another call.

As she emerged from the building, a flash of red caught the corner of her eye. Was that Art Papatonis's scooter? What was he doing here? The thought that he could have been the person arguing with Stan Barber crossed her mind. She hadn't seen him since the day she'd volunteered at the Government House gardens.

Funny, I didn't expect being a project manager would require so much extracurricular time. Here I am, volunteering yet again, all in the name of getting the project done. She'd better get moving on those appetizers.

☙

The team at Bellavista worked late into the night getting everything ready for the gala. Unfortunately, the gallons of tea Mallory had consumed made itself known a few hours after she turned in. Bleary-eyed and unable to fall back asleep, Mallory wandered into the kitchen, where Amira was punching dough into a bowl. By the looks of things, she'd been up for hours already.

"What are you doing up so early?" asked Mallory, making herself a cup of strong tea. Now that she was up, she might as well stay alert.

"I wanted to do a fresh start," said Amira, "Is that what you say? — no, *head start* — on the baking for the gala."

Amira gave the ball of dough a determined punch. Then she pulled it into a log and twisted off a section.

"Here," she said, putting the piece in front of Mallory. "Wash your hands and come join me."

Digging her fingers into the warm dough was strangely therapeutic. Mallory copied Amira's more expert movements, and together they punched and rolled the dough in companionable silence. The soothing rhythm of repetitive movement, plus the quiet that came before the rest of the world awoke, emboldened Mallory to ask a question.

"Amira, what was it like for you, starting over completely? I'm sure you never expected to end up on the west coast of Canada baking bread. That's a world away from the life you were living in Syria."

Amira didn't answer for a moment. Was that too personal a question?

Amira gave Mallory a rueful look. "I wasn't prepared to start over. No one is. I did not expect that I would leave my home and not go back to my old life. Even in war, daily life kept going. I took my son to school. I worked with my husband at the hospital. I went to the market, cooked, did laundry. Talked to our neighbors. All the ordinary things. When my husband was killed and I had to leave, even then, my plan was always to go back. Always. I could not imagine anything else."

Amira paused to show Mallory how to roll out the dough and braid it into rolls that they set out on oiled baking trays before slipping them into the oven.

"If I am honest," she continued as they wiped down the counters to prepare for the next batch, "I fought the idea that my life had to change. In the refugee camps in Turkey, where none of us could find work and we were completely dependent on others, I dreamed of returning. Even when I saw others who had lived for years in the camps, who left behind businesses, professions, entire lives. I met a friend in the camps who owned a garment factory with her husband and employed a hundred people. They had a very good life. She had to give it up, flee with nothing. The government sold all her equipment to Turkey. She was very bitter about that. My friend now lives in a tiny town in Sweden, in the north, with her parents, husband and children. There are very few opportunities for them to work except in menial jobs. She knows they will never get back the life they had."

Amira sighed. "I thought I would have more opportunities because I can speak English. Realizing that I will never be a doctor again, that has been very hard. But I am proud of the life my son and I have here. That friend told me, the best advice I can give you is not to look back, to let go and try to get into the new way of life."

As the room began to fill with the appetizing aroma of baking bread, Mallory reflected on Amira's story, and her own attempt at a fresh start. Was it time for Mallory to let go and not look back?

༄

A few hours later, Mallory greeted the small team of volunteers in the Government House ballroom.

"People, we've five hours to make this room look like a wonderland. You've each been assigned a specific task, so please check the list pinned up in the dining room for your name. Any questions, come talk to me right away."

The dining room had been commandeered as Gala Central, with the enormous dining table piled high with place cards, table settings and floral centerpieces designed by Georgie awaiting setup in the ballroom. Amira was in the kitchen supervising the catering staff and figuring out how to work with what the caterer had left.

"Can't you imagine Princess Margaret waltzing with a dashing partner across the floor?" sighed Georgie, looking around in delight at the ballroom. Clad in turquoise paneling, with white medallion accents surrounding a honey-brown parquet floor edged in red carpet, and floor-length damask drapes, the ballroom was the epitome of 1960s interior decorating.

"Mmmhmm," responded Mallory distractedly, as she ran her eyes down the guest list. Some guests had purchased entire tables and so had a built-in seating arrangement, but she still had to work out where to seat individuals and couples. She was beginning to understand why the events planner may have called in sick. Every local dignitary would be in attendance, including the premier and the mayor of Victoria.

Round tables for ten were scattered about the ballroom; the dais was set up with a podium and microphone for speeches and the awards presentation. After learning about the gala from Raquel, Hope DeWitt had purchased a table for ten to the gala and invited the Bellavista crew as her guests. Cora was still having difficulty putting weight on her ankle, so she regretfully declined, but Georgie thrilled at the opportunity to swan around in a gown. Grumbling that she'd prefer to stay home with Cora, Etta let Georgie talk her into attending. Amira, Mallory and Saffron made up the other seven spots, along with Hope and Raquel, leaving three seats unoccupied. Mallory had suggested they ask Kiki to join them and had been pleasantly surprised to hear that Kiki would be bringing a date. That left one extra seat at the table.

"How about Simon?" Mallory had asked Saffron when she heard about the extra tickets. "Do you want to invite him as your plus one?"

Saffron had blinked. "Why would I want to do that?"

"Oh! I thought you and Simon… well, he invited you out for dinner…"

Saffron had snorted. "I'm not dating Simon Green! Pssh, the guy can't even dress himself." All the same, Saffron had smiled fondly to herself.

Recalling the conversation now, Mallory inwardly sighed. It would be easy to resent how Saffron dismissed a very cute, potential suitor. To the Saffrons of the world, there was no such thing as a "diminished dating pool." Saffron, however, appeared oblivious to the effect her beauty had on others, her entire focus being on her career.

Not wanting the ticket to go to waste, Mallory had impulsively invited Art Papatonis, partly out of curiosity and partly out of self-interest. Art Papatonis would be excellent company. He'd texted her back that he would be delighted.

"Mallory!" One of the volunteers brought her attention back to the present. "The caterer didn't provide enough forks and we don't know where the teaspoons are."

Dropping the seating list on the table, Mallory hurried away to deal with the latest crisis.

༄

By some miracle, everything came together in time for the opening of the gala.

"Nice work," murmured Saffron approvingly, pointing to the prominent addition of the Bellavista Housing Cooperative to the list of event sponsors. A couple of guests might raise their eyebrows when they spotted the cooperative's name, but so far, no one had made any negative remarks. While she was supposed to be off now, Mallory kept on her headset so she could coordinate with the volunteers who were working with the catering staff. It made an interesting accessory to her simple, black A-line dress. To appease Georgie, she had added a rhinestone bracelet, but drew the line at wearing heels. Ballet flats were good enough for Audrey Hepburn, so they were certainly good enough for her.

At their table, Georgie, in a sparkly red evening gown, was chatting with a young man who looked familiar. When he leaped to his feet, Mallory couldn't hide her surprise that Kiki's mystery date was none other than Detective Grover. "Ms. McKenzie-Chu!" he exclaimed. "Thank you for inviting me this evening."

"You're most welcome," said Mallory, smiling at Kiki, who, decked out in pink tulle, winked back. "Please enjoy yourselves."

Etta was sporting a beautiful, beaded shawl over her habitual grey-hued layers. "Georgie insisted," Etta grumbled, but Mallory caught her looking contentedly at her finery.

Amira's voice came through her headset. "Mallory, we're all set in the kitchen," she announced. "Appetizers will circulate now. Dinner will be served in thirty minutes."

"Great. I'll let Stan know." She wove her way through the tables, looking for the director. He wasn't in the ballroom. Venturing out, she spotted him in the foyer in front of the enormous hearth, deep in conversation with a sandy-haired man in an ill-fitting tuxedo.

"I'm telling you, no more, okay?" Stan was saying in a furious whisper. He broke off when he spotted Mallory.

"Mallory! The place looks great! Thank you so much!" Stan said, shaking her hand.

"Yeah, thanks," echoed his companion. He looked familiar; Stan was talking to Brad Jobson.

Brad gave Mallory a curt nod, then walked away. Stan watched him leave, a hard expression on his face, but he thanked Mallory again after she had shared the catering staff's timing with him. As Stan made the rounds, smiling and clapping acquaintances on the back, Mallory couldn't help wondering: *What did Stan's comment to Brad mean?*

"Mallory!" She looked up to see Metchosin Barnes, looking stunning in a cream silk, halter-neck gown.

"Metchosin! You look amazing! How are you?"

"I heard how the cooperative stepped in at the last minute to save the gala," Metchosin said warmly. "Excellent work."

"We were happy to pitch in," said Mallory. "It's good to have the co-op associated with something positive for a change."

Metchosin shot her a sympathetic look. "Makes sense after all you've been through. How's Cora doing? What a nasty fall. Especially at her age."

"Cora's doing great," said Mallory. "Thanks to her regular yoga practice and swimming, she's in great health and healing well."

"That's a relief," said Metchosin. "I wasn't sure if I was going to come tonight, but then Kiki said she was coming, and Becca Gill said she'd be my date, so I thought I would support the foundation. While Nate had his faults, the foundation is his true legacy; he really believed in giving youths a head start in the trades."

"You're here with Becca Gill?" asked Mallory puzzled. Weren't the two women supposed to be sworn enemies?

"Becca and I sit on a couple of boards together. We decided we could both put up with Brad Jobson pontificating for one evening to toast Nate's memory. So long as we have enough sparkling wine, we'll be fine."

Before Mallory could follow up on Metchosin's comment about Brad, she felt a tap on her arm. She turned to see Art Papatonis, nattily dressed in a red blazer and matching bowtie. "Art, you look so dapper!" she said to him, then introduced him to Metchosin before letting him escort her back to the table.

"This is some shindig," remarked Art, looking about with interest. He had a slight limp but was able to navigate his way through the tables.

Mallory took her seat, only to bounce back up when Amira's voice came through on her headset again. "Art, I'm so sorry. I have to take care of one more thing."

He waved her away graciously and started chatting with Hope, who had arrived with Raquel. The first half of the evening went much the same way, with Mallory hovering near the table before being called to manage the next hiccup. Luckily, Papatonis didn't seem to mind, keeping the table enthralled with his stories. Hope and Raquel looked vastly entertained, and Etta couldn't hide her chuckles. Mallory was so busy she didn't have time to think much further about Metchosin's comment about Brad Jobson or wonder about what she'd overheard between Brad and Stan.

Mallory and Amira sank into their seats as the servers were clearing the entrees and serving tea and coffee.

"I thought I'd checked everything off my list but there was so much still to do!" Mallory told Kiki.

"Working the event is a whole different experience from being a guest," said Kiki sympathetically. "I saved you both some dessert." She slid two slices of chocolate cake toward them.

"You are an angel from heaven," said Mallory fervently.

Brad Jobson strode across the dais toward the podium and leaned into the microphone. "Ladies and Gentlemen, honored guests, thank you all for coming. Tonight, the Wheelbarrow Foundation is celebrating its fifth year in operation!"

A round of applause met his remarks.

"As you know, Nate Narkiss was the heart and soul of the foundation. I'm sure you'll agree with me that Nate would be thrilled to see the support of his community tonight. Now I'd like to introduce you to the new director of The Wheelbarrow Foundation, Stan Barber. Stan, come on up!"

"Stan Barber?" whispered Papatonis to Mallory, as Stan took the stage. "I've heard his name somewhere."

"Stan Barber took over from Nate Narkiss," Mallory whispered back. As Stan Barber cracked a few jokes, Art's puzzled frown grew deeper.

"And now we come to the highlight of our evening," said Stan. "These ten hardworking men and women — yes, we let in a couple of women" — a murmur of obligatory laughter rose from the audience — "have earned fully-paid spots in our upcoming apprentice training program. Over the next year, they'll apply their skills on actual projects while being overseen by masters in the trade. Please join me in celebrating our new candidates!"

Music played over applause as each of the candidates was introduced and made their way across the stage to accept their scholarships. Suddenly, Art bolted out of his seat. "That's him!" he cried, pointing at Barber. "He's the plant on our condo owners' association board!" Before anyone at their table could react, Art rushed toward the stage, teeth bared in a snarl.

But he didn't make it there. He sank to the floor with a groan as his right leg gave way underneath him. Detective Grover was the first by his side, helping him up. As Art struggled to his feet, he locked eyes with Stan Barber and shook his fist at him, yelling. "You rigged the votes on our condo board! You gave away the contracts to Sand Dollar and nearly bankrupted me!"

Stan staggered back from the edge of the stage, breathing heavily. "I-I don't know w-what you're talking about!" he stuttered.

Art let out a low growl and tried to lunge at the stage again while Detective Grover held him back. Almost immediately, two security personnel came running up, and together they hauled Art toward the door. Mallory stood and ran out after them. When she reached the foyer, Detective Grover was speaking to Art in a low, calming voice. The older man resisted, but then the fight went out of him, and he let the police officer walk him to the front door. Before he left, Art turned to Mallory.

"He was the guy on the condo owner's association board, Mallory! Stan Barber!"

Mallory tried to catch up. "You think Stan was the one who convinced the board to give the remediation work to Sand Dollar?" she asked.

"I don't think it, I know it!" Art insisted. "He's behind all those purchases forcing owners to sell below market." He scowled at the security guards who blocked his way. "Hold your horses, I'm not going to do anything. But I'm going to see that Stan Barber pays for what he did!" With those parting words, Art disappeared into the night.

Detective Grover raised his eyebrows. "Someone's had his feathers badly ruffled," he said to Mallory.

Mallory walked back to their table, mulling over Art's accusation against Stan Barber. It couldn't have been Art arguing with Stan the other day since he didn't recognize Stan until tonight. And what was tonight's argument between Stan and Brad all about? *Was it Brad I overheard at the office?*

"What was that about?" whispered Saffron as Mallory took her seat. "I'm not sure," she whispered back. Kiki gave her a look full of meaning, clearly wanting details at the first opportunity.

Brad Jobson was once again at the podium, having finished handing out the scholarship awards to the candidates. Stan stood next to him, looking pale and sweaty. Despite the murmurs rustling through the crowd like wind through a wheatfield, it looked like they were proceeding with the evening's events as if nothing had happened.

"Now we come to a special part of our program, where I'd like us all to take a few moments to reflect on the wonderful life of our founder, Nate Narkiss," said Brad as the lights dimmed.

A slideshow began of Nate's involvement in the Wheelbarrow Foundation programs over the years, working on construction sites, hanging out with Brad, handing out past scholarships. As the music swelled, another sound interrupted the presentation: the sound of a hundred phones receiving an alert at the same time. Mallory's own phone beeped; she glanced down and saw a text from an unknown number:

Barber embezzled from Wheelbarrow!

Mallory compulsively read the rest of the text. Stan Barber was accused of stealing thousands in donations from the foundation; the text's author alleged that Nate found out about the embezzlement and confronted Stan, who killed him to hide his crime.

As exclamations drowned out the slide presentation, she looked up to see Brad and Stan also glued to their phones. Stan's face took on a terrified expression.

"It's not true!" Stan gasped, looking up. "It's all lies! I didn't do it!"

Brad shook his head sorrowfully at Stan's blustering denials. "Stan, the game's up. You can't hide. Everyone knows what you did now."

"No!" Stan yelled. "It's not true!" He turned and ran off the dais. Detective Grover sprang to his feet and gave chase. Seeing the police officer and security guards coming towards him, Stan froze, then rushed up the staircase to the upper balcony and out of sight. As the crowd watched in horrified fascination, Detective Grover and the guards pounded up the stairs after Stan. A cry rang out, followed by breaking glass and an ominous thud. Several people screamed.

Mallory stumbled to her feet and ran toward the back doors of the ballroom that were open to the night air. She found Stan Barber lying prone on the pavement, having tumbled from the upper story through the window onto the ground. Looking up, she spotted Art Papatonis looking straight at her!

"I didn't do anything!" cried Art, as he was being hustled into the back of a patrol car. His eyes met Mallory's. "You gotta believe me!"

☙

As Stan was taken away in an ambulance, unconscious, Detective Grover promised he'd keep them posted on his status. After the intense events at Government House, all Mallory wanted to do was crawl into bed. Her companions excitedly rehashed Art's arrest and protestations of innocence as they walked from Government House back to Bellavista.

"Too bad Art's now a felon," Georgie said with a sigh. "With his natural dramatic flair, he'd be the perfect addition to my theatre group."

Mallory's head pounded. Saffron took one look at her and sent her upstairs to bed. As she was about to turn in, the empty cage on the landing caught her eye. She'd forgotten it was her turn to bring in Gregory Peck for the night. Despite her initial misgivings over being responsible for the little rooster's care, Mallory had grown fond of GP; a morning person by nature, she didn't mind his early morning crowing, and the little rooster enjoyed following her around while she went through her morning routine. Saffron still pulled a pillow over her head and let out a string of unmentionables every morning.

It was quiet and dark by the chicken coop. Mallory unlatched the gate and let herself in, careful to close the gate behind her. But as she turned, a dark form rose up in front of her. She gasped, staggering back. The form grabbed her arm but before she could scream, a gloved hand covered her mouth.

Chapter 23

> **"The truth always come out. Be ready for it."**
> **- Raquel DeWitt,** ***The Smart Woman's Guide to Getting it Done.***

Fear made Mallory go rigid, her heart battering. Then a familiar face swam in front of her eyes. Lucas!

"Please, Mallory, don't scream, okay? I'm not going to hurt you." His eyes pleaded with her to believe him. "If I take my hand away, will you hear me out?" Lucas asked.

She nodded. Lucas removed his hand, and she fell back, gasping for air.

"What's going on, Lucas?" she whispered fiercely. "You've got two minutes, then I'm calling the police!"

"I didn't do it. I didn't kill Nate!"

When she didn't say anything, his words tumbled out. "Brad Jobson was the one who was here that night. I saw the whole thing. Brad and Nate got into a fight, and Brad pushed Nate. I don't think he meant to hurt him, but Nate fell and hit his head on the fountain edge and got knocked out. I - I panicked and took off in my truck. Then I made myself turn around and come back to see if Nate was hurt. I couldn't leave him like that. But when I got back, Brad was gone and I couldn't find Nate, so I went to check the coop and that's when I heard the sirens."

"What were Nate and Brad doing here that night?" asked Mallory. It was the question no one had been able to answer.

Lucas hesitated.

"Two minutes," said Mallory in a warning tone.

"Brad had convinced me that Cora needed to sell Bellavista to Nate," he said hurriedly. "Brad and I, well, we did some stuff to the house to make her want to sell."

Mallory's eyes narrowed. "What kind of stuff? Wait, were you the reason things kept breaking down all the time?"

Lucas hung his head, avoiding her eyes. "Yeah, the lights going out, the roof tiles, I did that. The plumbing's an old problem; it wasn't hard to make it worse. We were planning to mess with the sprinkler system while you guys were at the council meeting. Nate found out and tried to stop Brad. That's when they had the big fight." Lucas looked miserable, but she wasn't about to let him off the hook.

"Why would you do that to Cora?" she asked, her voice rising. "And why tell me now and not her?"

"I've been waiting for Cora all day, but she never came out to the garden."

"She's had a bad fall. She's in hospital."

At Lucas's devastated look, Mallory relented and said, "She fell trying to replace a lightbulb. She's going to be fine, but her ankle needs surgery before she can come home."

Lucas let out a shuddering sigh. "For a second I thought..." He took another deep breath. "Brad took a chance on me when he knew I had a prior record. I believed him when he told me Cora would lose Bellavista if she didn't sell to Nate and that we needed to put a little pressure on. I got so frustrated by how slowly everything was going. I thought it would help her if she made a deal with Nate. At first it was little things, like a couple of roof tiles, tinkering with the lights, nothing dangerous. But then, after Nate was killed, Brad got bolder."

"He kept it up after Nate died?" Mallory was appalled.

Lucas looked wretched. "Yeah, he wanted me to keep pressuring Cora to sell, this time to him so he could finish the Rock Cliff Resort. I told him I didn't want to do it anymore, but he wouldn't listen."

"The open house," she muttered, understanding dawning. That was why everything that could have gone wrong went wrong that day.

Lucas nodded. "I told Brad that I was done helping him. He laughed and said he didn't need me. Then he told me to make a run for it because he'd set me up and was calling the cops on me. I went straight home and cleared everything out."

She remembered Detective Blair's warning about dealing with Lucas; how could she have forgotten that he was a suspected drug dealer! Lucas saw the change in her expression and said, "I'm telling the truth! Brad set me up! Yeah, I did the runs to Nanaimo and back, like he asked, but I didn't know it was drugs! I never checked the bags!"

She gave him a searching look. *Could Lucas really have been that naive? He had bought into Brad's outlandish scheme to force Cora to sell Bellavista.* She didn't know what to think.

"Brad's bad news," Lucas said urgently. "Tell Cora and the others. Stan Barber told me Brad's been pressuring him about the foundation's finances; he wants access to the accounts. Stan thinks he wants to cook the books. Brad's a bully and he won't stop until he gets what he wants."

Lucas didn't know. The news probably wouldn't be public until the morning. "Lucas, Stan Barber is in the hospital. He fell from the Government House balcony at The Wheelbarrow Foundation gala tonight."

The outside lights came on, spilling light into the coop. Lucas jumped back into the shadows, but not before she saw the fearful expression on his face.

"I gotta get out of here! Please, tell Cora I'm so sorry!"

"Lucas, wait!" But he was gone.

ෲ

Mallory lost no time in running back into the house to grab her phone and take it back outside to call Detective Blair. She didn't want the others to overhear her conversation. While she empathized with the position Lucas had found himself in, the fact remained that Nate Narkiss was dead and the police ought to know what Lucas had told her.

Detective Blair was curt. "You should have called us as soon as you saw Lucas."

"He would have run," said Mallory, "if I didn't promise to hear him out first."

Detective Blair grunted. "Ms. Chu — er, McKenzie-Chu — I don't need to remind you that this is an active investigation and that there are consequences for aiding and abetting."

"I didn't aid and abet anyone," she protested. "But I need to tell you that Lucas said Brad Jobson was the one who assaulted Nate. He told me..."

"Stay out of this, please." Detective Blair abruptly hung up, leaving Mallory to stare at her phone in disbelief. *Were the police going to ignore critical information?*

"What was that about?" asked Saffron, who'd come out to look for Mallory when she wasn't in bed.

"Come with me, and I'll tell you," said Mallory, turning back toward the chicken coop. "I don't want the others to hear." As she collected Gregory Peck and put the little rooster into his cage, she told Saffron about Lucas's sudden appearance and his confession.

"Unbelievable!" cried Saffron. "He abused Cora's trust and now he's blaming it all on Brad Jobson? How convenient. Don't fall for it, Mallory. Lucas is guilty."

"He felt terrible about what he did to Cora," said Mallory, as she carried GP back to the house.

"Lucas was smuggling drugs," said Saffron. "How do we know if he's telling the truth about anything? Maybe he's trying to confuse things by accusing Brad Jobson. I believe him when he says Brad is bad news, but we need to stay out of it. After last night's gala, I don't want anything more to do with Sand Dollar or The Wheelbarrow Foundation. Bad things keep happening around these people. Don't get involved!"

Gregory Peck let out a squawk in agreement.

"Do you think Brad had something to do with Stan's accident?" asked Mallory. "I can't believe Art had anything to do with that."

"Mallory!" Saffron was in full mother hen mode. "Listen to me! Will you please stay out of it? People are getting hurt! I don't want you to be next."

Chapter 24

> "Don't wait for others to come to you."
> - Raquel DeWitt, *The Smart Woman's Guide to Getting it Done*

Despite Detective Blair's warning and Saffron's concern, Mallory was convinced Lucas was telling the truth. All roads led back to Brad Jobson. If Brad really was responsible for Nate's death and the problems at Bellavista, her innate sense of justice refused to accept that he would get away with it. It wasn't enough that Cora and the others weren't suspected. She wanted to see Brad pay for what he did. She remembered Lucas's look of terror when he heard about Stan's accident. *Could he know something about that? Was Brad responsible for Stan's accident too?*

She also couldn't forget the beseeching look Art Papatonis had sent her as he was driven away in the police cruiser. Art hadn't put a finger on Stan, she was sure of that. If Stan Barber really was the plant on Art's condo board, Mallory could understand the rage that propelled him to rush the stage, but in the brief time she'd known him, he didn't strike her as someone who could chase another person through a window to their death.

She couldn't shake the memory of Lucas's warning about Brad. His words played over and over in her mind. She had to do something. Mallory still had the enormous event planning binder Stan had given to her. A built-in excuse to visit Brad Jobson's office and return it since she expected Stan's office at the Wheelbarrow

Foundation to be closed. Saffron would try to talk her out of going to see Brad, so she reached out to Kiki for a ride.

As sometimes happened in early May in Victoria, the day had turned unexpectedly warm; the parking lot asphalt reflected serious heat as they walked toward the row of low-rise buildings that housed Sand Dollar's satellite office and The Wheelbarrow Foundation's headquarters. Kiki vibrated with excitement while Mallory had to work at controlling her nerves. *We're just returning the binder*, she told herself. *If we happen to come across some useful information…*

The faint outline of a red, spray-painted message was visible under the hastily painted-over business sign for Sand Dollar Developments. They took the exterior staircase up to the second-floor office. Traces of painter's tape stuck to the edges of the door and the interior smelled of fresh paint, cigarettes, and fast food. A sullen-faced receptionist with stringy hair sat behind the front counter eating a burger. On the wall behind her, a calendar displayed the month of January and an agitated fly buzzed behind slatted window blinds. Trapped heat vibrated off the walls.

The receptionist eyed them. "Can I help you?" she asked reluctantly, putting down her burger.

"We're looking for Brad Jobson. Is he available?"

"He's at a site. Won't be back for the rest of the day. Do you wanna leave a message?"

Mallory was reluctant to leave the binder without seeing Brad, since it was her only excuse to connect with him. "Could you tell us where the site is? I've something to return to him in person."

The receptionist's eyes flickered, and she reached over to grab a notepad and pen to scribble a note.

"Here's the address. Evergreen Apartments. Know where that is?"

"We can find it, thanks."

They hurried out of the office, glad to escape the stifling atmosphere.

᠃

Evergreen Apartments did not live up to its name. The nondescript, four-story 1960s complex had a dried-out, yellowing front lawn and not a single tree. Scaffolding obscured the entire building, where construction workers hammered, sawed and shouted instructions to one another to the syncopated beat of rock music from a radio dialed to maximum volume. No one took any notice as Kiki took out her phone and snapped a few pictures— "for evidence"— she told Mallory.

"I'm going to check out the rest of the building," Kiki said.

Mallory spotted Brad standing by the site office, talking to a worker in a hardhat, tool belt and steel-toed boots. Neither looked happy with the way the discussion was going.

"Just do it. I don't want excuses," said Brad. The worker turned and walked back to the site, his mouth set in a grim line.

Brad noticed Mallory staring. "Yeah, can I help you?"

"Brad Jobson? Do you have a moment? I'm Mallory McKenzie-Chu — I was at the gala last night."

"Oh, yeah," Brad rubbed the back of his head. "Stan mentioned you helped out. Thanks for that."

"I brought back the event-planning binder," said Mallory, handing it over. "With Stan's accident, I wasn't sure where to return it."

"Thanks." Brad took the binder and looked uncertain what to do with it.

"It was really awful what happened to Stan last night." Genuinely upset about the director's accident, Mallory teared up.

Brad thrust his hands into his pockets and pursed his lips. "Yeah, who knew he was stealing from the foundation the whole time? The guy sure had me fooled."

"You think the rumor is true, then?" asked Mallory. "That Stan stole donations and that he killed Nate to cover it up?"

Brad nodded. "The police took the foundation's account books this morning. Stan was taking a cut right off the top of every donation. When he wakes up, he'll face embezzlement charges, maybe even murder charges. We were all taken in by Stan."

If Lucas hadn't told Mallory about what Brad had been up to, she would have thought Brad was sincerely devastated by Stan's "betrayal". Maybe he was.

"This must be very difficult for you," said Mallory, forcing an empathetic expression.

Brad lowered his brows and blinked a few times. "Yeah, it is. I keep asking myself, 'why, Stan, why?'"

"But if Stan killed Nate, what were the two of them doing at Bellavista? Why would Stan kill Nate in the chicken coop? It doesn't make sense," said Mallory in a puzzled tone. If she hoped to provoke a response, she succeeded.

Brad was immediately suspicious. "What are you, a reporter? A cop? Who sent you?"

Mallory pretended to be confused. "I'm sorry, I thought I told you, I'm with the Bellavista Housing Co-op. Why, have the police been asking you questions about Nate's murder?"

"Why would they?" Brad straightened up, looking wary. "I wasn't even in town that night. I was in Campbell River on a fishing trip. Cops asked me this already. A friend and I chartered a fishing boat and were out on the water that evening. I didn't get back to shore until the next day."

He trotted out his alibi without much prompting, indicating he was confident that it checked out. All the same, Brad's sorrowful mask had slipped, showing a man on edge.

"Why are you asking all these questions?" he demanded.

"Sorry, I didn't mean to upset you," said Mallory. "I just wanted to return the binder."

She walked quickly away, feeling Brad's eyes boring into her back, and hurried over to where Kiki was taking photos at the front of the building.

With about ten workers on the scaffolding and more on the ground, the remediation project looked like an extensive undertaking. Art's condo remediation had almost bankrupted him. How much were the residents paying for this work? Mallory felt a tap on her shoulder and turned to see a short, elderly man with alert black eyes.

"You with the city?" he asked, his straw fedora tipping back.

"No, sorry."

The man pointed at Kiki, who was taking photos of the site with her phone.

"What about her?"

"No, she's not with the city either."

"I called the city many times to do something. They're useless! Last week, a guy got high, went inside the porta-potty, crashed around. I called police and they came, but he was gone. It's not safe here for kids with people like that!"

"Mr. Kwan." Brad Jobson came striding toward them. "I told you we took care of it."

Mr. Kwan pointed a bony finger at Brad. "You took care of nothing."

Brad noticed Kiki's camera. "What are you doing?"

Kiki turned. "Taking some pictures."

"Give me that!" Brad's face flushed as he tried to grab her phone. Kiki darted out of his reach.

"Hey!" Mr. Kwan barked. "Leave my granddaughter alone!"

Brad backed away, his hands raised. "Sorry, I didn't realize."

He brushed past Mallory and walked back to the site. As he passed, Mallory wrinkled her nose at his pungent blend of aftershave.

Laughing, Kiki gave Mr. Kwan a hug.

"*Is* he your grandfather?" asked Mallory, confused.

"Never seen him before."

"All Asians look the same, right?" said Mr. Kwan with an impish grin.

Mallory grinned back. "Quick thinking, Mr. Kwan. What was that about a guy in the porta-potty?"

"Half the workers on this site are on drugs. I see them come to work with their eyes bloodshot and they leave the place a mess. I told the building owners, but they don't care. They just want the remediation done fast and cheap."

Drugs again and poor remediation work. They were the common thread running through everything. Lucas had said that Nate went to Bellavista to confront Brad about the sabotage. Could he also have confronted Brad about drug use on the work site?

Mr. Kwan said, "I gotta go make a call. City needs to do something about this."

As he stepped off the sidewalk, a truck came racing around the corner and narrowly missed him. Mr. Kwan staggered and fell. While Mallory ran to him, Kiki pointed her camera at the truck and started snapping furiously.

"I got the license plate!" cried Kiki.

"Mr. Kwan, are you okay?"

Mallory helped him up to his feet.

"I'm ok, I'm ok." He was shaken, but not hurt. "Dang idiot driver!"

Kiki scrolled through her photos. "I managed to get a few shots of the back of the truck. Rats. I can only make out a few numbers." She showed the clearest photo to Mallory.

Mallory glanced at the photo. "That truck was red, like the one Lucas uses to pick up supplies. It's the same make too."

Mr. Kwan looked over Mallory's shoulder. "That truck belongs to Brad, the guy who tried to take your friend's camera." He snorted in disgust. "Dang idiot tried to drive over me!"

Mallory and Kiki exchanged looks before Mallory asked to see the photo once again. Now she could make out Brad's flat cap and scowl. Did Brad try to run them down? Brad had a red truck like Lucas's. Mallory's mind stretched to give meaning to that piece of information, but the reasoning eluded her.

All the same, the police should know about the near hit-and-run. She called Detective Grover directly at the number Kiki shared, while Kiki drove them back to Bellavista. The young detective was more sympathetic than his senior colleague.

"Did anyone get hurt?" he asked anxiously. "Is Kiki okay?"

"We're all fine," Mallory reassured him, "but Brad Jobson was trying to scare us off."

"I won't ask what you were doing at Sand Dollar Development's work site. Please, from now on, leave the investigating to us."

"Wait, do you have any news about Stan Barber?" she asked anxiously. "Is he okay?"

"We've been told we have to wait and see as he hasn't recovered consciousness yet."

"What about Art Papatonis?"

"We let him go this morning," said Detective Grover. "The security footage showed that he was nowhere near Stan Barber when he fell."

What a relief. "Did the footage show anyone else nearby when Stan fell? Did Stan fall or was he pushed?"

"Mallory, you know I can't tell you anything," answered Detective Grover. "Look, please stay out of this. You don't know what you're dealing with, and it could get dangerous." He hung up.

"Drat!" Mallory couldn't hide her frustration. Kiki looked over at her with concern. "Did Neel shut you down?" she asked.

"Stan's not conscious yet, and I can't get anyone to take my concerns about Brad Jobson seriously! They're not even interested in what Lucas had to say! It must be because he has a watertight alibi."

"Neel's a real stickler for the rules," said Kiki. "He won't tell me anything about the case. I totally respect that, but it's beyond frustrating!"

Mallory knew she had no choice. If the police weren't investigating him, it was up to her to collect enough evidence for the police to be convinced to take a closer look at Brad Jobson.

Chapter 25

> *"Ask the right questions."*
> *- Raquel DeWitt, **The Smart Woman's Guide to Getting it Done.***

Mallory called Metchosin Barnes to follow up on the grant applications she had offered to provide and to see if Metchosin might have anything further to say about Brad Jobson.

"I'm in the middle of my campaign so my office is a disaster," said Metchosin. "Do you mind meeting at my place?"

Metchosin's townhouse was near Willows Beach, a highly coveted stretch of waterfront in the tony neighborhood of Oak Bay. Casually chic in a cream cable-knit sweater and leggings, Metchosin welcomed Mallory warmly.

"Come in! It's chilly today so I turned on the gas fireplace. I'm making us some tea."

Mallory entered an inviting space done in warm, beachy tones. She took a seat at the kitchen island while Metchosin fetched the teapot and two mugs. Outside the large picture window, dogwalkers jostled with kids on their scooters and lululemon-clad mums pushing jogging strollers. In the distance, a couple of boats sailed serenely out of the small, protected harbor to the surrounding islands.

"This place is stunning, Metchosin," said Mallory. "I could stare at that view all day."

"Being this close to the beach is a nice perk, for sure," agreed Metchosin. "You should be here when it's stormy, though — that's a whole different experience. Sometimes the waves toss the driftwood logs right onto the road. I'm worried that one day, a log will crash through my picture window!" Metchosin placed a mug of lemon ginger tea in front of Mallory.

"How've you been doing?" Metchosin asked. "We were all really shaken by Stan's fall. Didn't you know the guy who was charged? What was his name...Papadopoulos?"

"Art Papatonis," said Mallory. "He was released. The police said he had nothing to do with Stan's fall."

"I'm glad to hear that. It was an accident, then," said Metchosin. "I hope Stan's going to be okay."

She pulled over the stack of paper. "Here are the grant applications I've put together. The online guides to the grants are useful, but I think you'll find the notes my staff compiled more helpful on the factors the province and the city consider most important. Use your own judgment, of course, as you know your project best."

"Thanks so much. This will help a lot." Mallory tucked the folder of applications into her bag. "Speaking of the gala, do you mind if I ask some questions about Brad Jobson?"

"Brad?" Metchosin looked surprised. "We didn't interact at the gala. It's been years since we've spoken."

"We found out that Brad has been actively sabotaging Bellavista to force Cora to sell."

"What?" Metchosin looked genuinely shocked. "What did he do?"

Mallory told her about the problems with falling roofing tiles, vermin infestation, plumbing issues. "It was all manufactured by Brad, with Lucas's help. He was trying to get Bellavista for Nate's Rock Cliff Resort development."

Metchosin shook her head. "Why am I surprised? Brad always played dirty. I should know. When I was running for city council, a nasty story came out on an online gossip blog attacking my campaign and painting me as "anti-business." Ridiculous, because I'm a business owner myself. I suspected that Brad was behind it — the story had his fingerprints all over it. I'd seen him try that kind of smear before on another businessperson in town, spreading innuendo. Nothing slanderous, but enough to cast a shadow."

"What did you do about it?" asked Mallory, feeling slightly guilty. She'd become addicted to checking out the *Vic in the Know* blog.

"He denied it, of course, with a smirk. When I confronted Nate, he swore he knew nothing about it. I realized then that not only was Nate unsupportive of my career, he was willing to stand by and allow his friend to smear me. That's when I knew that our marriage was over."

"Did you mention this to the police?" asked Mallory.

"I didn't think what happened with my campaign was relevant, and I had no proof, only suspicions. The *Vic in the Know* blog is anonymous and no one knows who moderates it. But I knew Brad had to be involved."

"Lucas told me that Brad was the one who assaulted Nate at Bellavista," said Mallory. "He was there that night."

"Oh my gosh!" Metchosin's eyes went wide. "That's unbelievable! Brad and Nate were so tight; they've known each other since they were kids. Nate didn't talk about his past very much, but I know he was in foster care with Brad and that's why they were so close. I wonder what caused them to fall out so badly."

"Nate found out about Brad's sabotage attempt and went to stop Brad," said Mallory. "At least, that's what Lucas told me, but I think there must be more to the story. I read that Brad and Nate owned one company together, Sand Dollar Developments, and were going to do a merger of their separate leasing and remediation companies, but nothing came of it. Before he was killed, there were rumors that Nate was considering a partnership with Jacob Prentiss. Could that have been the reason for their fight?"

Metchosin frowned. "I know that Nate wanted to move in the same circles as J.P.; he asked me to sponsor him to the same golf club. And when Nate offered in exchange to accept a lump sum payout for alimony, I agreed. If Nate was separating his business interests from Brad's, I can see that upsetting Brad."

The mystery of the $100,000 payout to Nate resolved! "Brad's businesses seem to be all kinds of messy," said Mallory. "Cutting corners, alleged drug use on-site, workplace safety issues. But he's like Teflon, nothing so far has stuck to him. I tried to tell the police what Lucas told me about Brad assaulting Nate, but they weren't interested. I think it's because Brad apparently has an alibi and Lucas has zero credibility now that he's believed to have been trafficking drugs. But I believe Lucas!"

Metchosin went quiet for a minute. Then she said, "I know about another situation where Brad may have crossed the line. I don't know if it's enough to get the police to look at him more closely. But it's not my story to tell. If you want to know more, I suggest you talk to Becca Gill."

As she left, Mallory looked up to see Metchosin standing on her balcony watching her go. Metchosin was already on the phone.

༄

Catching Saffron before she left to pick up title and zoning documents from Becca Gill's office, Mallory asked if she could tag along, and quickly filled her in on her conversation with Metchosin about Brad Jobson. Saffron wasn't thrilled that she was still investigating, but her curiosity got the better of her and she agreed to let Mallory join her.

Becca was nervous. That much was clear to Mallory the moment they walked into her office.

"Yvonne has your documents ready for pick-up at her desk," the lawyer told them.

"Yes, thanks, we have them," said Mallory. "Do you have a minute to chat about something else?"

"What can I do for you?" asked Becca briskly. "I should let you know that I can only spare a few minutes."

"It's about Brad Jobson, Nate's business partner."

Becca's lips tightened. "I told you, I don't really know…"

"We know you and Nate were dating for a while and broke up a couple of months before he was killed," said Saffron.

Becca sat back. "How did you find that out? I only shared that with the police."

"*Vic in the Know* had an article about last year's Wheelbarrow Gala and there was a photo of you with Nate and Brad Jobson," said Mallory.

Becca let out a frustrated breath. "That stupid blog! It's made so much trouble for so many people. Okay, I did date Nate, but it was for a short time, less than a year. I don't see what that has to do with anything."

"If we told you that Brad was sabotaging Bellavista and that Lucas told us he was the one who assaulted Nate, would that make things more relevant?" asked Saffron.

Becca stared. "Is that true? Did Brad go after Bellavista and Cora? And Nate?"

Mallory nodded. "We know he created issues at Bellavista to try to force Cora to sell. Lucas saw Brad assault Nate, and we believe Lucas is telling the truth. The problem is, the police aren't taking our suspicions seriously. If you know anything about Brad that might be important, please tell us."

When Becca said nothing, Mallory added, "Please. If Brad's responsible, we can't let him get away with it."

"If I tell you what happened with Brad, will you promise not to bother my grandfather about this?" asked Becca. "He's had enough to deal with and I don't want to stir things up again for him."

Mallory and Saffron promised, and Becca began her tale.

"Shortly after Nate and I started dating, a blind item appeared in *Vic in the Know* that said that a well-established developer with the initials BG was colluding with sub-trades by fixing pricing. It was a parcel of lies that targeted my grandfather, Basinder Gill. There's no other big-name developer in Victoria with those initials. I was furious and confronted Nate, but he denied that Brad was involved."

"Why did you suspect Brad?" asked Mallory.

"I had heard from Metchosin Barnes that a similar smear had happened to her on the blog and she suspected Brad was behind it. Metchosin and I are friendly. I do some volunteer work for The Land Trust, so we're often at the same events. When I started seeing Nate, she found out through mutual acquaintances and invited me out for coffee. She told me what to watch out for, one woman looking out for another. I respect Metchosin— she calls it like it is— and it didn't seem like she was trying to get back at him by talking to me. I know many people saw Nate as an arrogant blowhard, but there was more to him than that. He was smart, ambitious and could be incredibly charming. Metchosin wanted me to be aware of Nate's failings and to stick up for myself; she also wanted me to be prepared in case Brad started interfering. She told me Brad was very possessive about Nate and really resented anyone taking Nate's attention."

"Then other stuff happened that caused me to break things off with Nate. I suspected that the primary reason he was dating me was to get information about my grandfather's business, so he could use it against him or have an advantage in deals or construction bids. That and the blind item trying to discredit my grandfather were too much for me."

Mallory asked, "What was the other stuff that happened. Did it involve Brad?"

Becca hesitated, then got up and went to the door. "Yvonne, do you mind joining us?"

When the receptionist came in, Becca introduced her. "This is Yvonne Desjardins. She knows the whole story, so I'll let her tell you what happened."

Yvonne took a seat, tucking her feet underneath, and sitting upright as if for a deposition. "Several months ago, I suspected that someone had been accessing our confidential client files. I maintain a strict logging system for file access in our file cabinets. I could tell that someone other than myself had been in our client files."

"Was there a break-in? Did you report it to the police?" asked Saffron.

Yvonne shook her head. "There wasn't enough to take to the police the first time, just my own sense that someone had disturbed the files. Things that only I would notice, such as a file's papers being out of order or a folder being misfiled. I keep the files locked in the filing cabinets and the key is kept in my desk drawer. The office has an alarm system and there were no alerts about a break-in or tamper. When armed, the system keeps a record of every time the office door or window is opened or any movement within the office. We would know if someone had been in here after hours. There was no evidence of a break-in beyond the file disturbance."

"Yvonne's a drill sergeant when it comes to file protocol. I'm not allowed to pull any files myself," said Becca.

"And you suspected Brad"? asked Mallory. "Why?"

"We're sure it was Brad. One time Brad dropped by to meet Becca and Nate for lunch. I went to use the restroom and when I came back, he was behind my desk hovering over my computer. He jumped back and pretended he wasn't doing anything. As I log out every time I leave my desk, I wasn't concerned that he saw anything confidential, but I told Becca about the incident. And I started wearing the key to the filing cabinet around my wrist. Two weeks later our alarm system reported a breach to the police, but they found nothing when they arrived."

Becca continued. "The following week, Gill Construction was outbid on a property my grandfather needed to finish a development. He ended up having to buy it from the new purchaser for a much higher price than the property was originally valued at. We suspected that Brad had accessed information in our land transaction files."

Yvonne took up the tale again. "I set a trap for Brad by planting a mocked-up land title transfer document with a fake seller's name and Becca's grandfather listed as the buyer. If he was going through our client files, I expected he would contact the seller and try to outbid Gill Construction on the property."

"Did Brad fall for the ruse?" asked Saffron.

Yvonne nodded. "A week later someone called the number I had listed for the seller on a disposable cellphone I bought for that purpose. Becca didn't want to report the matter to the police because of Nate and because we couldn't confirm it was Brad who made the call. I felt I had enough to confront Brad with my suspicions, but when I did, he denied everything. I told him I would go to the police if he tried anything again with Becca, the firm, Gill Construction or me."

Yvonne looked fierce. "No one messes with our files or our reputation. Not on my watch."

"Nothing was taken from the files," said Becca, "But I reported the security breach to the Law Society and told all my clients. However, I didn't tell the clients who we suspected. As Yvonne said, reputation matters. I admit I was afraid of the hit my professional reputation would take if word got out about the security breach. I knew that Cora wouldn't say anything, and I felt confident in my existing clients, although I did lose a few."

"Did you tell Nate about Brad accessing your client files?" asked Mallory

Becca exhaled. "He played it down and said that Yvonne must have been mistaken. I saw that he wasn't prepared to take our side against Brad. That's when I broke things off with him."

"What do you think Brad was after?" asked Saffron.

"Information. Brad likes the feeling of knowing stuff about other people. We suspect he was after dirt on my grandfather, any kind of inside knowledge that would give Nate and Brad's companies an advantage in deals. It looks like another target could have been Cora, if Bellavista was at stake."

ɑ℈

"Could Brad have been involved in blackmail?" asked Saffron. They were grabbing a quick lunch at The Daily Bun after their meeting with Becca.

"He was involved in something shady. Breaking and entering for sure, but Becca only has suspicions, no concrete proof. The timing of the blog post discrediting Becca's grandfather and then the thwarted property purchase seems suspicious. Is there a link between Brad and the blog? Could he be the author?"

"But if Brad was blackmailing people, wouldn't he be the one with enemies, not Nate?" asked Saffron.

"That's true. It would make more sense. I think the *Vic in the Know* blog has some connection. It can't be random that every time Nate was involved with someone there was a smear against that person on the blog. Ugh, this is so frustrating! Unless Lucas is willing to turn himself in and make a statement against Brad, the police are not going to act on what we tell them."

What did they know about Nate? Charming and attentive, he attracted successful women like Metchosin and Becca. At the same time, he resented their success if they outshone him. He was ambitious and wanted to grow his companies, yet he tolerated shoddy workmanship and let his tenants down. He sought social acceptance through the golf club membership and becoming a patron of the arts; he demonstrated generosity and paying it forward with his scholarship program and charitable foundation, yet he encouraged anti-social actions by his best friend if he benefited from them. Who was Nate Narkiss, really? Readily adapting to the interests of whomever he was around, he was a walking mass of contradictions.

Brad Jobson was more straightforward to read; he was bad news through and through, no grey zones, except possibly his enduring friendship with Nate. And if their suspicions were correct, that obsessive friendship culminated in a violent end when it no longer served Brad's interests.

Una came by with their warmed-up rolls and beverages. "Hey, you guys. I hope you parked round the back. Pierce has been going ballistic on anyone daring to park in front of his store."

"Thanks for the warning. We're good," said Saffron. "Speaking of our favorite antique, I noticed that he hasn't been bothering us about the chickens for a while."

"That reminds me," said Mallory. "With the hearing in a couple of days, I expect that the heritage society will be attending. I'd like to chat with Pierce to see if I can persuade him to support our application. I'm confident of our success, now that we have J.P. on board and a list of potential buyers, but it would be good to know that the society isn't going to object. With everything that's been going on, it fell to the bottom of my list." She wasn't looking forward to another encounter with the cantankerous businessman.

"Good luck with that," said Una dubiously. "Pierce only supports what supports Pierce. Unless there is some advantage that the redevelopment can bring him, Pierce will find a way to complain about it."

An advantage..."Una!" said Mallory, perking up. "Thanks, you've given me an idea."

Chapter 26

"Nothing risked, nothing gained."
- Raquel DeWitt, **The Smart Woman's Guide to Getting it Done.**

Saffron needed to go back to Bellavista for a work call. She wasn't super optimistic about Mallory's strategy, despite Amira's confirmation when Mallory called her, but agreed that it was worth a try.

"Can you catch an Uber back to Bellavista?" asked Saffron. "Amira's taking Georgie and Etta to see Cora at the hospital this afternoon. She's able to come home later today."

"No problem. It's a lovely day. I think I'll walk back up the hill," said Mallory.

As Mallory entered The Seasoned Connoisseur, the tinkling of the bell alerted Pierce to her presence. He was behind the counter, clutching a corded phone receiver to his ear and scowling.

"Would I be able to pick up the suite next week? I won't have room until then."

He listened for a minute, his scowl growing deeper. "That's most unfortunate," he said. "I'm afraid I must decline then."

He hung up and frowned at Mallory.

"Hi, Pierce," she said with a smile, refusing to be cowed by his surly expression. "Do you have a moment?"

"I suppose so, now that I won't be driving to Oak Bay to collect Doris Everall's nineteenth-century living room suite. I don't have room to store it until after the auction. If only Nate had given me instead of Metchosin the lease next door!"

It was the opening Mallory needed to make her pitch.

"Pierce, have you thought about turning part of Downton into a salesroom and warehouse?"

Pierce sniffed. "I already have a small workshop for furniture refinishing, but I don't have the permits or zoning for a full-scale business operation. Don't tell me, you're planning to open a commercial hatchery at Bellavista?"

Mallory ignored the sarcasm. "Amira discovered that there is an old zoning bylaw in place that allows for a broader scope of commercial operations at Bellavista. The Vandervoss family used to operate a bottling factory on their property and the zoning has never been changed. She checked the plans, and it appears that the zoning extends over your property too."

"Really?" His whole demeanor changed. "Does this mean I could run my store out of Downton? I've been thinking about moving to a more online presence."

"If Bellavista's redevelopment plan gets approved, we'll be asking council to confirm the zoning status quo. We're hoping that we'll have the community's support, including that of your heritage society."

Pierce frowned. "The society is opposed to extensive changes to heritage properties out of sync with preservation and true renewal."

"It would be a shame if there couldn't be a middle ground between preservation and renewal," said Mallory. "The Bellavista redevelopment wants to create work/live units for small business owners. Imagine the foot traffic that would be attracted to a tastefully curated collection of turn-of-the-century antiques in a bucolic setting, minutes from downtown. If council decides to repeal the commercial zoning due to the society's objections, all that commercial potential would vanish."

Pierce pursed his lips, weighing up the personal benefits against the society's objections. "I'll reconsider the Bellavista proposal and advise the society accordingly. After all, we don't wish to be anachronistic, but to preserve what we value. What could be more valuable than continuing the commercial enterprises of our city forbearers?"

"What indeed?" answered Mallory, with a relieved smile. "I'll make sure to email you a copy of the development proposal."

"Do you have a hard copy?" asked Pierce. "I have a difficult time reading documents on screen. Tell you what. I'll close up the store and give you a ride back to Bellavista and you can print out a copy for me."

Mallory agreed, wanting to stay on Pierce's good side. She hoped he'd stay true to his word and support Bellavista before council. In keeping with his love of all things vintage, Pierce drove an ancient white Renault circa 1966, in surprisingly good condition. When she admired the pristine state of the vehicle, Pierce said, "It helps that we have much less salt on the roads in the winter, so less rust. There's a whole community of vintage car collectors on the island for that reason."

He parked in front of Bellavista and pulled out his phone before she could unbuckle.

"Look at this 1934 Timmis Ford V8 Roadster! I spotted it the other day." Pierce enthusiastically scrolled through more photos of vintage cars. "There was a 1966 Pontiac Parisienne 'Veronica' a few weeks ago! Now where is it?"

He scrolled through more photos before stopping, his scowl reappearing. "There's a vehicle I'd be happy never to see again! Brad Jobson insists on parking his red monstrosity in my commercial zone!"

Red truck? "Can I see that?" she asked. Pierce handed his phone over.

"You're sure this is Brad's truck?" It looked exactly like the one that had tried to run them down.

"Yes. He always parks in my delivery zone, which makes my blood boil."

Mallory looked at the date and time of the photo. "8:10 p.m. 24/04. Is that April 24?" She looked up at Pierce. "You saw Brad Jobson the evening of April 24?"

"I don't recall. I was coming back from...I had an appointment that evening and that's when I saw Brad's truck. Scroll through, I took more photos because I was planning to file a complaint with the city."

She flipped through the photos and found a couple that showed the truck's license plate clearly. "Pierce, April 24 was the night Nate Narkiss was killed! Brad was supposed to be out of town on a fishing charter in Campbell River, but you have a photo showing he was still here in town!"

Pierce's eyes widened. "Really? Are you saying that this photo breaks Brad's alibi?"

"If this license plate number matches his, then yes, I think it does," said Mallory. "Can you text me this photo? I'm going to send it to Detective Blair."

"Of course, of course!" said Pierce, his fingers trembling as he quickly typed a text and attached the photo. "There, I've sent it to you. Oh my, who would have thought I'd be the one to contradict his alibi!"

"Did you actually see Brad that night?" she asked.

"I saw him come out of his office, get into his truck and drive away. It was about ten minutes later."

"We've got him then. Even if he drove straight up island, it would still take him at least four hours. Who takes a fishing charter out at midnight? He must have faked his alibi."

☙

Mallory said goodbye to Pierce and dashed into Bellavista. Where was everyone? Oh right, Saffron had a work call, and the others were visiting Cora. After she'd printed off a copy of the development plan for Pierce, she delivered it, then quickly typed out a note to Detective Blair, attaching Pierce's photos and sent it. Then, to make doubly sure, she called both officers and left a message so that they would know to check their emails. The photo was proof that Brad was still in Victoria when Nate died. Surely with that evidence, the police would move swiftly.

Half an hour later, Saffron and the others had not yet returned. She put aside the grant applications she was working on and checked her phone to see if there were any updates on the *Vic in the Know* blog. To her astonishment, Pierce's storefront photo of Brad's truck popped up as a new blind item on the site with the caption:

Guess who was in town when they were supposed to be somewhere else? Were they checking out a *beautiful view*? Luckily, a *seasoned* expert had the foresight to snap a photo.

The post had to have come from Pierce. What was he thinking? It was about as subtle as a hammer to the head. Detective Blair would go ballistic if he knew Pierce was tipping off Brad Jobson. She needed to talk to Pierce and tell him to pull the post down immediately.

Her phone pinged.

This is Pierce. Can you come over?

I've something important to show you.

Mallory typed a response.

Heading over now. Take down that post!

She sent a brief text to Saffron letting her know she would be at Downton and ran next door.

The large carved front door of Downton was ajar. Mallory knocked and called out, "Pierce? It's Mallory." No one answered. She hesitated before pushing the door open.

Other than the dignified ticking of an imposing grandfather clock, the house was silent. No sign of Pierce. She slipped off her shoes and padded down the thickly carpeted hallway to the kitchen, where she found a half-eaten croissant and a bowl of red leaf salad, but no Pierce.

Pierce had said he had a workshop on the property. Perhaps he was there. Outside, the grounds were still quiet but for the cawing of the peacocks. Guessing that Pierce used the former carriage house as his workshop, Mallory knocked. There was no response. She pushed open the door and went inside. An astringent whiff of lemon polish and varnish hit her nose as she peered into the dark interior.

"Pierce?" she called.

Two hands grabbed her roughly from behind. She screamed and struggled against their grip, terror rising in her throat. Instinct taking over, she slammed the heel of her shoe down, catching her attacker's toes, and thrust her elbow back into their ribcage. Her attacker swore and let go. Mallory raced out of the carriage house and back toward Bellavista.

Her heart thudded in her ears as she ran. The smell of aftershave lingering in her nose had told her exactly who her assailant was. Snatching her phone out of her back pocket, Mallory autodialed. "Saffron," she hissed, "Brad attacked me! I think he has Pierce! Call Detective Blair." Saffron let out a torrent of questions, but Mallory didn't have breath to answer them. She thrust her phone into her pocket with shaking fingers and ran through the kitchen side door, flinging it shut behind her and locking it. Her chest heaved as she tried to catch her breath. The police were coming. He couldn't get in here.

The heavy front door rattled and crashed open.

Not looking behind her, Mallory sprinted up the carpeted stairs to the second floor. Her mind raced, trying to stay one step ahead. She dashed into an unoccupied bedroom covered in drop cloths and scanned it with increasing desperation for a hiding spot. A set of French doors led onto a Juliet-style balcony. She turned back, grabbed hold of a ladder left by the painters and lodged it under the handle of the door, hoping the barrier would slow her pursuer down. Then she flew out onto the balcony, running on instinct to put distance between herself and Brad. A quick check over the edge of the balcony showed at least a twenty-foot drop to the terrace below. The hard flagstones below offered little reassurance. If she jumped down, she would be lucky if she didn't break most of her bones.

    She fought down her fear by reminding herself that help was on the way. She could hear Brad pounding up the staircase. In desperation, she reached for the drainpipe hugging the side of the balcony. It was now or never. Taking a deep breath, Mallory flung her leg over the side of the balcony.

Chapter 27

"Let what you fear drive you."
– Raquel DeWitt, *The Smart Woman's Guide to Getting It Done.*

Mallory made it over the edge as Brad burst through the makeshift barrier and into the room. She had angled herself off the balcony by grabbing the drainpipe. Praying it would hold, she swung her body toward it and twisted herself to the right so she could get her foot onto the wooden trim that covered the top half of the house. The trim was barely deep enough for her to grab a toehold, but if it bore her weight, she could edge across it and move further out of arm's reach. She managed to make it onto the thin ledge as Brad exploded out onto the balcony.

He swore under his breath when he saw Mallory precariously clinging to the drainpipe and stared at her, his eyes huge, sweat pouring down his face. Mallory's stomach clenched.

Recognition flickered in Brad's eyes. "You! You're the one who was at the gala and snooping around my work site. Did that dried-up old prune put you up to it?"

"Where's Pierce? What did you do to him?"

"Don't worry about him. I took care of him. Interfering old fool."

Brad lunged, but he fell short of reaching her. Mallory sucked in her breath in relief, silently thanking the skilled craftsmen who had built the house so solidly.

"What are you doing out there?" demanded Brad.

"Getting away from you." *What did he think she was doing? Auditioning for Cirque du Soleil?*

"Come back here," he wheedled. "I'm not going to hurt you."

"I'll stay where I am, thanks."

"Pierce said you have the photos. I want to see you delete them."

"It's no use, Brad. The photo has already gone to the police."

He swore loudly and furiously.

"What did you do to Pierce?" cried Mallory.

"Your nosy friend is going to have a little accident. Too bad he was overcome by varnish fumes before the fire took down his workshop."

Mallory felt sick, and then a flame of anger burned in her belly. "It's over, Brad. Lucas told me everything. You were here the night Nate was killed. You hit him and left him in the chicken coop for dead."

Brad's face turned dark. "It was an accident! Nate fell and hit his head on the fountain edge. He wasn't supposed to die!"

For a moment, he lost focus on Mallory as he relived his memories of that night.

"He wouldn't back off. I told him I had it all under control, but he had to keep poking his nose in. He wanted Bellavista so badly and I was going to be the one to get it for him. Why did he have to show up and ruin everything?"

Mallory needed to keep Brad talking until she figured out how to get to a safer position.

"You mean, ruin your attempts to sabotage Bellavista?" she prodded. "How did Nate find out?"

She tightened her grip on the drainpipe and tried not to look down. If she made it across the trim and grabbed hold of the peaked part of the gable, she might be able to squeeze herself through the opening of the window.

Brad rubbed his face with his hands. "It was a stupid mistake! Lucas left a voicemail for me on Nate's line saying we needed to break the sprinkler system while you guys were at the council meeting. Nate panicked and rushed over. He was worried the sabotage could be linked back to him. Nate Narkiss growing a conscience." Brad let out a harsh laugh. "For years I did the dirty work, got what he needed to clinch his deals. And now, because he wanted to be in tight with Mr. Perfect Prentiss, he was so concerned with his reputation? Didn't want to associate with me? He didn't care at all what would happen to me. I was dispensable. I saw red and I punched him – hard – and he went down."

Brad took a shuddering breath. "I tried to wake him up, but he didn't move. Then Lucas took off and I panicked. I dragged Nate into the chicken coop to try to buy time. But when I heard someone coming, I ran to my truck and drove away."

"You left your friend for dead?" This guy was a total coward.

"I only took off because those crazy chickens wouldn't leave me alone! I was gonna go back and get him out but then someone came."

Amira going to fetch Gregory Peck for the night. Mallory's arms ached. Her strength waning, she fervently promised to take up upper-body strength training if she survived this. I will do reps, she vowed silently, I will do weights. I will take up hot yoga and fencing like Metchosin. Tightening her grip on the drainpipe, Mallory pressed as close as possible to the siding and tried to reach the gable roof with her other arm without attracting Brad's attention.

"How did you fake your alibi?" she asked. "Your fishing trip."

Brad scowled. "If Pierce hadn't been policing his parking spot, I would have been fine. I had to go back to the office to delete Lucas's voicemail from Nate's phone. Then I drove straight up to Campbell River. My friend owns a fishing charter, so I got him to fix the charter logs to show I took the boat out that afternoon. My friend wasn't happy about it, but what was he going to do, rat me out?"

Brad likely had dirt he used on the fishing charter owner to get him to fake the time entries.

"Why set up Lucas? What did he do to deserve that?" she asked.

"Lucas came by my work site and threatened to tip the police off. That's when I sent a tip of my own to the police about his drug dealing and his connection to Nate and he had to scram."

There was another person who had ended up hurt. "What about Stan? How was he involved?"

A sneer came over Brad's face. "Stan was the weak link. Liked the kickbacks he received from the remediation contracts, but when Nate died, he got all squiggly about it, didn't want to help me. I always have a back-up plan; when he threatened to sell me out to the cops, I rigged the foundation accounts, so it looked like Stan was stealing."

While Brad talked, Mallory edged her way closer to the gable.

"Stan got in the way too. Too bad he had that accident."

Another accident. Lots of people ended up dead from accidents when Brad Jobson was around. The level of Brad's self-delusion was jaw-dropping. He really didn't think he was responsible for anything. He saw himself as the victim. Everyone else was to blame.

She was so close now. If she looped her fingers into the edging, she could swing herself into the open window.

Brad saw what Mallory was doing. "Where are you going? Come back here."

"No, thanks. I don't want to be your next "accident."

Brad grabbed the edge of the balcony, pulled himself up onto the ledge and lunged. Mallory launched herself through the open window as a shadow swooped over Brad's head. Brad threw up his arms, trying desperately to bat the peahen away, and Mallory watched in horror as Brad lost his balance and tumbled to the ground.

Chapter 28

> "Know when to wrap it up."
> - Raquel DeWitt, *The Smart Woman's Guide to Getting it Done*

Mallory crashed onto the floor with a painful thump. "Mallory! MALLORY!" Someone was shouting. Then a pair of arms took hold of her.

"What were you doing on the roof?" cried Saffron, beside herself with anxiety.

"Brad —he fell — he's on the ground," gasped Mallory.

"The police are down there — don't worry, they'll get him. He's not going anywhere."

Mallory closed her eyes as the room went dark.

When she came to, she was lying on the sofa in the library, and Saffron and Amira were hovering over at her with very worried expressions on their faces.

"Pierce!" she exclaimed, struggling to sit up.

"Easy there," said Saffron. "Pierce is fine. We found him tied up in his workshop. The fall broke Brad's leg but not his mouth. He was ranting about how it was all an accident, and he didn't mean to do it. The police have him in custody now."

Mallory tried to tell them what she knew. "We have proof that Brad was here the night Nate was killed! Brad set up Lucas and Stan! I think he scared Stan so much that he fell from the balcony!"

"Shhh, you need medical attention right now," said Amira. "You can tell us all about it later."

❦

Once the paramedics checked out Mallory, Detectives Blair and Grover asked for an interview.

"You took a big chance, Ms. — er — McKenzie-Chu," grouched Detective Blair, but he looked relieved, as did Grover. "You were very lucky you didn't fall off the roof. What were you and Mr. Wexford thinking, posting public messages on that blog — you might as well have hung out a sign saying, 'come and get me.'"

"You know about *Vic in the Know*?"

Detective Blair scowled. "Please give us some credit. We've been investigating Mr. Jobson this whole time. There was no need for heroics."

"It wasn't on purpose. I was trying to get away. Brad admitted that he hit Nate and dragged him into the chicken coop and left him. And I think he was involved in Stan's accident! He can't get away with it."

"He won't, not if we can help it," said Detective Grover. "Now that Stan Barber has regained consciousness, he's been sharing some interesting information about Mr. Jobson. We've also been talking to his friend up in Campbell River and he's singing like a canary." Detective Grover wasn't giving up his bird metaphors any time soon.

Detective Blair rolled his eyes.

❦

There was a great deal to unpack after the arrest of Brad Jobson. As Detective Blair explained, the police had had their sights on Brad since uncovering a convincing motive; Brad had been siphoning funds from the Wheelbarrow Foundation for years, and Nate had discovered the embezzlement. While Brad still claimed that Nate's death was accidental, the evidence was mounting against him.

Saffron filled Mallory in on what she had learned from Detective Grover.

"Brad saw Pierce's post and realized once he saw the photo that his alibi no longer held up. Brad knows the *Vic in the Know* blog moderator and pressured them to take the photo down. He was able to figure out that Pierce had sent the picture – not difficult to do given the obvious clues in the comment. When Pierce told him you were emailing the photo to the police, Brad lost it and tied him up in the carriage house, then forced him to text you to come over."

"Brad was going to set fire to the workshop and let Pierce die," said Mallory. "Everyone would have thought it was an accident."

Saffron grimaced. "Brad really is a nasty piece of work. It has come back to bite him. Brad's friend in Campbell River gave the police everything he had on Brad. It turns out Brad got inside Bellavista more than once. As he had a key courtesy of Lucas, all he had to do was monitor the place and see an opportunity."

"Those odd phone calls," said Amira. "Brad was checking to see if anyone was home before he broke in. Brad used Lucas to spy on us and sabotage Bellavista, so that Cora would feel pressured to sell."

Mallory shivered, remembering how she had felt observed many times. "That's why there were so many problems that we couldn't explain. That's how he came after me."

Saffron continued. "Lucas turned himself in and got a plea deal with the police, and they're taking into account that he tried to stop Brad. Since he's moving back to Ladysmith to be closer to his mother, we need a new handyperson."

"What about Kiki?" suggested Mallory. "She's been helping us out, and I know she's saving up for school. Perhaps there can be a rental discount in exchange for maintenance services?"

"That's a brilliant idea!" said Amira.

"To think Brad almost got away with pinning Nate's murder on Stan," said Saffron. "Until you discovered that alibi-busting photo. Brad had no idea Gregory Peck caused Nate's death, so he believed he was going to be charged with murder. Simon says he's looking at manslaughter at the very least in relation to Nate's death, and breaking and entering, and the police will be looking more closely at Stan's accident and the foundation's accounting discrepancies. What possessed him to burn it all down like that? Did he really think he could get away with it?"

Mallory had been talking over the case with her mother, and Fiona had some thoughts about Brad's mental state that Mallory shared.

"Brad couldn't get over Nate moving on without him. He viewed everyone who entered Nate's life as a threat to his relationship with Nate. Think of everyone who was targeted at some point. Metchosin Barnes. Becca Gill. Jacob Prentiss. I bet when the police investigate, they'll find that Brad was behind all those blind items on the *Vic in the Know* blog. The whole time he was convinced he was helping Nate. It was really twisted logic, but to Brad, it must have made perfect sense. When Nate wanted to distance himself, Brad couldn't handle it. He couldn't handle being left behind."

03

Mallory's muscles ached for several days due to the strain on her lower arms. Never again would she take the strength and capability of her body for granted. She had saved herself, with a timely assist from an indignant nesting peahen. Much to Saffron's disgust, the peacocks' morning shrieks were music to Mallory's ears.

Mallory admitted as much to Pierce when he came over to thank her for trying to save him. Pierce was deeply remorseful about his post on *Vic in the Know*.

"Brad tracked us down because of my post! I thought I was being so clever with it. He made me send that text to your phone number. I feel terrible."

"Don't beat yourself up. I roused his suspicion long before that with my visit to his work site."

"I heard that he broke into Metchosin's office to get dirt on her campaign."

Mallory discreetly did not mention that Brad had also broken into Becca's office to access confidential client information.

"How are you doing, Pierce? You went through your own ordeal."

Pierce shuddered. "I was absolutely terrified. When I heard your voice inside the carriage house, I couldn't say anything because of the gag. I felt so helpless."

"Thankfully, it all turned out fine and you and your workshop are still standing. Are you still thinking about setting up your business at Downton?"

"Oh yes! I've got a website now, and the online store will launch next week."

"I helped him with that." Kiki had arrived, carrying a bag of mandarin oranges and, to Mallory's delight, a take-out order from Dynasty Dumpling. Everyone was being so kind. Pierce had brought Mallory an assortment of buns from The Daily Bun, courtesy of Una, and the APHIDS had sent over several gorgeous bouquets. Even Art Papatonis had dropped off some reading material. He had confessed to vandalizing the signs at the offices of Sand Dollar Developments and was doing a stint of community service.

"Kiki has been indispensable in helping me set up my point-of-sale equipment and marketing materials. My carriage house is turning out to be the perfect spot for my business."

"That's great, Pierce." He looked happy, which boded well for continuing neighborliness.

Pierce said his goodbyes as Kiki unpacked the take-out dishes for Mallory.

"I wonder where Pierce was the night Nate was killed," murmured Mallory. "He never told us."

"Oh, I know where Pierce was," said Kiki. Mallory turned to stare at her. "On Thursday evenings at seven, I teach Jazzercize classes at the Fairfield Community Center. He was there that night for the class."

Mallory winced at the vision of a Jazzercising Pierce in spandex. "Kiki, you really are amazing."

"Aw, thanks, Mallory. Now..." Kiki said eagerly, pulling up a chair. "Tell me *everything*!"

☙

In the aftermath of the police investigation wrap-up, Mallory called Raquel and asked if they could meet for tea. Raquel being Raquel suggested The Empress. Once upon a time, she would have given in to Raquel's request, but the new Mallory calmly suggested a more casual alternative.

At Murchie's on Government Street, they met over a modest tray of warm currant scones, whipped cream and strawberry jam.

"Thanks for all the help you and Hope have given me on the co-op project," said Mallory. "We've made great strides because of Hope's contacts."

"I'm so glad! But are you sure this is the line of work you want to be in? Anytime you decide to come back to work for me, say the word. We all miss you— the staff, the twins, everyone."

"I miss you all too, Raquel, I really do. Being part of your household was one of the most meaningful experiences of my life. While I'll treasure forever those memories, my new business is my focus now. I'm not sure if I'll keep working as a project manager, but it's time for me to move on."

Raquel couldn't hide her disappointment. "I've been saying goodbye to so many parts of my life, and I'm not ready for the changes. When I realized that the twins were heading to university this fall, I panicked. I'm not ready to lose them to the world. You've been with me for the twins' entire lives, from babyhood on. I suppose that's why I've had a hard time letting you go too."

Raquel reached over to clasp Mallory's hands. "You'll always be very dear to the DeWitt family. No matter what, you're our people."

"You're my people, too," said Mallory, her eyes brimming.

"Would you like me to take a picture of the two of you?" offered one of the friendly servers, sliding over at this opportune moment.

"Look at us!" said Raquel, half-laughing, half-crying. "If you take my picture when I've got mascara tracks down my face, I'll never forgive you!"

"Oh, who cares what we look like!" Mallory handed her phone over to the server and pulled Raquel in for the shot. "Say Bellavista!"

Chapter 29

> "Home is anywhere you want to be."
> - Raquel DeWitt, *The Smart Woman's Guide to Getting it Done*

"Ta da! What'd you think?" Saffron pushed the door to the carriage house open and Mallory entered, in awe at the remarkable transformation Saffron had made in only a few weeks. After Bellavista's application had met with universal approval from city council, Saffron had set to work transforming the old carriage house into a rental suite. Gone were the dingy, cramped quarters covered in dust and cobwebs. The entire interior had been cleaned out and repainted in a soft dove grey, the natural oak floors sanded and polished to a warm sheen. Reframed windows let in sparkling sunshine that filtered through billowing muslin curtains. Mallory explored every corner, marveling at the copper, mid-century floating Scandinavian fireplace and the compact shower Saffron had managed to fit into a small bathroom on the main floor. Two of Etta's vibrant canvases added a splash of color to the otherwise neutral space.

Mallory ran up the sturdy new set of stairs leading to the loft, now remade into a bedroom with a double bed invitingly accessorized with Cora's Tuscan linens and framed by wraparound bookshelves. Paper screens ran around three sides and could be slid open or closed to block out the light and provide privacy. Off the fully equipped, efficient kitchen area downstairs, Saffron had created a nook set apart by additional sliding doors and fitted with a chair and a wooden desk, the perfect size for a laptop. A plush sofa covered in an array of blankets and cushions made for a cozy retreat.

"You've done an incredible job!" cried Mallory. "I absolutely love it! How did you get it done so quickly?"

"I have my resources. Pierce came through with the furniture, some odds and ends he had in storage, and with Kiki's paint job it all came together." Kiki had happily accepted the position as Bellavista handyperson, moving into Lucas's old apartment in the main house.

"As soon as the listing goes up on Air BnB, you're going to get a ton of requests. I'd stay here in a heartbeat," said Mallory wistfully.

"Say the word, and it's yours, if you want it."

Mallory looked at her in astonishment.

Saffron put on a beseeching expression, clasping her hands together. "Please, Mallory! I really want you to stay on to help Cora through this next stage, and if you agree, you can live here. We can figure out the rent and offset it with the hours you put into the co-op project. It would make me feel a lot better knowing that you were carrying on here when I go back to London."

"What does Cora think about that?" asked Mallory. "She's got a great team with Amira, J.P. and Metchosin taking over from me."

"I think it's a fantastic idea!" Cora came through the front door on crutches. "Mallory, please say yes. I know that you want to take your consulting business in a different direction, but I would very much appreciate you helping us over the bumpy parts of the process. The more people who can work with us, the smoother it will be. What if we agreed on a set number of hours? You could choose when and how much you'll work with us, and we'll adjust to your not being available 24/7."

Mallory could see that the carriage house would work well as both a workspace and a living space. She'd be part of the community that she cared about and still have the privacy she craved with her separate living quarters. How could she say no to a deal like that?

"How about we try it out for the next six months? That way, we can see whether or not it's working for both of us, and if it isn't, I can find another place, no hard feelings."

Cora broke into a huge grin. "She said yes!" she yelled, startling Mallory. In poured Amira, Georgie and Kiki, exclaiming with excitement and hugging Mallory.

"Clearly, you were all on pins and needles," commented Mallory dryly as Amira handed out ice cream sandwich treats from a portable cooler and Kiki uncorked some sparkling elderflower cordial. Georgie placed a huge vase of flowers on the counter as Mallory unwrapped a mint chocolate chip ice cream sandwich and took a bite.

"We were *cautiously* optimistic," conceded Saffron. "I put a lot of faith in that floating fireplace."

"I adore it," confessed Mallory. As her friends chattered and laughed, excitement bubbled up. Who would have thought her unexpected detour to the west coast would end with her putting down roots and becoming part of a community? This really was a new beginning, and she couldn't wait to see what happened next.

Epilogue

One month later

The sun hovered on the horizon of the clear blue morning. Seagulls and shorebirds bobbed gently on the surf and little waves rolled into the shoreline. On the pebbly beach, a small army was setting up what looked like a base camp from the volume of tote bags, coolers and gear they had trekked in. Amira helped Etta take a seat on a large driftwood log while Kiki placed a throw over her lap. Etta waved them both off, but she accepted a hot mug of tea poured from a thermos. Etta had recently taken up Tai Chi with Georgie, who had read that the practice was very beneficial for people with Parkinson's, but Etta drew the line at Jazzercise. Georgie, swathed in a cashmere wrap against the early morning chill, waved to Mallory and the others already in the water. The components of a lavish picnic were spread out for when the swimmers emerged, frozen and blue from the ocean.

Kiki ran down toward Mallory, aiming her phone.

"Mallory, smile please!" she called. Mallory obediently smiled. Kiki snapped a volley of photos. "You'll look great on my Instagram!"

As ice-cold water lapped around her toes, Mallory geared herself up to take the plunge. The wetsuit borrowed from Kiki was insurance against the temperature. Saffron, wearing a dramatic gold two-piece and a knitted polar bear hat, splashed about with Cora and the other members of the Polar Bear Swim Club, exuding more Miami Beach than Oak Bay.

"This is incredible!" Saffron yelled. "I feel so alive!"

"Mallory, come in!" called Cora. "It's amazing!" This was Cora's inaugural swim to celebrate the removal of her cast.

Amira came up beside Mallory, dressed in a wetsuit and headscarf. She smiled encouragingly before splashing into the water. Taking a deep breath, Mallory plunged in after her. At the shock of the cold water, she gasped, trying to catch her breath as her senses went on hyperalert. Everything looked brighter, sharper when she resurfaced.

Ducking her head under the water again, Mallory entered a Zen-like bubble of calm as the water muted the shrieks and laughter around her. So much had happened in a short time. J.P. had mapped out the master plan for the redevelopment, and construction would break ground next month. The Bellavista project was happening. In addition, her family had taken her decision to relocate to Victoria surprisingly well. Her mother had sent her more material on ADHD and Mallory had listened to a couple of ADHD podcasts geared for women diagnosed in mid-life. In that community, Mallory received the affirmation and sense of finally being seen she hadn't known she needed. As a housewarming present, Kiki had gifted Mallory a bullet journal, promising the trendy alternative to agendas would solve all her time management and scheduling issues. After watching dozens of Youtubers demonstrate their bullet journaling preferences, Mallory was officially obsessed.

As she drew near Saffron and Cora, Mallory reflected on strong women, on how community could be created with hope, optimism and commitment. Mallory emerged next to Saffron, who threw one arm around her and the other around her aunt.

"We've more than earned that hot chocolate!" Saffron shouted. "Save some for us!"

Shivering and laughing, the trio splashed their way back to the shore to their waiting friends.

THE END

EGG RECIPES FROM BELLAVISTA
(SERVES ONE OR TWO)

CORA'S GOVERNMENT HOUSE CURRIED EGGS

My dear friend, Professor Herbert Franklin, discovered this recipe in an old cookbook from the Government House kitchen of the Lieutenant-Governor of British Columbia, who is the King of England's representative in B.C. It speaks to the Anglo-Indian origins of the first Government Houses in the British Empire.

    2 hard-boiled eggs
    pat of butter
    2 Tbsp flour
    1 Tbsp curry powder
    1 chopped up apple
    ½ cup hot broth or water
    salt and pepper

Boil the eggs, cool, peel and slice them. Add the butter to a small saucepan and melt over medium heat. Add the chopped apple and stir until softened. Whisk in the flour and curry powder until a thick paste is formed, stirring constantly. Watch that the mixture doesn't burn. Immediately add some of the broth or water in stages, stirring in between additions, until a sauce is formed to the desired thickness. Season with salt and pepper to taste. Serve the sliced eggs with the sauce on top. This is delicious over steamed rice.

GEORGIE'S PASTA ALLA CARBONARA

I first tasted this dish on a sunlit piazza while visiting La Bella Roma in 1966.

>   2 cups leftover pasta (any kind)
>   2 eggs
>   2 slices chopped bacon (regular or turkey)
>   Olive oil
>   Salt and pepper
>   Parmesan or Romano cheese, grated

Make fresh pasta or re-heat cold pasta in the microwave. Meanwhile, sauté the chopped bacon in a non-stick frying pan. I said two slices but use as much as you want. Once the bacon reaches your desired level of crispiness, dump in the warm pasta and stir so the pasta is coated in the fat. Add a drizzle of olive oil. Crack in the two eggs and quickly stir to cook the eggs for about a minute or two. You'll know when it's done. Grate some cheese right over the hot pan. Stir everything together, season with freshly ground pepper and serve in a big bowl. *Mangia!*

AMIRA'S GREEN OMELETTE

I ate this dish often as a child on my grandmother's roof-top terrace in Damascus.

>   2 eggs
>   2-3 Tbsp chopped herbs or greens (parsley, cilantro, romaine, other lettuce, whatever is on hand)
>   Chopped nuts (almonds are good, also walnuts; use a mortar and pestle if you have one)
>   Olive oil

Salt and pepper

Beat the two eggs until blended in a small bowl. Chop up the greens and nuts. Heat some oil in a non-stick frying pan. Add the eggs once oil is hot. When the egg sets but isn't cooked through, add the herbs and nuts in the center and fold over the egg. Cook to your liking. Season with salt and pepper. Serve immediately.

KIKI'S VEGGIE FRIED RICE

Most families don't have a recipe. This is how we use up leftovers.

2-3 cups leftover rice (cold, from the fridge. Break it up with a spoon; never use fresh rice, as it will be too sticky. If you must use fresh rice, put it in the fridge for a couple of hours first so it can dry out)
2 Tbsp vegetable or peanut oil (don't use olive oil! It will taste weird)
Diced onion (about a handful)
Diced vegetables (celery, carrots, broccoli, about a handful — use up whatever bits of leftover cooked vegetables you have in the fridge or use fresh, but remember, this is supposed to be a left-overs recipe. I grate the carrots if using fresh)
Sliced scallions
1 egg, beaten
Frozen peas, defrosted (frozen corn is also good)
Grated ginger or fresh ginger minced
Soy sauce or oyster sauce
Salt and pepper
Sprinkle of sesame oil (optional)
Dash of sriracha sauce (optional)
Add a sprinkle of furikake and sliced nori for Japanese-style fried rice.

Heat a wok or a large frying pan. Add some oil and cook your beaten egg until set. Put the egg in a clean dish and wipe out the wok with a paper towel. Add some more oil, then your diced onion. Once the onion starts to soften, add other raw vegetables (if you don't have leftover vegetables) or your cooked vegetables and stir-fry for a few minutes until cooked or warmed through. Add the rice: make sure to break up the clumps with your fingers or a spatula. Add more oil if it looks sticky. Add the peas (you can defrost them in the microwave or hot water) and stir in. I like to add a tablespoon of soy sauce or oyster sauce, or sometimes sriracha sauce for a spicy kick. Grate in some fresh ginger or shake in some grated dried ginger, some salt and pepper. Give it a taste and adjust seasonings. Sprinkle sliced scallions on top. *Sic fan!*

MALLORY'S ASIAN-SCOTCH EGGS

My mum makes these for our annual Gung Haggis Fat Choy celebration when we celebrate both Chinese New Year and Robbie Burns' Day.

    large eggs, hard boiled and peeled
    1 pound ground chicken or ground beef
    2 teaspoons sugar
    2 teaspoons soy sauce
    2 teaspoons rice vinegar
    Black pepper
    1 teaspoon ground ginger
    2 scallions, finely chopped
    1/2 cup flour
    1 teaspoon kosher salt
    1 cup panko breadcrumbs
    Flavorless oil, for deep-frying, about 1 quart
    Heat the oven to 350 F (175 C).

Cook the eggs until hardboiled and let them cool before peeling. Mix the ground meat gently with the remaining ingredients except the flour, salt and breadcrumbs. Shape the meat mixture around each peeled egg until it's about a half inch thick. Mix the flour, salt and breadcrumbs into a shallow plate and pat the breadcrumb mixture around each egg ball. Heat the oil in a deep pan suitable for deep frying. When the oil reaches 375 F or 190 C, fry the egg balls until golden, and then put them in the oven for 10 minutes. Serve sliced in half.

SAFFRON'S EGGS BENEDICT WITH SMOKED SALMON

Almost every restaurant in Victoria has a version of a smoked salmon eggs Benny. I like the ones at John's Diner and Shine Café.

ETTA'S HARD-BOILED EGG

Boil an egg.

Edit. Note: We were not able to obtain any additional instructions from Ms. Hopkins. We suggest that you use the following boiled egg recipe to prepare eggs for Cora's Government House Curried Eggs and Mallory's Asian-Scotch Eggs.

Put eggs in a saucepan and fill with cold water until the eggs are just covered. Do not put on a lid. Set the heat to boiling and watch the pot. Once the water boils, immediately take the saucepan off the heat and put the saucepan lid on. Set a timer for 15 minutes (12 minutes if you like the yolk firmer but not completely set). Once the timer goes off, drain the eggs and pour in cold water to cool the eggs.

As an enthusiastic reader of cozy mysteries for many years, I have always thought that my hometown of Victoria, Canada would be the ideal location for a cozy mystery series. So I decided to write one. Some iconic landmarks are referenced by their real names and locations, while I've changed the names and locations of others. For locals, I hope you enjoy the local references and inside jokes; for visitors to Victoria, I encourage you to discover the treasures of this delightfully quirky waterfront capital city. If you're interested in the continuing adventures of Mallory and the Bellavista residents, please email me at ionalam306@gmail.com to be notified when the next book in the Bellavista Cooperative Mystery series is published. And thank you for reading!

Manufactured by Amazon.ca
Acheson, AB